THE
GOOD SON

THE
GOOD SON

YOU-JEONG JEONG

Translated by Chi-Young Kim

Little, Brown

LITTLE, BROWN

First published in South Korea in 2016 as *Jongui Giwon* by
EunHaeng NaMu Publishing Co.
First published in Great Britain in 2018 by Little, Brown

13 5 7 9 10 8 6 4 2

A CIP catalogue record for this book
is available from the British Library.

Hardback ISBN: 978-1-4087-1123-1
Export ISBN: 978-1-4087-0974-0

Typeset in Bembo by M Rules
Printed and bound in Great Britain by
Clays Ltd, St Ives plc

Papers used by Little, Brown are from well-managed forests
and other responsible sources.

MIX
Paper from
responsible sources
FSC® C104740

Little, Brown
An imprint of
Little, Brown Book Group
Carmelite House
50 Victoria Embankment
London EC4Y 0DZ

An Hachette UK Company
www.hachette.co.uk

www.littlebrown.co.uk

I

A CALL IN THE DARK

The smell of blood woke me. It was intense, as though my whole body were inhaling it. It reverberated and expanded within me. Strange scenes flitted through my mind – the fuzzy yellow light of a row of street lamps in the fog, swirling water below my feet, a crimson umbrella rolling along a rain-soaked road, a plastic tarpaulin shrouding a construction site snapping in the wind. Somewhere a man was singing and slurring lyrics: a song about a girl he couldn't forget, and about her walking in the rain.

It didn't take me long to figure out what was going on. None of this was reality or even the remnants of a dream. It was a signal my head was sending my body. Stay lying down. Don't move. It's the price you have to pay for not taking your medication.

Not taking my meds was a quenching rain in the desert of my life, even if it sometimes caused a seizure. Right now, I was experiencing the unsettling hallucinations that warned me a storm was imminent. There was no safe harbour; I could only wait for it to arrive. If past experience was any indication, when it was over, I wouldn't remember what had happened. It would be simple and intense, and afterwards I would be tired and depleted. I deserved this; I knew full well what I was getting into when I chose this path. It was an addiction; I kept doing it again and again despite understanding the risks. Most addicts get high to chase after a fantasy, but for me it was a different route: I had to get *off* my drugs to reach a heightened reality. That was when the magic hours opened up – my headaches and tinnitus disappeared, and my senses became acute. I could smell like a dog, my brain whirred quicker than ever, and I read the world by instinct instead of with reason. I felt empowered and superior.

Even then, I still had tiny dissatisfactions. I never felt superior to Mother and Auntie. These two women treated me like a seat cushion – something to be suffocated and smothered. I knew what the chain of events would be if Mother were to witness me having a seizure. As soon as I recovered, she would drag me straight to Auntie, the famous psychiatrist and director of Future Paediatric Clinic. Auntie would look into my eyes and talk to me kindly to try to get me to listen to her. *Why did you stop taking your pills? Tell me honestly, so I can help you.* Frankly, though, honesty is neither my strong suit nor something I aspire to. I prefer to be practical, so my answer would be: *I forgot to take it one day, then the next day I forgot that I'd forgotten the day before, and while I'm at it, why don't I just say that I've forgotten about it every day until this very moment?* Auntie would declare that I was falling into another dangerous pattern, and Mother would order me to take the pills at each meal under observation. They would drill into me the steep price I would pay for a few thrilling days, making it clear that as long as I continued to behave this way, I would never be free of their gaze.

'Yu-jin.'

Suddenly Mother's voice popped into my head. I had heard it, soft but clear, right before I woke up. But now I couldn't even hear her moving about downstairs. It was so quiet. A deafening stillness. It was dark in my room; maybe it was still early, before the sun was up. She might still be asleep. Then I could have this seizure and be done with it without her having to know about it, like last night.

Around midnight, I'd stood panting near the sea wall on my way back from a run to the Milky Way Observatory in Gundo Marine Park. I ran when I got restless and felt my muscles twitching with energy. I thought of it as 'restless body syndrome'. Sometimes I ran in the middle of the night; it wouldn't be exaggerating to call it a mad urge.

The streets were deserted, as they always were at that hour. Yongi's, the street stall that sold sugar-filled pancakes, was closed. The ferry dock below was shrouded in darkness. Thick fog had swallowed the six-lane road by the sea wall. The December wind was biting and powerful, and a torrential rain was falling. Most would consider these adverse conditions, but I felt as though I was floating in the air. I felt fantastic. I could float all the way home. It would have been perfect if it hadn't been for the sweet smell of blood perfuming the wind, suggesting an impending seizure. A girl got off the last bus to Ansan and tottered towards me with her umbrella held open, pushed along by the wind. I had to get home; I didn't want to crumple to the ground and roll around, contorted like a squid thrown on the grill, in front of a complete stranger.

I couldn't remember what happened after that. I must have lain down as soon as I walked into my room, without bothering to change. I probably fell asleep snoring. It had been the third seizure I'd had in my life, but this was the first time I'd sensed another one coming so quickly after the last. And this smell was a different beast altogether: my skin was stinging, my nose was tingling and my mind was foggy. The episode that was about to come felt like it could be the most intense one yet.

I wasn't anxious about the seizure's severity; whether it was a drizzle or a downpour, I'd still get wet. I just wished it would come quickly so that I could be done with it before Mother woke up. I closed my eyes and stayed still. I turned my head to the side to prevent any possible breathing distress. I relaxed my body and breathed deeply. One, two ... When I got to five, the cordless phone on my bedside table began to ring, jolting me out of my preparations. I flinched, knowing it would be ringing downstairs in the living room too. Mother would startle awake. What bastard calls in the middle of the night?

The phone stopped ringing. The grandfather clock took over and chimed just once in the living room. As well as ringing out on the hour, the clock chimed once every thirty minutes. I reached over to the alarm clock by my bed and peeked at the display: 5.30. Waking early was a legacy from my years of competitive swimming. No matter what time I fell asleep, I would wake up one hour before practice. That meant that Mother must be sitting at the writing desk in her room, reciting Hail Marys to the statue of the Virgin Mary.

After she prayed, Mother would take a shower. I listened for a dragging chair or running water, but all I could hear was the loud ringing of the phone. This time it was my mobile. Maybe the earlier call had been for me too.

I raised a hand above my head and felt along my pillow for my phone. Where was it? On the desk? In the bathroom? The ringing stopped. Then the landline began going off again. My head jerked up and I grabbed the receiver.

'Hello?'

'Were you sleeping?'

It was Hae-jin. Of course. Who else would be looking for me at this hour?

'I'm up.'

'What's Mother doing?'

What a weird question. Did he not come home after his meeting with the movie studio yesterday?

'Aren't you home?' I asked.

'What? Why would I call if I'm home? I'm in Sangam-dong.' The director of *Private Lesson*, which Hae-jin had worked on last summer, had found him a new gig, he said. To celebrate signing the contract, they'd gone out for *makgeolli*, then they'd gone to a friend's studio to edit a sixtieth birthday party video he'd filmed during the day, and fallen asleep. 'I just woke up and saw that Mother had called in the middle of the night. I thought it was a little weird – she should have been asleep.' He added that he'd thought we would be up by now, but that he'd got worried when nobody picked up. 'Everything's okay, right?'

Just then, I realised that something stiff was crusted all over me. 'Why wouldn't it be?' I replied absently as I touched my hardened, tangled hair.

'Why isn't she picking up, then? She didn't answer the home phone or her mobile.'

'She's probably praying. Or in the bathroom, or out on her balcony.' I felt my chest, then my stomach, then my legs. I was still wearing the same clothes from last night but they felt completely different. My soft, airy sweater was stiff. My trousers were hard, like raw leather. I raised my foot; that was caked with something too.

'Oh. So everything's fine?'

I murmured in annoyance. What could be wrong, other than the fact that I was apparently covered in mud? 'If you're so worried, just give her a call later.'

'Nah. I'll be home soon.'

'Okay.' Why was I muddy, though? Had I fallen on my way home? But where was there mud? Had I gone the long way round, past where the new flats were being constructed? Had I slipped, maybe, as I tried to leap over a flower bed?

'I'm going to take a shower. I'll be home by nine at the latest,' Hae-jin said, and we hung up.

I sat up, placed the phone back on my bedside table and turned on the overhead light.

'Yu-jin!' Mother's scream rang in my ears. But it wasn't real – the flat was silent.

I looked around the room. My breath caught in my throat and I began choking and coughing, pounding on my chest as I fell forward on the bed, tears springing to my eyes.

Once, after I'd won gold in a 1,500-metre race, a journalist had asked me, 'What would you say your strengths are?' Modestly, the way Mother had instructed me to, I answered that I had relatively stable breathing. When the same question was posed to my swimming coach, he'd said, slightly less modestly, 'He has the most extraordinary lung capacity of all the kids I've ever coached.' There were few things that could affect my extraordinary lung capacity; they included the two women who used me as a sofa cushion, and the torpedo that seemed to explode in my throat as I looked around my room now.

Bloody drips and footprints were smeared all over the silvery marble floor. They started by the door, crossed the room and stopped at the foot of the bed. Assuming that the person leaving the prints hadn't walked backwards, whatever had happened had occurred outside my bedroom door. My bed was drenched in blood – the sheets, blankets and pillow. I looked down at myself. Clots of the stuff hung all over my black sweater, sweatpants and socks. So the tang of blood that had made me lurch awake wasn't a sign of impending seizure; it was the real thing.

Were those my footsteps? What had happened outside my room? Why was I covered in blood? Did I have a seizure? If so, it must have been bad. Did I bite my tongue? Could you bite your tongue so that the blood covered your whole body? Given the amount, it would make more sense that someone had spitefully thrown a bucket of pig's blood over me, or stabbed me. Neither seemed likely.

Where had Mother been while all this was happening? She must have been sleeping. Mother kept strict routines for most things in life, from eating to going to the bathroom to exercising. Her sleeping habits were another such thing. Each night, she went to bed at nine after taking one of the sleeping pills Auntie had prescribed. I had to be home before then. The only time she didn't follow her nightly routine was when I was late.

This rule didn't apply to Hae-jin. Mother justified this discriminatory practice by saying that she didn't need to worry about him having a seizure on the streets late at night. It was unfair, but I had to accept it; I didn't want to collapse in front of people, fall onto the tracks while waiting for a train, or flail around in the street and get run over by a bus. Nevertheless, it was my curfew that led me, from time to time, to run in the middle of the night, sneaking out via the steel door on the roof like a person starved of darkness.

I had done it just last night. I'd arrived home at 8.55 p.m., having had to leave in the middle of drinks with professors to make it back in time. I'd had three or four glasses of *soju* mixed with beer, even though I normally didn't drink, and had walked home from the bus stop in the rain, hoping it would cool my flushed face. The heat subsided but I was still buzzed enough to feel happy. Maybe I was a little more than buzzed – I forgot that the front door to the flat didn't work unless you punched in a code followed by an asterisk, so I waged a hopeless battle with the door for twenty minutes. All the flats in this building had keyless locks. After a while, I just stood there with my hands in my pockets, glaring at the malfunctioning lock. My mobile pinged several times. I knew they were texts from Mother. I didn't have to read them to know what they said:

Have you left?

Where are you?

Are you close?

It's raining. I'll pick you up at the bus stop.

Five seconds after the last message, the door flew open. Mother, who dressed elegantly even to go to the supermarket, appeared with her car keys in her hand, looking stylish in a baseball cap, white sweater, brown cardigan, skinny jeans and white trainers.

Annoyed, I pursed my lips and looked down at my feet. *Let me be*, I wanted to snap at her.

'When did you get here?' She secured the half-open door with the doorstop and stood in the opening. No way was she going to let me in without a fuss.

My hands still in my pockets, I glanced down at my watch: 9.15 p.m. 'A while ago . . .' I stopped short, realising I was digging my own grave. My head felt like lead. My face was on fire. I must have looked like a ripe tomato. I kept looking straight ahead so she wouldn't notice. Then I carefully and slowly rolled my eyes towards her. My gaze met hers. 'I couldn't get in. The door wouldn't open,' I added quickly.

Mother glanced at the lock. She pressed the seven-digit code, her fingers a blur. The door unlatched with a beep. She looked at me again. What was the problem?

'Oh . . .' I nodded, trying to convey that I understood

nothing was wrong with it. Water rained down from my wet hair. A drop slid past my eyes and dangled at the tip of my nose. I blew upwards to make it drop. Mother's eyes were boring into me. More precisely, she was staring at the small scar in the middle of my forehead as though that was where all my lies were generated.

'Have you been drinking?'

Well, that was an awkward question. According to Auntie, alcohol brought on seizures. Drinking was the ultimate rule I couldn't break. 'Just a little. A teeny bit.' I showed her with my thumb and forefinger.

Mother's gaze didn't soften. My scar burned.

'Just one beer,' I added, hoping it would turn the situation.

Mother blinked. 'Oh, is that so?'

'I wasn't going to, but my professor offered me one ...' I stopped. Here I was, in trouble for having a few drinks at the age of twenty-five! All because of the damn front door. If it had worked, I would have slipped inside and run upstairs, calling, 'I'm home!' as I passed Mother's bedroom. I wouldn't have missed my curfew, Mother wouldn't have come out to accost me, and I wouldn't have been caught drunk. My legs grew weak and my left knee buckled. I swayed.

'Yu-jin!' Mother grabbed my elbow.

I nodded. *I'm okay. I'm not drunk. It really was just one drink.*

'Let's go inside and talk.'

I did want to go inside but I didn't want to talk. I brushed Mother's hand off my elbow. This time, my right leg gave

12

way and I tipped towards her, catching myself by hanging onto her shoulders. Mother drew in a quick breath, her small, thin body stiffening. Maybe she was surprised, or moved, or thought it out of character for me to touch her. I held onto her, thinking, *Let's not talk. What's the point? I've already been drinking – it's too late to stop me now.*

'What's going on with you?' Mother said, sliding out from under my arms and regaining her usual calm.

As I stepped inside and took off my shoes, I felt deflated.

'Did something happen?'

I didn't bother to look back. I shook my head. As I walked through the living room, I nodded lightly at her. 'Goodnight.'

She didn't stop me. 'Want me to help you upstairs?'

I shook my head again and climbed up the stairs, not too fast or too slow.

I remembered taking off my clothes as soon as I got to my room, lying on my bed without washing, and hearing Mother go into her room and close the door. As soon as I'd heard that click, I sobered up. After that, I probably looked up at the ceiling for forty minutes or so, until I got too antsy and slipped out through the steel door on the roof.

I just woke up and saw that Mother had called in the middle of the night. I thought it was a little weird – she should have been asleep. That was what Hae-jin had said on the phone. I hadn't thought anything of it, but now I wondered … Why did she call him? Because I was acting strange? Did she know I'd gone out again? What time did she call him? Eleven? Midnight? If she was up for a while after that, did she hear me come back?

13

If she'd heard me, she wouldn't have left me alone. She would have made me sit down and grilled me, just the way she got me to confess to my transgressions when I was young. She wouldn't have let me go to bed until I told her everything. *Where are you coming from at this hour? When did you leave? How long have you been sneaking around?* Though I'd graduated from punishment a long time ago, it could have been back on the table – kneeling in front of the statue of the Virgin all night and reciting Hail Marys. If she'd seen me this bloody, prayers wouldn't have been the end of it. No, the fact that I woke up in my own room was evidence that she hadn't seen me looking like this.

I got out of bed. I needed to figure out what had happened. Taking care not to step in the bloody footprints, I inched towards the door. I stopped still in front of my desk. Behind the desk, in the sliding glass doors to the roof deck, I saw a man. His hair was standing up like horns, his face was red and raw, and the whites of his eyes glinted nervously. I felt faint. That red beast was me?

I couldn't see anything outside, thanks to the fog coursing in from the ocean. Yellow light flickered faintly from the pergola Mother had built when she'd created her roof garden. I would have turned it on as I left last night. I should have turned it off on my way in.

I noticed that the sliding door was open a crack. It locked automatically when it closed, so whenever I went out to the roof deck, I left it open a little. I should have closed the door behind me when I came back in. I wouldn't have opened it again no matter what state I was in: it was December, and my room was on the second level of a duplex on the tenth floor of a building by the ocean. I wouldn't want cold air flooding in, unless I was Mother, who was going through the menopause.

That meant I hadn't come back in through this door last night. I'd returned through the flat's front door, judging from the direction of the footprints, the open sliding door and the pergola light. But why would I come in through the front door? Why did I look like this? What did the state of my room signify?

I looked over at my bedside clock again. Three red numbers were glowing against the black background: 5.45. I didn't hear running water, but Mother could still be in the bathroom. In ten minutes she would come out of her bedroom and go into the kitchen. I had to see what things looked like before she emerged.

I opened my door and went out into the hall. I flicked on the light. Bloody footprints stretched from my doorway down the hallway, all the way to the stairs. I leant against the door. The optimist in my head whispered to me: *It's a dream. You haven't woken up yet. There's no way something like this could happen in real life.*

I forced myself to move away from the door, and followed the footsteps reluctantly. I stepped onto the top of the darkened stairs, triggering the motion sensor. The light turned on. Bloody handprints were smeared all over the railing, with footprints stamped on each step. Dazed, I looked down at the blood-splattered wall beside the stairs, and the rivulets and puddles of blood pooling on the landing below.

I looked down at my blood-drenched hands, sweater, trousers and feet. Had I got covered in blood on the landing? Who had done this to me? I began to panic, unable to think, hear or feel.

I went downstairs sluggishly. I passed the puddle of blood on the landing and turned to continue down the next flight. I gasped; my head jerked up and I stepped backwards. I closed my eyes. My mind suggested an acceptable option. *Nothing's wrong. This isn't real. Go back to your room before Mother comes out. Get some sleep. Once you wake up again, it'll be like any other morning.*

The realist in my head disagreed. *No. You can't gloss over this. You have to find out if it is a dream or not. If it isn't, you have to figure out what happened downstairs and why you woke up looking like this. If it turns out to be a dream, you'll still have plenty of time to get back to bed.*

I opened my eyes. Downstairs, the lights were blazing. Blood had pooled along the dividing wall between the stairs and the kitchen. In the puddle was a pair of bare feet, heels resting on the marble floor and toes pointing up towards the ceiling. The wall blocked my view of what else was there, as if the feet had been cut off to be displayed like sculpture.

Whose feet were these? A doll's? A ghost's? Looking down from above didn't provide any answers. I had to figure out what was going on.

I gritted my teeth and continued ahead. Blood and footprints were on each step; the rivulet of blood had coasted down the stairs and reached the living room. When I got to the last step, all I could see was the physicality of real, human feet – bumpy toes, high arches, an anklet with a dangling charm hanging from the left ankle. My stomach flipped and I began hiccuping. I wanted to go back to my room.

I forced myself to continue. I hesitantly turned to the right, towards the front door. Blood formed an oblong swamp from under the stairs to the kitchen entrance. A woman lay neatly in the middle of it, her feet closer to the stairs and her head pointing towards the kitchen. She was wearing a voluminous white nightgown. Her legs were straight, her hands were clasped on her chest, and her long hair covered her face. She looked like a hallucination straight out of a delusional mind.

I took a step towards her, then another, stopping near her elbow. Her head had been jerked back and her neck was severed. Someone strong must have done this in one swift motion, with a sharp knife. The flesh around the wound was red, like a fish's gills. For a moment I thought I saw it throb. Dark irises met my eyes from under the tangled hair, ensnaring me, ordering me to come closer. I obeyed. I bent my stiff legs to crouch next to her. I reached out and pushed her hair out of the way, my hand trembling. I felt as though I were committing a crime.

'Yu-jin!'

Mother's voice again, the same one I had heard in my dream. This time it sounded faint. I couldn't breathe. Everything in my mind was crashing down; everything swam before my eyes. My spine crumpled and my feet slipped on the blood. I sat down heavily, breaking my fall with my hands.

The woman's eyes were bulging like a startled cat's. Droplets of blood clung to her long dark lashes. Her cheeks were thin and her jawline was pronounced. Her mouth was open in an O shape. Mother. The woman who had lost her husband and elder son sixteen years ago, who had clung to me and me alone since then, who'd given me her DNA.

Everything turned dark. I felt sick. I couldn't move. I couldn't breathe. Hot sand had filled my lungs. All I could do was wait for the light to turn on in my dark brain. I wanted it all to be a dream; I wanted my internal clock to ring its alarm and pull me out of this nightmare.

Time crawled by. Everything was chillingly quiet. The grandfather clock began to chime – six o'clock. Thirty minutes had passed since I'd woken up. This was when Mother would finish clattering in the kitchen and head up to my room with a smoothie made of milk, banana, pine nuts and walnuts.

The clock stopped chiming, but Mother was still lying next to me. Was this not a dream after all? Had Mother really called out to me last night? Was she calling for help? Or begging for her life?

My knees began knocking. My lower abdomen suddenly grew heavy. A sharp pain stabbed below my belly button. My bladder swelled, and I felt an urgent, intense need to pee. It was the same pressure I'd felt as a boy when I dreamed I couldn't move and the freight train was bearing down on me. I sat on my knees, pressed my thighs together and leant on them with both hands. Cold sweat trickled down my back.

*

Cold sweat trickled down my back. I felt stupid. My blankets and sheets were soaked through, my pyjamas were plastered to my bottom. Everything pulsated with the stench of urine. I'd made the same mistake three nights in a row. Mother would be annoyed. *What are you, a baby, wetting your bed all of a sudden?* She might sit us down and interrogate us. *Tell me honestly. Where did you go after school two days ago? What happened?*

My older brother, Yu-min, and I were in the first grade at a private elementary school near Sinchon. Mother drove us to school every morning on her way to work as an editor at a publishing house, which was nearby, behind Yonsei University. After school, we went to an art studio near her office, which was more of a day-care facility. It was close enough to school that we always walked. We often stopped to buy snacks and got distracted on our way there. Mother always worried about us. 'Don't go near the train tracks,' she would admonish. 'Stick to the main roads, okay?'

'Okay,' we said, but we didn't. Sometimes – no, often – we walked along the Seoul–Uijeongbu Line rails, our ankles sinking into the weeds. Of course, we didn't just walk. We came up with games and competed to see who would win. We played Scarecrow, where you spread your arms out and walked along the rail as you looked up at the sky; we did long jumps, where the person who leapt over the most cross-ties won. The best was Survival. We always tied, since we had the same weapons: Mother-approved toy sub-machine guns that made loud rat-tat-tat sounds without doing much else.

But three days ago, we had packed our backpacks with goggles and BB guns with plastic pellets that Father had brought for us from a business trip to America. Mother didn't like them, but the pellets didn't leave marks on our bodies, and she was more relaxed in the days when Yu-min was around. We were thrilled. We didn't pay any attention in class that day, as we were both thinking of Sinchon station.

As soon as school finished for the day, we put our goggles on and roamed the tracks and the adjacent wasteland that overlooked the station, shooting at each other; the one who was hit the most would lose. Mother and the art studio receded in our minds and we didn't realise how much time had passed. We'd used up all the bullets and the game was a draw but we weren't ready to call it quits, so we came up with a tiebreaker: a race to the station; the first one there would win.

One, two, three, we counted, and I shot ahead. I was a little ahead of Yu-min to begin with, but soon we were side by side. Near the end, I was behind him by a few strides. By the time I got to the last hurdle, the tracks, he was already running down the slope on the other side. A train was barrelling towards us from a distance. I knew I'd already lost, but I didn't give up. I leapt over the tracks. My backpack hit my elbow as I jumped, making the gun slip out of my sweaty hand. On the other side, I rolled to a stop, shot up and looked behind me. The train was still rushing forward, steam curling upwards from the engine. It was going to grind my gun to dust. Without thinking, I bolted back onto the tracks. By now, the train was close enough that I could see it was a freight train. But I couldn't give up and lose my gun.

'Yu-jin!' Yu-min screamed.

The horn blasted, but I didn't look at the train. I threw myself forward, my eyes only on the gun. As the train clattered and whooshed by, I rolled back down the slope, my gun in my hand.

I heard Yu-min shouting, 'Run!'

I took off at speed, in case the conductor stopped the train to come back and catch me, or a station agent watching from somewhere called the police. I felt electrified, fully expecting someone to grab me by the scruff of my neck.

I caught up with Yu-min in front of the art studio. My uniform was torn, my face was covered in dirt, and my hair was standing on end. The art teacher mended my trousers and washed my face. We insisted that we'd fallen in the yard while we were racing each other; we didn't tell anyone what had really happened.

The problem started that night. The moment I fell asleep, I found myself on the empty waste ground next to the tracks. I grabbed my gun as the train rushed towards me. When I opened my eyes, my bed and my body were drenched. The same thing happened the next night too. On the third night, I took off my wet pyjamas and threw them on my bed, then went into Yu-min's room, hugging my pillow. I slipped under the blankets and sidled next to my brother. I could smell the grassy scent of that afternoon. The stench of urine clinging to me vanished. I closed my eyes. I had the same dream, but this time, Yu-min appeared beside me and yelled, 'Train! Train's coming!' right before I was about to run onto the tracks.

I slept in his room for the rest of that year and continued until the spring I turned nine, the year he died.

Now, I wished I could crawl into Yu-min's bed again. He would help me deal with this nightmare, if only I could just lie down next to him.

He died a long time ago, a voice inside my head reminded me. *You have to handle it yourself.*

Outside, the wind howled, its reverberations burrowing into my ears. I could feel my pulse behind my eyes. I swallowed the spit that had pooled in my mouth. Yu-min was gone. I pressed my knees together to suppress the urge to pee, and sat up straight. I lifted my hand to bring it to Mother's face, but the world spun and I felt as though I might vomit. My shoulders were so stiff that my elbows would not move. The tips of my fingers trembled in the air. My body was frozen. The distance between my hand and her face seemed to stretch; it would be a million years later by the time I touched her.

It's not as if you are going to rip into her and eat her, the voice in my mind snapped again. *It's just to check if she's really not breathing, if her heart has really stopped, if her body is cold. Just put your hand out and touch her.*

I exhaled. I placed my middle finger under her nose and waited. I didn't detect anything. Her cheek, coated with dark purple blood, felt cold, dry and hard, like touching a stiffening mound of clay. I felt the middle of her chest, then moved my hand to the left and then to the right. I couldn't feel her heartbeat anywhere among her twelve pairs of ribs. I didn't feel any warmth. She really must be dead.

My shoulders drooped as despondency settled over me. What was it that I was hoping for? That she might still be alive? That this might all be a dream? It wasn't. I was in the middle of a murder scene.

'Everything's okay, right?' Hae-jin had asked. If I had known that something like this had happened, I wouldn't have emerged from my bed until he came home. It wouldn't have changed this 'something' into nothing, but at least I wouldn't have been sitting by myself next to Mother's body, shell-shocked, lost, not knowing what to do.

My eyes flitted around the flat. Everything looked strange. Questions echoed in my head. Who had done this? When? Why?

Someone must have snuck into the flat. Perhaps there really were thieves and muggers running rampant in Gundo; it seemed believable, aside from the fact that I'd just made it up.

It was true that people had begun to move into the newly developed city, though nearly half the flats were still empty. The area didn't have much infrastructure yet, with no shops, public transport or communal facilities. Given that only one police patrol division oversaw the two districts it encompassed, it would make sense if all kinds of criminals were running wild through the streets. Among them would be the sort of intruders who entered your building by simply walking through the front door behind a resident. The top floors had their own private roof decks that could be accessed both from inside the flat and from another door leading straight to the central stairwell facing the lift; so there was a sliding door to the roof garden in the bedroom and then there was another door – made of steel – from the roof garden into the stairwell; those units would understandably be their primary target. Such thieves must have visited our home last night.

They would have come through the roof door off the main stairwell. It wouldn't have been that difficult to pick that lock. After all, I had snuck out through that very door just a few hours before, leaving the deadbolt unlatched. Having entered, they would have ransacked the place – my room, the downstairs bedrooms and the living room. Mother, who was a light sleeper even when she took sleeping pills, would have woken up. She would have known it wasn't me or Hae-jin; she had a keen intuition. If she'd got out of bed, then . . .

Would she have opened her bedroom door to look out? Would she have gone out into the living room, calling, 'Who is it?' Or maybe she'd called me on my mobile first, but I hadn't seen her request for rescue because I'd left my phone at home. She would have tried Hae-jin next. That would explain why she called him last night. The thieves, who had searched through all the other rooms by that point, would have come into her room. What would she have done? Maybe she had pretended to be asleep. She might have run into her dressing room or the bathroom to hide. Or maybe she'd dashed onto her balcony. Maybe she'd screamed, 'Don't hurt me, please!' She might have run into the kitchen to resist, perhaps looking for a weapon. They might have caught her in front of the island, and they would have struggled. However it happened, it was clear that everything had gone down in front of the dividing wall between the kitchen and the stairs. It would have ended in just a few minutes. No matter how quick Mother was, no matter how weak that old goat of a thief was, it was still a woman against a man.

Maybe that was when I arrived outside our flat. I would have been in that zombie state I went into right before a seizure. That had to be when Mother fell, moaning my name – the moment I remembered like something out of a dream. I would have run in through the front door. She would have collapsed already, and the intruder would have advanced on me with the knife. For a moment I imagined myself fighting with him. It would have been hard for a single man to subdue me. He would have run up the stairs to escape via the steel door on the roof deck, but I would have caught him. Then what?

I didn't remember anything that would support any of this. In my mind, nothing remained from the hours after midnight. It still made sense, though. If I'd had a seizure after fighting the thief off, if I'd fallen into a deep sleep after managing to crawl into bed, it was possible I wouldn't remember those events. So what now? I needed to report it. I *had* to report it.

I crawled to the living room table and yanked the phone off the hook. Who should I call? An ambulance? The police? My fingers kept slipping off the buttons. Numbers bounced and danced in front of my eyes. It took so long for me to punch them out that I was automatically sent to directory assistance. A grunt leaked out of my throat. I rubbed my palms on my thighs and started over. 1. 1. 2. Carefully, digit by digit, I dialled the emergency number. I went over what I would say. Then I raised my head and froze. I saw in the glass doors leading to the balcony the man I'd caught sight of when I first got out of bed – the man covered in red. The line was ringing. I looked back at Mother. I suddenly realised what the police would see. A dead woman with her throat cut, lying in a pool of blood next to her dazed, bloodied son.

'Incheon Police Department. How may I help—'

I hung up. What would I say to them? That when I woke up, Mother was dead; that it looked like an intruder had killed her; that for some reason both my room and I were covered in blood, but please believe me when I say I didn't do it? Would they believe me? The voice in my head said, *You might as well tell them that she cut her own throat.*

For me to prove that there had been an intruder, there had to be one of two things: the intruder himself, or his body. The only traces of him were on the stairs and the landing. If he had been injured in our fight, he would still be in the flat somewhere. Or if he had hidden and died overnight, his body would be here. Then everything would make sense: why I woke up covered in blood, why there was so much blood on the landing *and* in the living room, why I couldn't remember what happened after midnight, and all the rest.

I returned the phone to its cradle. Blood pounded through my veins. My thoughts began to advance rapidly. My hands and feet twitched. My neural circuits whirred. I thought of all the hiding places in the flat. It would be somewhere warm where he could lie down, somewhere hidden where he couldn't be found easily. There were at least ten places that met those criteria.

I stood up and tiptoed to Mother's bedroom door, holding my breath. I turned the handle, kicked the door open and rushed in.

The room was pristine. Nothing looked out of the ordinary: there was no blood, no footprints, no evidence of a fight. The double curtains hanging over the glass balcony doors were closed tightly. The bed didn't look like it had been slept in. The pillows were propped neatly against the headboard and the white wool blanket was taut and smooth. The lamp and clock were in their usual spots on the bedside table and the square cushions stood primly on the couch by the foot of the bed. It was orderly, the way it always looked after Mother straightened her room upon waking.

The only thing that was even a little bit disturbed was the writing desk. A single ballpoint pen was on the edge, and the tall leather chair had been pushed back. A brown blanket, still neatly folded, was on the floor below, as though it had slid off the arm of the chair.

I leapt over the bed and yanked open the curtains. Nothing. No one behind the curtains or outside on the balcony. I opened each of the built-in cupboards. The first had pillows, cushions and curtains; the middle one contained enough sheets and blankets to outfit at least ten groups of students on a school trip, and in the third were boxes holding small belongings. I opened the door to her dressing room, which led to the study and to Hae-jin's room, and turned on the light. It was the same as the bedroom.

The obsessively clean white marble floor shone like an ice rink, the obsessively neat dressing table had jars and tubes lined up in a neat row, the obsessively organised drawers had clothes stacked precisely on top of one another, and the obsessively orderly wardrobe had garments painstakingly separated by season and sheathed in individual bags. There was no hint of the thief. The bathroom was much the same. The floor was dry and spotless and the light scent of shampoo perfumed the clean air.

I opened the door to the study, which held some of Father's old belongings and Mother's books. It looked the same as it always did. I went back out through the living room and walked into the kitchen. That, too, was clean. No footprints or blood anywhere. The blood was only around Mother's body. If that was where she had been killed, everything nearby should have been sprayed with blood.

I looked around the rest of the flat. The balcony behind the kitchen, Hae-jin's bedroom and bathroom. Everything appeared normal. On my way out of Hae-jin's room, I glanced around one last time at his bed, television, wardrobe and desk, his workout gear hanging on his chair.

Outside of work obligations or travel, Hae-jin always came home to sleep, even on nights he went out, even though Mother didn't insist. But last night . . . last night of all nights, he'd stayed out. Then he'd called me around the time I usually woke up to ask if everything was all right. As if he'd known something was up. To lure me downstairs, perhaps.

A script wrote itself instantly in my mind. Hae-jin comes home after I fall asleep post-seizure. For some unknown reason, he attacks Mother. Mother flees, but he catches her and kills her. He comes upstairs, tracking footprints and blood all over the place, and covers me with blood to frame me for the crime. Then he saunters out of the flat.

I quickly backed away from that thought, and as I closed the door to his room, I put it out of my head for good. That wasn't possible. It was insane. I knew Hae-jin. We'd lived in the same flat for ten years. It was more likely that Mother would kill *him*; that was the kind of person Kim Hae-jin was. The most rebellious thing he had done in his entire life was to go and see an adult-rated move before graduating from middle school. But even then, he'd asked Mother to come along as a guardian, and invited me too.

I slid open the door to the entrance foyer. Four pairs of shoes were in a neat row: Mother's slippers, Hae-jin's slippers, Mother's white trainers, and my wet, muddy black running shoes. I never left those shoes by the front door. I hid them in the ceiling of my bathroom and retrieved them only when I went out through the door to the roof. If I'd come home via the roof the way I usually did, there was no way they would be here. So I *had* come in through the front door last night.

Strangely, Mother's trainers were also wet. Not just damp, but soaked. I tried to remember what had happened when I came back last night after the party. When I was struggling to unlock the door, Mother had come out wearing those trainers. Were they wet? I couldn't remember, but Mother wasn't the kind of person who would shove her feet into wet shoes. That meant she had gone out again afterwards. But she couldn't have taken the car. She must have run around in the rain like I had. It was the only way her shoes could be this wet.

I closed the door and turned around. I noticed a black Gore-Tex jacket and quilted vest crumpled in the corner. I'd been wearing those last night over my sweater. Why were they here?

Maybe this was what happened: I ran through the front door, hearing Mother's scream. I discovered her collapsed in a pool of blood in front of the kitchen. I took off my wet jacket and vest and placed them carefully by the entrance foyer door, then came inside. That made no sense. That made the least sense of all the things that had made no sense since I'd woken up this morning.

I was picking up the jacket and vest when I heard 'Hakuna Matata', the song from *The Lion King*. Mother had recently changed her ringtone. It sounded like it was coming from the living room.

I rushed in, jacket and vest still in hand, and spotted her phone on the edge of the coffee table. I hadn't noticed it when I'd called the police. She often left it there. An unexpected name was on the screen: *Hye-won*. Why was Auntie calling so early?

It rang half a dozen times. Then the cordless began to ring. Auntie again. It was 6.54. Hae-jin and Auntie were doing the same thing, separated only by an hour and a half. A thought popped into my head. Did Mother call Auntie last night, too?

I picked up Mother's mobile. I knew as much about her as she did about me, so I was able to unlock her phone. According to the call list, she had rung Hae-jin at 1.30 a.m., but they hadn't talked. She'd called Auntie at 1.31 a.m., and they had spoken for three minutes. So she had been alive at least until 1.34 a.m.

I thought back to last night, back to the point in time where my memory was the clearest. At midnight, I had been at the pedestrian crossing by the sea wall where I'd seen the woman getting off the last Ansan-bound bus. That crossing was about two kilometres from home. It would have taken me twenty minutes if I'd walked, fifteen if I'd alternated between running and walking, and ten if I'd run the whole way. I remembered running; if I'd run the entire way home, I would have entered our building around 12.10 a.m. and would have been at the front door of the flat by 12.15. Even if I'd walked up the stairs, which I didn't remember doing, it would have been before 12.30 a.m.

So I'd walked into the living room around 12.30 a.m., and Mother had died after 1.34 a.m. between the living room and the kitchen.

My brain felt tangled. It was impossible to figure out what had happened. The intruder disappeared from my conjectures. Maybe I'd missed something important, something that would tie all of this together.

With my jacket and vest and Mother's mobile still in my hands, I turned towards Mother herself, lying neatly in the pool of blood, looking as if she were asleep. For the first time I noticed something unnatural about the way she was positioned. A person who bleeds out from a massive wound to the throat wouldn't have time to rake her hair forward to cover her face and place her hands carefully on her chest before dying.

I went over to her. I now noticed things that hadn't registered before. It looked as though a big, heavy object had been dragged down the stairs, smearing the blood. An object like Mother's body. Next to the smears were footprints heading both up and down. Someone had murdered Mother on the landing and dragged her down to arrange her like this.

But why? Who had done this? If not an intruder or Hae-jin, the only other possibility . . . I looked at Mother, terrified, and shook my head. I remembered what my mind had thrown up earlier: *You might as well tell them that she cut her own throat.*

That *could* have happened, I thought. For some reason she cuts her own throat on the landing, and for some reason I can't stop her. Because I'm about to have a seizure. She collapses and tumbles down the stairs. I come downstairs and move her to where she is now, which is probably the bare minimum I can do before my seizure takes over. Maybe I put her in a sleeping position, since I'm dazed and unable to think, then bid her goodnight like I do every night.

I felt a glimmer of hope. If I could figure out why she cut her own throat and why I couldn't stop her, I could call the police without worrying about becoming a suspect. I could figure it out. Or at least I could make it make sense. I had always had a gift for reshaping a scene to make it comprehensible, though Mother disparaged this skill, calling it 'lying'.

I ran up the stairs, taking care not to step in the blood or footprints. The blood on the landing was beginning to congeal. The footprints were disorderly, stamped in every direction. Someone had paced around in confusion.

'Yu-jin,' Mother called from somewhere in my memory, in a low voice, suppressing emotion, the kind that forced a response. I stopped and looked over at the solid wood-panelled wall, now stained deep purple. I could see myself leaning back against it, cornered. I stopped breathing.

'Where were you?'

When was this memory from? Last night? When I came back from the sea wall? A faint light flickered at the bottom of my muddy consciousness, but when I blinked, my own ghostly form against the wall disappeared. Mother's voice vanished, too.

I continued up the stairs and followed the dried foot-prints along the marble floor of the hallway. Even though I placed my heels purposefully, I felt as if I were slipping and sliding. I turned the bloody door handle of my own room, walked inside, and stood at the foot of my bed.

'Stop right there.' Mother's voice came again.

I stood next to the footprints; they were the same size as my feet. I looked cautiously around the room, at the sliding door still open a crack, the blinds pushed to one side, the light on the pergola blinking in the fog, the neat desk, the chair draped with the comfortable clothes I wore at home, the cordless phone on my bedside table, the pillow and blankets drenched in blood. Mother's mobile slid out of my hand and fell to the floor. All the clues were pointing to one person. The 'intruder', the 'murderer', was me.

I perched stiffly on the edge of my bed. Why would I have done it? I came home around 12.30 a.m. last night. If

I'd bumped into her then, she probably held me hostage for a long time, pressing to find out what I had been doing. She would have figured out that I was on the verge of having a seizure, and she would have realised I wasn't taking my meds. Her speciality, gentle scolding, would have begun. But that still didn't explain why I would have killed her. How many mothers would still be alive if their sons murdered them when they got caught doing something they shouldn't?

I slumped over. Nobody would side with me. I needed someone who would believe me, no matter what anyone said, no matter what kind of evidence they could dig up. I looked down at the black Gore-Tex jacket, the words *Private Lesson* embossed on the back in blue. Would he believe me? Would he help me?

It was August, the day after I'd taken the exam to enter law school. I'd taken a Mokpo-bound train at Hae-jin's invitation. Since May, he had been part of a crew filming on an isolated island called Imja in Sinan County. Lonely and bored, he had called nearly every day to see what was going on. If he'd had something to drink, he'd call once an hour and ask, 'What's up?' Each time, he insisted that I should come for a visit after my exams. 'I want to show you something.'

'What is it?'

'You'll see when you get here.'

I didn't take him seriously. Everything annoyed me at the time, because I had the worst headaches and all I was doing was studying; I didn't have time to even think about

Imja Island. More than anything, I didn't want Mother on my back. Though I was twenty-five, I'd never travelled alone, not even backpacking or going abroad to learn a foreign language like everyone else. Mother went so far as to ensure that I went to work at the local government office instead of letting me escape for military service. All for the same reason that my curfew was 9 p.m. – to prevent my having a seizure out in the world all by myself.

I was at the dining table when Hae-jin called. 'Tomorrow's the last day of shooting,' he said. 'You have to come. You can stay over one night, and then we'll go home together.'

I hesitated and glanced at Mother.

Even though he couldn't see me, he understood instantly. He asked me to put Mother on the line. 'Let me try.'

Hae-jin was persuasive. Mother listened without pro- testing, then said, 'All right.' She didn't stop her nagging, though. *Don't forget to take your medicine, don't drink, don't get in people's way* . . . On the way to Gwangmyeong sta- tion, she added, 'Don't go into the deep water,' as if she'd completely forgotten that I'd once been a competitive swimmer.

Everything was fine all the way to Mokpo and on the intercity bus to Sinan. The symptoms started when the ferry left Jeomam Quay. For the twenty minutes it took to get to Imja Island, I was surrounded by a strong metallic scent, and I hallucinated that the sun was literally burning my eyes. I couldn't tell if I was about to have a seizure or not; maybe I was just getting sunstroke.

If I had been taking my meds, it would have been

obvious. But I'd stopped taking them two days before the exam, for the first time since the episode I'd had when I was fifteen. I was going to start taking them again the night after my exams, but I changed my mind when Hae-jin called. I decided I would wait until I returned home from Imja Island. What's two more days? I thought. I wanted to revel in my true self, freed from my usual constraints.

But by the time we docked at Imja Island, my hallucinations were so severe that I could barely keep my eyes open. I got in a cab, the metallic smell permeating everything around me. Sweat was running down my back, but I was freezing. I now understood that I was going to have a seizure but I was too far away to go back home. I had to get to Hae-jin's place as fast as possible. I told the driver to rush to Hauri Harbour.

'Let's give it a go,' the driver said.

I felt that I was drifting in and out of consciousness as the car flew along the roads.

'Excuse me.' The driver had turned around in his seat and was shaking my knee. 'We're here.'

I opened my eyes. We were at the harbour. I managed to pay and get out of the cab. I didn't have to go far; this was where they were shooting. Two men were running along the top of the tetrapod-covered sea wall as the camera followed them, a large truck spewing water over the actors. People were huddled around monitors. Villagers had gathered around the perimeter of the shoot to watch. I stopped about ten metres away. I needed to lie down, but I couldn't move. Hot white light trapped me. The world disappeared. The last thing I heard was Hae-jin yelling, 'Yu-jin!'

When I came to, I was lying down. My vision was still fuzzy but I knew right away that the brown eyes that met mine were Hae-jin's. 'Are you okay?'

'Yeah,' I croaked, and a headache gripped me. It wasn't the usual sharp stabbing from behind my eyes but a heavy pain pressing on my head.

'Can you see me?'

I saw the beach umbrella above his head. Something soft was under mine. My trousers were damp. I must have pissed myself during the seizure. A black jacket was draped over me.

'Are you hurt?'

Everything hurt, even my jaw; maybe I'd been grinding my teeth. It must have been a bad one. I could hear people on the other side of the umbrella. I could see myself collapsing in front of them, Hae-jin running over, grabbing the umbrella to give me privacy, a cushion to prop my head up, and clothes to conceal my lack of bladder control. I wanted to go home.

'Can you get up?'

I sat up. We went to Hae-jin's place, which was near the docks. I showered and changed, while Hae-jin packed his things and called a cab. I had arrived just as they were finishing the shoot, and the only thing left was the wrap party.

I knew what films meant to Hae-jin – this was what he'd dreamed of since he was twelve, maybe even younger. It had kept his spirits up while his alcoholic grandfather was raising him, and had given him something to live for when he'd lost his grandfather and become an orphan. These three months at Imja Island were the first step toward his dreams; he must have wanted to stay and celebrate.

I knew all of this, but I didn't stop him. I didn't want to go home by myself; I didn't even think I could go back outside. A strange chill settled under my ribs. I sat curled up in the corner of his room, wrapped in his jacket, until the cab came. The jacket smelled like something I hadn't smelled in a long time – the grass on the waste ground near Sinchon station, from back when I used to wet my bed.

An hour later, we were sitting on the deck of the old ferry, heading back to Jeomam Quay. We didn't talk much. When Hae-jin asked, 'Are you hungry?' I shook my head, and when he asked, 'Are you feeling better now?' I nodded. The evening sun hung between the rocky islands that flanked our passage home. Red waves blazed and bobbed under the orange sky. The spray of water behind us and the strong sea breeze were red, too. The ferry sliced through the flames like a speedboat.

'That sunset's killer, isn't it?' Hae-jin said.

I got up to look out over the ocean. I unzipped the jacket and breathed the hot wind deep into my lungs. The chill in my chest seemed to melt away.

Hae-jin came and stood beside me. 'Remember when I said I wanted to show you something? This is it.'

I turned and faced him. His eyes were smiling kindly. Hae-jin's smile was like a gift to me. While Mother poured endless fear into my bloodstream, Hae-jin warmed me like the sun, always on my side.

*

I wanted to believe Hae-jin would be on my side today, too. In fact, I believed he would be. I stood, picked up the home phone from my bedside table and dialled his number. It began to ring. Something that had fallen between my bed and the bedside table caught my eye. I bent down to pull it out – a straight razor with its blade open. Dark blood was crusted on the long wooden handle and the sleek blade.

'Hello? Mother?'

Hae-jin's voice receded. I stared at the blade, stunned.

'Yu-jin?'

With my fingernail, I scraped off the blood at the end of the handle. Familiar initials appeared.

H. M. S.

Han Min-seok. Father's razor. I had found it years ago in a box in the study and brought it up to my room. I had hardly any memories of him. I didn't remember his mannerisms or his voice, and even his face was fuzzy in my mind. I remembered only that his cheeks and chin were covered in dark stubble, and that every morning he shaved with this very razor in front of the bathroom mirror. A frequently constipated child, I would be on the toilet, straining, my chin in my hands, watching his stubble disappear with the suds. I liked the sound of the razor scraping and sliding along his flesh. Once, I asked him what shaving felt like. I wasn't positive but I thought he said something to the effect of: *It feels like you're pulling up the hair embedded deep in the skin, and it makes you feel clean and fresh.* He said you needed to learn how to use a straight razor properly – your chin wouldn't emerge unscathed until you figured it out – but that the feeling it gave didn't compare with any other razor, annoying as it was to keep the blade sharp.

I remembered what I said after that. I asked if I could have it after he was dead. I recalled his foamy reaction: a soap bubble flaring from one of his nostrils, his eyes turning round and big like full moons. He was laughing. Emboldened, I asked him to promise me. Father said: *Sure, I don't know when I'll die, but when I do, I'll definitely leave it to you.* We did pinky swears and even pressed our thumbs together to seal the promise. Mother couldn't have known about that, and when Father died, I didn't feel like explaining it. I just took the razor without telling anyone.

'Hello? Hello?' Hae-jin was getting louder on the other end of the phone.

'It's me,' I managed to croak.

'What ...' Hae-jin grew quiet, then annoyed. 'Why didn't you say anything? You nearly gave me a heart attack.'

'I'm listening. Go on.'

He snorted. 'Go on? You're the one who called me.'

Right. I'd called him. I was going to say I needed help, that I thought I was in serious trouble. I pointed the razor up so the blade stood vertically under my chin. I'd never once used it to shave. After all, I wasn't as hairy as Father, and I could make do with an electric shaver. In fact I only started growing light facial hair when I was twenty-one. It wasn't that I was saving the razor for a special occasion, either; I just kept it hidden in a panel in my bathroom ceiling, out of Mother's sight. I'd never taken it with me anywhere until last night, when

I went out of the roof door with it in the pocket of my sweatpants.

'Yu-jin?' Hae-jin prompted.

I found myself at a loss for words. Before I'd found this razor, there had been so many possible explanations. But now . . .

'Where are you?' I managed to ask.

'I just got to the train station. I'm not feeling that great, so I made myself some ramen before I left.'

He'd probably had two. He always had two ramen when he was hung-over, a habit he'd inherited from his grand-father, who was drunk seven days a week. So Hae-jin was still in Sangam-dong.

'Why, is something up?' he asked.

'No.' I changed my mind. 'Yes.' It couldn't hurt to buy some time. 'I have a favour to ask.'

Hae-jin was silent, waiting.

'Do you remember the raw fish restaurant in Yeongjong Island? The one we went to for Mother's birthday?'

'Oh yeah. Léon or something, right?'

'No, Léon was where we had coffee after. It's Kkosil's, about fifty metres further in. At the end of the beach.'

'Oh yeah.'

'So last night, after the drinks party, we went there for another round.' They say that a normal person lies on average eighteen times an hour. I probably come in a little higher than average, what with my difficulty with honesty. My extra output makes me very good at it, able to spin any kind of story in a believable way. 'I left my mobile there, but I can't go and pick it up right now. I have to send some documents to the dean this morning, and today's the day they announce the law school entrance exam results. I have to be home to check online.'

'Today's the day already?'

'Yeah.'

Hae-jin gave me the answer I wanted. 'No problem. I'll swing by on my way home.'

'They won't be open until after ten, though.'

'I'll just wait at Léon and get some coffee.'

'I'm happy to pay for a cab,' I said, in the hope of finding out how Hae-jin would return.

'Are you insane? A cab from Yeongjong Island?'

Good. He would rather get the bus. Just as I thanked him and was about to hang up, Hae-jin asked, 'So, is Mother up yet?'

I pressed the end button, pretending not to have heard. I thought about Mother lying in the living room. The blood could be explained in different ways, but the discovery of the razor was proof of a singular truth. It had been in my jacket last night, and now it was under my bed. How would Hae-jin take this? How would he take Mother's death? Would he be shocked or sad or enraged? Would he believe me? Would he still be on my side?

Eleven years ago, I was fourteen and Hae-jin was fifteen. We were about to graduate from middle school. Following Mother's wishes, I had selected a humanities high school where I could continue swimming alongside my studies. Hae-jin, whose grades were good enough to get him into an exclusive high school, instead selected an arts and culture vocational school. He'd decided on that path on his own, refusing to listen to his teacher, who tried to persuade him to aim higher. He was swayed by the fact that he would receive a full scholarship from the vocational school in addition to a living stipend, and that going there would help him achieve his dream of working in film. He didn't have much choice: at the time, he was basically on his own. His parents had died in a car accident when he was three, and his grandfather, who had taken him in and brought him up, had been in the hospital for several months with cirrhosis and renal failure; nobody knew if he would ever get better. Hae-jin was the busiest student in the world: he went to school every day, worked in the evenings at a petrol station for 2,900 won an hour, and slept in the hospital by his grandfather's side.

Hae-jin and his grandfather weren't well off even before the illness. They had been making ends meet with the government aid his grandfather received, and the little he earned collecting paper for recycling. Until recently, Hae-jin hadn't needed to get a job: though his grandfather was an infamous drunk, he wasn't so unconscionable as to rely on his young grandson to support them. In fact, he insisted, 'You focus on school, I'll take care of everything else.' But then he'd collapsed.

I was busy at that time, too. Having been selected as a member of the national swimming team, I was in a special winter training camp to prepare for the junior world championships in New Zealand, and because of my schedule, Hae-jin and I couldn't hang out much. Mother updated me on how he and his grandfather were doing each day when she came to the pool. It seemed that she was going to the hospital regularly with food.

On the last day of 2005, the coach cut the training session short and gave everyone the afternoon off. He told us to go home and get pampered by our mothers, and come back refreshed the next day at 9 a.m. I don't know how she'd heard, but Mother was already waiting for me outside. She looked happy and excited. Her straight hair was grazing the shoulders of a white overcoat I'd never seen before, and she was even wearing make-up.

I fastened my seat belt. 'Are you going somewhere?'

'Dongsung-dong,' she said, which didn't explain anything.

We arrived in front of the hospital where Hae-jin's grandfather was being treated. I was confused. Hae-jin ran out. I unbuckled my seat belt. I had read the situation to mean that Mother was going somewhere in Dongsung-dong, so I was to hang out with Hae-jin.

'No, don't get out,' Mother said.

Hae-jin grinned at me and got in the back seat.

'Happy New Year,' Mother said to him, a day early.

'You too, Mother.' Hae-jin pulled something out from behind his back and handed it to her. A heart-shaped red lollipop as big as her face, with a message written in white: *The apple of my eye.*

A smile spread across Mother's face as she took it, her cheeks flushing and her eyes downcast. As far as I knew, that was the first time Hae-jin had called her Mother. Maybe she was moved by that, or maybe she liked that she was the apple of his eye. In any case, I'd never seen that expression on her face.

'Did your grandfather give you permission to come?' Mother asked, carefully laying the lollipop on the dashboard.

Hae-jin grinned. 'He thinks I've gone to work.'

Mother smiled back, meeting his eyes in the rear-view mirror. There was still no explanation of where we were going, and why. I didn't ask; since she'd said Dongsung-dong earlier, I figured that was it. Hae-jin asked me about training camp and practice, but I was consistent with my monosyllabic answers: good, no, yeah. Then Mother took over the conversation, asking about his grandfather's illness and discussing books or movies that only the two of them knew about. The car weaved through hellish traffic before arriving at Daehangno. Mother circled a car park a few times before finally landing a spot.

'Let's go,' she said.

We got out and walked the streets, which were adorned with twinkling fairy lights. There were so many people on the footpath that it was difficult to walk side by side. Mother was jostled and almost fell. I reached out to help, but Hae-jin was already by her side, holding her up. When she was knocked back again a few steps later, he wrapped an arm around her shoulders and walked alongside her. I had no choice but to fall behind.

A little later, we arrived at a quiet Italian restaurant. I still didn't know why we were in Dongsung-dong, but I didn't ask. Mother raised her glass of juice and said it was bittersweet: she was one year older now, and Hae-jin and I were also growing older. I assumed we were just celebrating the new year. I don't remember what the food was like. It must have been mediocre. Or maybe it was my mood that was mediocre.

Hae-jin and I had met two years before, and ever since then, Mother had seemed to think of him as more than just her son's friend. She was always looking at him in moments that should have revolved around me – whether it was at my birthday party or a school event – watching him with soft, gentle eyes, the same eyes I'd seen every day of my childhood, aimed at my brother.

When it was just Hae-jin and me together, we were the best of friends. It was like that when it was just Mother and me, too. Like they both lived to be with me. But now that we were all together, I felt like the third wheel. I didn't like how this atmosphere had formed so naturally. I felt like a dick for resenting their bond, which only made me feel worse.

We left the restaurant about an hour later. The two of them led the way through the crowd, which seemed to have doubled since we'd gone inside. We stopped at a shop. Mother bought us each a checked scarf and slung them around our necks. Mine was green and Hae-jin's was yellow. She said they were New Year gifts. She said we looked great in them, but her gaze was fixed on Hae-jin.

Next, they stopped in front of the art-film cinema Hypertech Nada, which had a sign over the entrance: *Nada's Final Proposal*. Mother went to the ticket booth.

'What are we doing here?' I asked Hae-jin.

'What?' Hae-jin laughed. 'You came all the way here without knowing why?'

The air had turned warmer. My scarf felt tight. I took it

off and sat down. How was I supposed to know what we were doing if nobody said anything? Did they think I was a mind-reader?

Nada's Final Proposal was a film festival that played all of the year's best films that hadn't done well at the box office. That day it was showing a Brazilian movie called *City of God*. It turned out that Hae-jin had suggested coming here; he'd wanted to see the film when it opened, but had given up when he realised it was adult-rated. When he'd heard that it was being screened again at Nada, he said, he'd thought of Mother, who could accompany him as a guardian.

He was right about that: we settled in our seats without anyone stopping us. The movie was hilarious and effervescent; I soon forgot my gloominess. Set against the backdrop of Rio de Janeiro's favelas, which teemed with poverty, drugs and crime, the story followed a group of young gang members. It was also a coming-of-age story about two boys who went down different paths, one becoming a photographer and the other ruling the streets.

I started laughing from the opening scene, when a chicken escaped its certain death. I giggled throughout the film. When Li'l Zé ran into the motel and gunned everyone down, I even chortled out loud. That was when I noticed I was the only person in the cinema who was laughing. I realised that Mother was staring at me. Her eyes, glistening like water, were asking, *What's so funny?*

After the movie, she was quiet as we walked back to the car. Hae-jin also looked straight ahead without talking. I followed behind. I didn't know what their problem was.

'That was disturbing,' Mother said once she started the car. 'I can't believe that's based on a true story. Life can be so sad.'

So that was why she had been looking at me oddly in the cinema. It had been fun and exciting for me, but it must have been an unsettling and depressing movie. Which part was supposed to be unsettling or depressing? I wondered.

'Happy stories aren't usually based in reality,' Hae-jin replied after a moment.

I turned to look at him.

'Having hope doesn't make things less awful,' he continued. 'Things aren't so clear-cut. People are complicated.' He met my gaze. His eyes were asking, *Right?*

I didn't understand what he was talking about. He was a few months older than me, but he seemed ten years older and a foot or two taller at that. It was almost as though he was Mother's peer.

'Do you think the world is unfair?' Mother asked.

Hae-jin paused again. 'I have to believe that it will become more equal at some point. I mean, if we work towards it.' He looked out of the window.

Mother watched him through the rear-view mirror. I turned back to the front.

'How did you like the movie?' she finally asked him, when we were waiting at a red light near Gwanghwamun.

'I read a review saying that if Tarantino had done the *Godfather*, it would have been something like that. I think I know what they meant,' Hae-jin said.

Did that mean he liked it? Or hated it?

'So you liked it?' Mother said.

'Yes.' Hae-jin didn't say anything after that. Maybe he was still thinking about the film.

As we drove on, the bell at Bosingak began to ring, marking midnight. It was quiet in the car, each of us immersed in our own thoughts, until we pulled up at the hospital.

'Thank you for today,' Hae-jin said as he opened the door.

Mother followed him out of the car. From inside, I watched as Hae-jin bowed. She held out a hand for a handshake, as if they were equals. Hae-jin hesitated before taking it. The interaction couldn't have lasted more than five seconds, but they seemed to be confirming something inexpressible, something I couldn't understand.

Mother returned to the car. Hae-jin stood there, his yellow scarf fluttering in the dark. I realised that I'd lost mine. I had held it in my hand after I took it off, but I must have let go of it at some point during the movie. Maybe it was when I was laughing but then met Mother's eyes, the moment when Li'l Zé gunned people down in time to samba. A line from the film came to mind: 'The exception becomes the rule.'

I was Mother's only son. That was the rule. The exception happened soon afterwards. Hae-jin became her adopted son the following March, taking Yu-min's place. The exception had become the rule.

I looked back down at the razor in my hand. Clues to who had killed Mother were all over the place, including the decisive evidence of the murder weapon. Without a single clue pointing to a different conclusion, I would be implicated. How would Hae-jin take this? No matter what he asked me, I could only answer one way – I don't remember a thing. The time-worn excuse made by thousands of criminals over thousands of years.

Would he believe me? Or would he call the authorities? Would he tell me to give myself up? I couldn't do that. But all of that would come later. What I needed now was time to think. I needed to find evidence that made sense. If I really had killed my mother, shouldn't I at least know why?

'I should have done away with you.' Mother's voice. It wasn't in my head; it was coming from behind me. I turned towards the sliding door to the roof deck. I saw her standing out there, her hair in a ponytail, wearing a white nightgown, her feet bare. The way she must have looked before she died. I remembered now. She didn't have a speck of blood on her. Her throat was intact.

'You ...' She glared at me, her eyes burning. Scarlet veins popped in the bluish whites of her eyes. 'You, Yu-jin ...'

I flinched and stepped back towards my bed.

'You don't deserve to live.'

My pulse thumped at my temples. My hand gripped the razor tightly. 'Why? What did I do?'

She didn't answer. Fog coursed forward like an avalanche and swallowed her. I looked around my room at the blood, the footprints, the stained blankets. All of this happened after she died. The words I'd just heard – Mother had spat them out when she was still alive. Was it because I'd gone out in the middle of the night? Why would something so inconsequential make her tell me I didn't deserve to live?

My head began to pound. Heat flared up the back of my head. Black spots danced in front of me. I felt dizzy. I turned round and went into the bathroom. I tossed the razor into the sink and filled it up with cold water. I dunked my head into the water to cool it down, so that I could keep my focus and not get discouraged or angry.

'Tomorrow, Mum. I'll tell you everything in the morning.' That was my voice. I looked up and met my own eyes in the mirror. Tell her what in the morning?

I stared at my blood-crusted head and the blood that had dissolved in the water and was now streaming down my face. The sink turned scarlet and the razor shimmered like the shadow of the moon. A thought glimmered in the pitch-black darkness of my head. Maybe . . . I looked down at the razor, aghast. It couldn't be. I blinked the bloody water out of my eyes. But maybe . . . I shoved my hand into the cold water and fished the razor out. Maybe.

I ran out of the bathroom. Before I could change my mind, I opened my bedroom door and stepped into the hallway. I went down the stairs as slowly as possible. One, two, three, I counted, my gaze fixed on my toes. Four, five, six. Counting usually helped me to keep control and cut through distracting thoughts, but it wasn't working this time. My whole body was alert to the orders being issued by my sympathetic nervous system. It was as if a beehive were stuck to my forehead: my thoughts bounced around, and noises of all frequencies funnelled into my ears – the sound of the river swirling, the spray of water, the wind rattling the door to the roof, Mother's voice lowering into a moan, 'Yu-jin . . .'

There were countless reasons why I should toss the razor aside and return to my room. I was tired, my eyes hurt, my head pounded, my thoughts were muddled, I was scared that I was actually going crazy. But I forced myself to continue down the stairs. I held my breath and stepped into the living room. Mother greeted me, her eyes wide and staring, her mouth open, her cheeks and jaw smudged in red, her neck clotted with blood.

I clutched the razor, which kept slipping out of my hand. I knelt next to her. The razor had been something to remember Father by, but now it had morphed into something completely different. It threatened to open a door I wasn't sure I wanted to go through. I swallowed hard. My throat was scratchy. My mind taunted me: *Are you shaking right now?*

I was. A blue chill pressed on the nape of my neck; I felt like it would suffocate me to death. I wanted to run away. I wanted to take fistfuls of aspirin and sedatives and lie down. Fuck. What was I supposed to do?

Run, my mind offered. *Nobody knows she's dead yet. You know where her bank card is, and what her PIN is, from doing all those errands over the years. Take out a load of cash. You have more than a year before your passport expires. If you run to the other side of the world right now, no one will stop you. Whatever happens after that isn't your problem.*

But I had to know. A conclusion arrived at via clues had no meaning; I had to hear it from myself. Was there someone inside of me other than the 'me' I believed I was?

52

I couldn't continue living the way I had without knowing what that someone had done, even if my life would be turned completely upside down because of it.

I studied the wound below Mother's jaw while trying not to meet her fixed gaze. Reddish-black film covered the incision from under her left ear to her right. I wiped it away with a finger. A long, deep wound appeared.

I closed my eyes, taming my leaping breath, and summoned the boy from long ago. I brought out swimming champion Han Yu-jin, bent over at the starting block, waiting for the signal. The boy beyond the reach of Auntie and Mother's watchful eyes, focusing only on the moment of flinging his body into the air over the water. My heartbeat began to slow. The goose bumps on the back of my neck settled back into my skin. The breath that had been trapped at the top of my throat moved easily in, then out.

I didn't hesitate any longer. I opened my eyes. I grabbed Mother's jaw with my left hand. I shoved the blade under her left ear, where the wound started. The incision sucked the razor in without resistance. It was as if the wound itself had moved, gripping onto the blade. The din in my head vanished. Quiet came over me.

My hand moved automatically, without hesitation, following the gaping wound fluidly. Each motion felt perfectly familiar – the soft resistance of the inner flesh, the smooth passage of the blade. The razor slid past the chin and arrived under the right ear in one easy swoop.

My visual field narrowed, as though a dark screen had lowered at either temple. Fragmented images and expressions came to me: long dancing hair, a cheek contorting, pupils dilating and contracting, lips moving as if to say something. Soon, reality was completely snuffed out. Heavy darkness pressed in from all sides and loomed over me. The door to my memories, which had been so firmly closed, was opening.

From inside that door, Mother called, 'Yu-jin.'

'Yu-jin,' Mother called from the front door, her voice low and flat. I stood silently in front of the steel door to the roof. I didn't have the strength to make a sound. Exhaustion weighed me down. I felt as if I were asleep on my feet.

'Yu-jin!' This time her voice was two pitches higher, as though she knew I was standing there.

From the seventh floor, Hello, that stupid dog, was barking, as he did every single time I used the main stairwell.

'Yes,' I called. I pocketed the key to the roof door and went down the stairs.

She was standing with her arms crossed, leaning against the railing of the main stairwell, watching me come down. The front door was half open. A yellow glow from inside the flat illuminated her from the side. Hello kept yapping downstairs.

'Where were you?' Mother's thin lips looked blue and cold. She was in a white nightgown and slippers, her spindly legs bare.

I stopped four steps from the bottom. 'I went for a run.' My tongue felt thick, as though I had woken up from an anaesthetic.

'Come down here. Take off your mask and answer me properly.'

I took the mask off and put it in my jacket pocket. I shoved both hands in my pockets and went down the rest of the stairs on shaky legs.

As Mother scanned me from head to toe, it felt as though her gaze could skin me alive.

'I said I went for a run.' I looked back at her.

She pressed her lips together, seemingly troubled. Agitated, perhaps, or maybe angry or sad. The one thing I knew was that whatever she was feeling, she was tamping it down before it exploded. 'Why were you sneaking in via the roof terrace?'

'I didn't want to wake you up,' I answered, though I didn't expect her to accept that explanation.

'Come inside.'

My toes twitched inside my muddy shoes. Below my waist, I felt my organs settle lower. Mother's scream that had shaken the dark streets echoed in my ears. Did I hallucinate that? I wanted to run away. I might have fled right then if I hadn't been so drained, if I hadn't been shivering so much, if I hadn't been worried that I was about to have a seizure.

'Why don't you come in?' Mother's voice softened a little and her eyes turned gentle, as though she could read my thoughts. 'Hello's going crazy.'

He was. The only way to shut that annoying dog up was to go into our flat. I walked past Mother and stepped inside. She followed right behind me and closed the door. The click of the lock echoed in my mind. I paused in the foyer. I had to take my hands out of my pockets to yank off my sopping shoes. Something dropped to the floor and rolled away. I didn't have a chance to look down to see what it was. Mother was so close behind me that I could feel her breath on the back of my neck. I stepped into the flat as though being pushed.

'Stop right there.' Her voice shifted. Cold, hard, low.

I stopped in front of Hae-jin's room and turned my head. Mother was standing there staring at me. Her complicated expression had disappeared and only one emotion was left in her eyes. Anger. She was livid.

'Take that off.' She held out her hand.

I took off my jacket and vest and handed them over. She started going through the pockets. She yanked out my iPod, earphones, mask and roof key, then shoved them back in. She dropped the clothes by the door and came right up under my chin. She moved aggressively, as though charging at me with her horns lowered. I flinched and leant back. Before I knew what was happening, she'd shoved her hands into the pockets of my sweatpants and taken them out in a flash. By the time I'd moved my own hands, saying, 'Uh . . . ' it was already too late. Mother took a step back. She was holding the razor.

'Give that back.' I swiped for it.

She was faster. She blocked me with her arm and lunged at me. I was completely caught off guard. It was as if she were fighting off a rapist, she was so determined. I lost my balance, stepped back and fell; my head snapped backwards and banged on the stairs. Everything darkened and shook. I felt clammy and I couldn't breathe. I managed to brace myself against the stairs and raise my head. Our eyes met.

I opened my mouth but nothing came out. My vocal cords were locked away. Mother's eyes were wide open, red with veins. She was like a burning tree. The air crackled.

'Mum, I—'

She cut me off. 'You . . . ' She pointed the blade straight at my face.

Something quaked in my abdomen.

'You, Yu-jin . . . ' Her voice was wobbly. The hand holding the razor was shaking as well. She was panting. 'You don't deserve to live.'

I teetered to my feet. With unfocused eyes, I watched her come at me. I couldn't feel a thing. I couldn't think of anything to say. The inside of my mind was dark, as though a switch had been turned off.

'I should have done away with you.' Mother stood right in front of my chest. Her eyes were like blades.

I felt behind me with my foot and climbed up a stair.

'We should have died back then. You and me both.' She shoved me hard with the hand that held the razor.

I was so stunned by this ambush that I didn't have the chance to deflect it. I fell backwards again. I didn't have time to dwell on the searing pain that flared up my back. I couldn't even breathe. I had to escape this razor-wielding grim reaper. I felt behind me again and pushed myself up another stair. 'Mum, tomorrow. I'll tell you everything in the morning.'

'Tell me what?' Mother shrieked, following me.

I dragged myself up a few more steps.

'What is there to say?' she demanded.

'All of it. Whatever you want.' I was starting to panic.

There were still two steps to the landing. 'I'll tell you everything. From the beginning. Please ...' I finally reached the landing, but she shoved me again.

The back of my head banged on the corner of the wall, but I managed to regain my footing and stay upright.

'Do it.' Mother closed in on me. She grabbed my wrist. 'Do it while I watch. I want you to do it in front of me.' She tried to place the razor into my palm.

I yanked my hand away.

'What, are you scared?' She grabbed my wrist again and stepped closer. 'Or do you think it's unfair to have to die alone?'

Standing against the corner of the wall, I shook my head. I wanted to yank my arm away, but there was no room. I couldn't escape without pushing her aside.

'Don't worry. When you're gone, I'll go too.'

My breathing was shallow. My chest felt heavy, as though my lungs were filling with water. I was standing on dry land and yet I felt as if I were drowning. I ripped Mother's hand off my wrist and squeezed it. With my newly freed hand, I twisted the hand holding the razor.

'Let go!' Mother began writhing. She pushed me and butted me on the chin with her head. 'Let go, you piece of shit!' Her head bobbed and danced in a dark blur under my chin. She roared, 'How dare you ... how dare you take your father's ...'

I had to raise my chin so that she wouldn't get me, but that meant I couldn't see what she was doing. Still holding onto both of her hands, I was whipped back and forth and dragged all over the landing. Mother, who had at first been trying to give me the razor, was now fighting to keep it. She began to swipe at my throat with it. I moved to slam her right hand into the wall, hoping she would let go of it.

Just before her hand made contact, Mother's face burrowed under my arm. I screamed. She was biting me as hard as she could in my armpit. 'Mum!' Pain ripped through my flesh, my muscles, and into my head. It snapped something inside me, the thing that had dragged me home in the first place, that had held me back from responding to Mother's attacks, that I'd thought was stronger than a steel cable. Control. Consciousness. It leaked out of me. 'Please . . . Stop.' My voice grew faint. Everything became muffled. Darkness pushed in from behind and took over my peripheral vision. I let go of Mother's left hand. I grabbed her by the hair and pulled backwards. Growling, she bit harder, deeper, working into my flesh. Her teeth released only when her head was yanked all the way back. All I could see was her thin, branch-like neck, its bones bulging under her pale skin. Blue veins were pulsing like angry snakes. I pulled her right hand, which still held the razor, up to her neck.

Everything slowed. The chill freezing my head, the heat scrambling my innards, the shiver of each nerve ending, the sound of my thumping heart, the blade that glided from under the left side of her jaw to the right. Hot blood spurted and covered everything; my face, the wall, the floor. I closed my eyes and shoved her away from me. She thudded to the ground. Her crumpled body tumbled down the stairs. It became quiet.

I wiped away the blood from my face with my hands. I looked downstairs. Everything was blurry. I could see Mother's body, slumped at the bottom of the stairs like an empty sack. Her eyes glistened. With those eyes as coordinates, I found my way downstairs. I stood dully next to her. I heard the clock chime. Once, twice, three times.

You're about to have an episode; it's coming soon, a voice whispered. I dragged Mother by the armpits and laid her down in the hall, with her feet towards the stairs and her head towards the kitchen. I raked her hair over her eyes so that she couldn't see me go up to my room. I folded her hands on her chest. I stood up. 'Goodnight,' I said automatically.

Morning had arrived. The fog was still thick, but it was bright outside and the rain seemed to have stopped. I could hear the cars whizzing along the road in the distance. If I hadn't gone out last night, it would be like any other day; I would be running along that road right now, passing occasional joggers or cyclists or pedestrians. I would run past a pretty girl and wonder where she was going, who she was meeting, what she would be doing later.

All kinds of people lived together in this world, each doing their own thing. Among them, some people became murderers, either by accident, or from a fit of anger, or for the fun of it. I'd never imagined that I could be one of them. Or that Mother would be my victim. I'd only imagined my future, when I could do whatever I wanted. I'd anticipated what I would do when my real life started, after Mother was dead and no longer meddling with my choices. But I'd never wanted her to die this way, though I couldn't say I hadn't fantasised about killing her.

My throat tightened when I looked down at her now. I glanced at my hand, still holding the razor I'd found beside my bed. My bones felt as though they were contracting. I raised my head. *It's you. You're the murderer. It's you.*

My pulse quickened. Despair burned in the pit of my stomach and surged up my oesophagus. Grunts burst out of my mouth. Soon they turned into laughter that echoed throughout the blood-soaked flat. Something trickled down my cheek and dripped off my chin. Sweat? Blood? Tears? I was a murderer. I'd killed my own mother. After all that panic and anxiety and effort, this was the fucking truth I'd unearthed.

Wait. Wait. Look down, my mind said. I saw myself from above, a madman kneeling over his mother's body, rocking back and forth in laughter. I turned my head to the side. My dead mother greeted me with troubled, glistening eyes, asking, *What's so funny?* just the way she did ten years ago in the Dongsung-dong cinema.

'How dare you ... how dare you take your father's ...'

I looked down at the razor in my hand. Father's initials bothered me. I remembered how her black pupils had widened in an instant, how her eyes had bulged, how the anger had radiated from her. All because of that? Just because I had dared to take my father's razor?

'You ... You, Yu-jin ... You don't deserve to live.'

How did taking Father's razor merit death? Why would that make her decide I should kill myself? Was that really why she had held the razor to my throat? In the end, it was her life that had been cut short. But now my life was effectively ruined too, and all because of a dead man's razor? I shook my head. That would be akin to finding a rat in the house and killing it with an intercontinental ballistic missile. If I had hidden the razor before Mother yanked it out of my pocket, if I had been able to tuck it into my palm or my sleeve, could this have been avoided?

I shook my head again. It was too late now. I couldn't turn back time and change life's trajectory. The only thing I could do was consider what had happened from a different angle. What could explain all of this? I shook my head a third time. I couldn't begin to guess. The whole thing was so surreal. I glared into Mother's eyes, my fingers twitching on the razor. I wanted to grab her by the shoulders and shake her. *Explain yourself, instead of just lying there! How does it feel? Controlling your son's life for twenty-five years before finally destroying it completely?*

The clock began to chime. I counted to eight. The gears in my head shifted and reality slid into focus. Bottomless fear returned. My gaze circled the house clockwise, like an electron in a magnetic field. The kitchen, the stairs, the door to Hae-jin's room, the key cabinet in the corner, the clock ... The clock. It had chimed last night. Once, twice, three times.

I stopped breathing. I'd left the sea wall at midnight, but I'd gone up to my room at 3 a.m.

It couldn't have been more than thirty minutes from when Mother caught me in the stairwell outside to when I headed up to my room. That meant I'd arrived home around 2.30 a.m. How did it take me two and a half hours to get home? The hair on my arms stood on end. Now I understood something. That was why Mother was able to call Hae-jin and Auntie around 1.30 a.m. But what was I doing from midnight to 2.30? Where had I been?

'Mum, tomorrow. I'll tell you everything in the morning.' My voice leapt out from my memory.

'Tell me what?'

What was I going to tell her in the morning? Now that it *was* morning, I had nothing to say. But what had happened? I was feeling great until midnight, when I started smelling blood. Did I have a seizure in the street, or by a construction site? That would explain why my trainers were muddy. But why was Mother awake when I came home? Why did she search my pockets as soon as I stepped into the flat? And why didn't I rebuff her over-the-top interrogation? Questions brought on more questions until I arrived back at the fundamental mystery. Why was Mother acting so crazy last night? Was it really all because of the razor?

It was clear what had happened, but the reason behind it all was still in hiding. The fucked-up truths I had managed to unearth so far were only the half of it.

The back of my eyes began to throb. I wanted to lie down. A part of my mind was agitated, telling me that instead of trying to fix this mess, it would be easier to give up and go to prison. Then I remembered: Hae-jin would be on his way back soon; I was expecting him around 11 a.m.

That gave me three hours. Would I be able to get to the bottom of things by then? A voice in my mind advised the following: *Hae-jin should walk into a home, not a murder scene.* First, I needed to clear up; then, once I'd figured out why everything had gone down the way it had, I would be able to make the decision – confess or flee? – that vexed murderers the world over. I put the razor on a side table and went into Mother's bedroom.

Some things never changed. Mother's room was one of those things. It looked the same now as it had in our Bangbae-dong house when Father and Yu-min were alive, and in the commercial building in Incheon where we lived for fifteen years after they died. The furniture and its arrangement were identical. The oldest piece was the writing desk, which Mother had had since she was a girl.

I stopped next to it and looked at the statue of the Virgin Mary. It was a combative figure; belying the moniker Our Lady of Mercy, her bare foot was stepping on the neck of a snake. Next to it were a small clock, a ceramic cup with pens and pencils in it, and two books Mother had taken from the study.

Even after she left her job, Mother spent a lot of time at this desk, reading, writing and praying. She'd probably sat here last night, too. The pen was on the edge of the desk; maybe she had been writing. She must have pushed the chair back and not noticed that the brown blanket had fallen to the ground when she rushed out.

The blanket from under the chair was a little too small, so I opened the linen closet and took out a dark blue one that was several times larger, with the thickness of a bath towel.

Outside the bedroom, I spread the blanket out.

What are you going to do to me? asked Mother's eyes, black and damp like rocks on a riverbed. I wanted to flee, but I couldn't turn away from her gaze. My body was frozen. She continued to berate me. *Don't you have any other thoughts beyond how you should bury me? Don't you feel anything? Don't you understand this is different from spilling coffee?*

I know that! I thought. *Of course I know that. Please stop. Say something useful. Tell me why you wanted to kill me, or something that could help me figure out why; give me a hint at least.* I shook my head to clear my thoughts. I tried to focus on the tasks at hand and the order in which I needed to perform them, so I could do them efficiently and mechanically.

I ripped my gaze away from hers and fixed it on her chest. I swiped aside the congealed mass of blood so that I wouldn't slip, and sat with a knee next to Mother's shoulder. Other than the fact that her eyes were open and glaring, she looked exactly the way she did when she was sleeping. Maybe that was why I'd said goodnight to her?

I thought of a day, not long after Father and Yu-min died, when we were still living in the Bangbae-dong house. It must have been a Saturday, since I wasn't at school and Mother wasn't at church. She cleaned all day. In the evening she went into Yu-min's room with a bottle of liquor. She didn't come out for hours. Through the closed door I heard her weeping. From time to time I heard her mumbling.

I lay on my stomach on my bed, my eyes closed, swimming in an imaginary pool. In my daydream, I'd just overtaken the future of Korean swimming, who had started training when he was three. I believed I could beat him, even though I had only been swimming for two years. I hit the touchpad just before he did, then heard something crash in Yu-min's room across the way. I paused and cocked my head. It was quiet. But I got up anyway, because I thought I knew what had made that sound.

I was right. The bottle had shattered. Mother was lying down, holding her bloody wrist. The family photo album, her indoor slippers and several hairpins were strewn about the room, and there was blood on Yu-min's bed and desk.

'Mum!'

Mother opened her eyes before closing them again. I ran downstairs to call the emergency number. 'My mum's collapsed!'

I sat on the edge of the couch in the living room, waiting for the paramedics to arrive, ready to open the door as soon as the bell rang. I was wearing a jacket – I had hesitated only for a moment before sliding my new Rubik's cube into my pocket – and I'd remembered to take Mother's wallet out of her handbag.

The nurse at the hospital asked me all kinds of questions. 'When did you find her like this?' 'Where is your father?' 'No other adults?'

There was Auntie, of course, but I shook my head. Even then I didn't like that woman. 'Just me and Mum. It's just the two of us.'

Mother woke up around dawn. I must have solved the Rubik's cube at least thirty times by then. She asked to be discharged immediately. The nurse tried to stop her, but she got out of bed, tottered out of the hospital barefoot and dishevelled, and hailed a cab. She didn't give me a backward glance as I clambered in after her. At home, she went straight to bed without bothering to shower. Her head landed on her pillow and her bandage-wrapped wrist dangled off the edge of the bed. I moved to leave the bedroom, then came back to her side: I'd remembered the nurse's instruction to make sure her hand was higher than her chest.

I placed it on her chest and she opened her eyes. I pulled a blanket over her. The tip of her nose was red. Her eyes, staring up at the ceiling, filled with tears. I felt disappointed. I'd thought she'd say 'thank you,' or 'you saved my life'. I didn't think she would cry. Shouldn't I be praised in this situation? Maybe she had forgotten all that I'd done. 'I thought you'd died,' I reminded her. 'I was so scared. Don't do that again, okay?'

Mother's lips moved. I stood there, waiting for her to say something. She clenched her jaw. A blue vein fluttered under her chin. It was as if she could barely restrain herself from hitting me. What had I done wrong? My mind advised me to get out of there. I backed away and paused in the doorway. 'Goodnight.'

That was the first time I strategically said goodnight to defuse her anger. Afterwards, I used it often when I needed to calm her down, when I wanted to stop talking to her, when I'd done something I didn't want her to find out about. I said goodnight to her instead of telling her to stop harassing me, to stop interfering. Maybe last night I meant to say: *Wait here, I'll take care of all of this later.*

Now I slid my arms under her and stood up. I swayed. She was heavy. How could she be so heavy when she was the size of a school-age child? Her head flopped against her chest, her bent elbows jabbed me in the stomach, and blood clots fell off her body like bird shit. I took a step towards the blanket but slipped on the blood. I had to practically throw her down.

I crouched and caught my breath. My legs were shaking, even though all I'd done was move a body barely half my weight about a metre. Just last week, as we'd spring-cleaned the flat, Mother had told me that ants could pick things up that were fifty times heavier than themselves, and bees three hundred times heavier. She'd pointed at the fridge as she told me that. Hae-jin would have moved it before she even had to ask, but I was the only one at home. I'd started to walk away from her, pretending not to hear as she said, 'So a man who is a hundred and eighty-four centimetres tall and weighs seventy-eight kilograms should be able to pull a nine-ton trailer,' but this dazzling feat of mental arithmetic stopped me in my tracks and forced me to move the fridge to the side. None of her talents were useful to her now, though; all she could do was lie on the old blanket. I suppose that's what happens when you die.

I closed her eyelids. I pressed down on her bent arm and straightened her neck, hearing the bones crunch. I forced her chin up to close her mouth, nearly breaking her teeth. I pulled down the hem of her nightgown, which had ridden up her thighs.

It was the nightgown I'd bought for her fifty-first birthday last spring, I realised. She didn't like it. She was annoyed that I'd bought her a 'granny nightgown'. I never saw her wear it, so I'd assumed she'd thrown it out. I'd even forgotten that I'd given it to her. What was she doing, wearing this nightgown last night?

I spotted something in the front pocket. Something small and long, like a lighter. Her car key. That was strange. She didn't leave her things just anywhere. The key should have been in her desk drawer. And in this nightgown, of all places? She wouldn't have gone out in a nightgown, even in the middle of the night.

I placed the key on the counter and wrapped her body up in the blanket. A rope would keep the blanket from falling open, but I didn't feel like going to find one; why waste time and leave bloody footprints everywhere? Just dealing with the existing bloodstains was plenty.

I slid my arms beneath her body again, drew in a deep breath and stood up. My heart rate spiked and the veins in my forehead bulged. Her body had somehow become even heavier. I moved carefully towards the stairs, avoiding the puddles of blood on the floor, one foot at a time, as though walking on a frozen lake. I stepped onto the first stair and the world quieted. I took another step and sound fell away completely. I started sweating and grew dizzy. My feet squelched. Sticky, slippery clumps of blood oozed between my toes. Mother's voice echoed endlessly in my head. 'Yu-jin.' Low and trembling. I stepped onto the fourth stair. 'Yu-jin!' A sharp, stabbing scream. The fifth stair. 'Yu-jin . . . ' Her voice pulled my shoulders down. My feet seemed to sink into the stairs. I pulled them up slowly, step by step.

I stopped for a moment on the landing and leant against the wall to take a breath, but my arm slipped on the blood smears. I gasped. Mother's voice vanished. Her weight vanished as well.

When I collected myself, I was sitting in a puddle of blood. Mother was lying between my legs, the blanket open. I felt faint. I couldn't believe I had to wrap her up again, pick her up and climb the remaining steps. I wanted to lie down. I might have given up and done just that if a shout hadn't rung out from my mind to remind me that Hae-jin was due home soon.

I got up. I threw the blanket around Mother and lifted her from between my legs. I went up the rest of the stairs and reached the sliding doors leading to the roof, thinking all the time about Hae-jin's imminent arrival. I managed to slide it open and went out onto the deck. The sharp marine wind greeted us. Seagulls cried in the fog. The pergola swing shrieked in the wind. We'd brought the old swing with us from Bangbae-dong. Mother liked to take breaks on it while she gardened. She would pretend to drink tea and spy on me in my room.

I walked along the paving stones to the pergola and laid her down on the swing. Also under the pergola were two benches, a table with room for eight, and a barbecue. Mother had designed the table herself. If you pushed the top of it, it slid open to reveal a deep storage space, where she kept all the things she used up here: a blue tarpaulin, clear plastic sheeting, a bag of fertiliser, a hoe, pruning shears, a trowel, a saw, empty planters and small pots, a coiled rubber hose.

I took everything out and spread a sheet of plastic in the empty space. I picked Mother up and placed her inside. I felt suddenly lost. I didn't remember a thing from when Father and Yu-min were buried. Mother had told me that I'd slept until the day the coffins were interred. Even if I did remember, what would it matter?

I didn't think Mother would want me to mark her death in any way; she would probably just ask why I was trying to make it better when I was the one who'd caused it all. I pulled the tarpaulin over her body and started shoving everything else back inside. I put the pots and planters by her feet and the fertiliser and hose near her head. I picked up the saw.

'I should have done away with you,' I heard her say.

My face burned.

'We should have died back then. You and me both.'

What did she mean? I never knew she'd hated me so much that she would want to kill me, her own son. I didn't realise she'd pretended to love someone she hated so much. My blood boiled with rage. I tossed the saw in, shoved the tabletop back into place and stalked away from the pergola without a backward glance. I didn't want to pull out my dead mother and shake her to bits; Hae-jin was on his way home and I didn't have much time.

I slammed the sliding doors shut. Quiet rolled over me like storm clouds. I couldn't hear Mother's voice any longer. I shut off those thoughts. I had to focus on the things I needed to do. I'd wanted to open the windows, but I changed my mind. The wintry wind would flood into the flat, which would neutralise the smell, but small, light objects might fall onto the floor and be dragged around. Then the whole place would be covered with new bloody traces.

71

I decided to wipe up the blood first. I took off my blood-caked sweater and trousers. Naked, I went into the kitchen and found red rubber gloves. I took rubbish bags and clean rags out from under the sink, along with bleach and two buckets. I found a plastic broom, dustpan, mop and steam cleaner and gathered them by the island. Then I began to clean with military precision. I swept the blood puddle Mother had been lying in into the dustpan, poured it into a bucket and flushed it down the toilet in Mother's bathroom. I flushed the puddle on the landing down as well. Then I began to mop. The upstairs hallway and living room floor were marble and cleaned easily, but the wooden stairs were a problem. They were laminated, so most of the blood came off, but some of it had seeped between the cracks and wouldn't budge. I didn't know how to get rid of it, and I didn't have the time to figure it out. I moved on, hoping that Hae-jin and his eagle eye wouldn't notice it.

Once the floors were clean, I put on slippers so that my crusty feet wouldn't make new prints. I cleaned the walls and the banister, scrubbed everything on the second floor, and finally went over the whole lot with the steam cleaner.

By the time I'd finished, it was 10.30. I leant the steam cleaner against the wall and straightened up. I threw the mop pad, rags, slippers and rubber gloves into the bin bag, then shoved the broom, dustpan and mop into a bucket with my clothes and placed it all in my room. The razor and Mother's car key went into my desk. Finally, I opened all the windows. The windows at the back, the kitchen window, all of them. Sharp, cold wind careened into the living room.

Outside the front door, a soulless female voice declared, 'The door is opening.' It was the lift. The only person who would get out on our floor was Hae-jin; the flat opposite ours was still empty, and non-residents had to be buzzed in to get past the main doors of the building. I looked at the clock: 10.55.

The keypad on the front door lock beeped. I looked around quickly. I hadn't tidied Mother's room or mine. Bloodstains remained on the roof deck. And I was naked and covered in blood. In less than five seconds, Hae-jin would open the door and walk in.

I dragged the steam cleaner behind me as I ran into Mother's bedroom and closed the door. I heard the entrance foyer door sliding open. I heard footsteps entering the living room. Silence. Hae-jin was probably standing by the stairs, looking confused. He'd gone all the way to Yeongjong Island to pick up a mobile phone that wasn't there, the person who'd sent him on a fool's errand was nowhere to be seen, all the windows were wide open, and the smell of bleach was lingering in the air. Maybe he could even detect the tang of blood. Damn. I should have aired the place before doing anything else.

'Yu-jin?'

II

WHO AM I?

It was February, at dawn, ten years ago. We were in the car on our way to swimming practice when Hae-jin called.

Mother pressed the speaker button. His voice was teary and trembling. 'It's Hae-jin.'

Something must have happened.

'Where are you?' Mother asked. She seemed to know what was going on, since she hadn't asked what was wrong.

'I'm at Yonghyon Hospital,' Hae-jin said. 'Grandfather . . . he just passed away.' The doctor had asked for a guardian who would handle the next steps, and he couldn't think of anyone else.

Mother opened her mouth, then stopped. She didn't usually choose her words this carefully. She always knew what to say before she opened her mouth. I was growing frustrated. Why wasn't she answering? All she had to say was that she was on her way.

'Come on, let's go,' I murmured.

She glanced at me as if to make sure it was okay to skip practice.

I nodded.

She turned on her hazards, crossed two lanes and made a U-turn at breakneck speed. 'We'll be there in five minutes,' she said.

Hae-jin's grandfather was on a gurney, covered by a white sheet. Hae-jin sat beside him, looking down at his feet. He was dazed and limp. He didn't notice us even when we were right in front of him.

'Hae-jin,' Mother said.

His shoulders stiffened and he looked up, his eyes unfocused. Could he even see us? He didn't say, 'You're here,' as I'd expected; instead he said, 'I'm sorry.'

Mother opened her arms without a word and embraced him, gently patting his back. I stood to the side. Mother had deep frown lines on her forehead, her nose and cheeks were turning red, and she swallowed hard. Her expression was complicated and unfamiliar. Was she sad? Was she feeling his pain? Or was it that she understood what he was going through? Was she showing him that he didn't have to worry, she would take care of everything? Was it all of the above? Or none of them?

Hae-jin, for one, seemed to understand what her gentle pats conveyed. He let out a noise through his clenched lips, and as he raised his arms hesitantly to hug Mother back, the sound turned into keening. Though she was nearly a foot shorter than him, he buried his face in her shoulder and wailed.

Although I could sense how sad Hae-jin was – my ears

were ringing with his sobs – I didn't feel anything. Mother was crying, the nurse's eyes were turning red, but I stood there alone, shielded from emotion. I wasn't able to say anything reassuring to him.

Mother talked to me about the adoption three days after the funeral. 'What do you think?' she asked, after she reminded me that Hae-jin didn't have any relatives and didn't want to go to an orphanage, that he and I got along well, and that we had a spare room at our place. 'What do you think?' wasn't a request to hear my thoughts; it meant 'You don't have a problem with it, do you?' Even if I did have a problem, I knew she wasn't interested in hearing about it. But in this case, I really didn't have any objections. As Mother had said, Hae-jin was my friend, and she had enough money to support two teenagers.

Two days later, on our way to early-morning practice again, Mother announced, 'Hae-jin's coming home today.'

At the time, we were living in a five-storey commercial building in Yonghyeon-dong, Incheon. Mother owned our flat; the entire fifth floor was our home. The bedroom in the hallway was reserved for my dead brother. Mother had furnished the room with his furniture, his books, and even the curtains from his room in the Bangbae-dong house. Every time I went in or out of the flat, I walked past that room. I always considered it Yu-min's. Maybe that was why I was shocked when I came home later in the day to find that no trace of Yu-min was left in it. Instead of curtains, it had double blinds, and there was new furniture, a white coverlet on the bed, a home cinema system, and a *City of God* poster on the wall.

I looked at the room, amazed. It was clear that everything had been carefully thought through. It felt as if it had been dreamed about and planned over a long period of time. The colours, the furniture, and the arrangement of the room were different from before, but none of it seemed out of character; it was exactly to Mother's taste, except for the poster. This was the kind of room she would have put together for Yu-min if he were still alive and now a teenager.

When had she begun thinking about doing this? I was genuinely curious. When she first met Hae-jin? Or when we went to see *City of God*? Or was it when we were in the hospital last week? I never knew what Mother was really thinking about anything, but I had never been as confused as I was that day. I hadn't realised she would switch her allegiance so swiftly. I hadn't known that two days after mentioning the adoption, everything would be ready. Hae-jin had taken Yu-min's place in Mother's heart. He didn't even have to change his last name; like Mother, he was a descendant of the Kimhae Kims. That was how he became her firstborn son. Later, I realised that I was the only one with a different last name – my father's.

'Yu-jin,' Mother called from the front door. She had returned with Hae-jin.

'Hey, Yu-jin,' Hae-jin said. His voice suggested to me that he would come further into the flat only if I answered.

I went out. He was standing by the front door, his shoes still on, a bag and suitcase next to him.

'I'm here,' he said, sounding uncomfortable and shy. His cheeks were turning red, as though he had just revealed a secret. Mother stood behind him, watching me, looking a little tense.

I had to clear the air and say it. I faced Hae-jin. 'I'm not going to call you *hyeong*.' However Mother felt about it, the only person I could call 'elder brother' was Yu-min.

Hae-jin took it well. He nodded, still looking uncomfortable, and stepped into the living room.

That was how the three of us became a family. The portrait now hanging in the living room was taken that day in a nearby photo studio to celebrate.

'Are they twins? They're practically identical,' the photographer had said. And for the last ten years, we really had lived like twins, peacefully coexisting despite trivial conflicts, the way all siblings did. That was our relationship even until just yesterday.

Would it still be possible after all this? Even though Mother was lying on the roof and the murderer, namely me, was hiding in her bedroom, covered in blood? I thought of Mother embracing the orphaned Hae-jin ten years ago. Maybe now I could identify the chill pressing down on my throat. Maybe it was loneliness.

I heard Hae-jin running up the stairs, rat-tat-tat like gunfire.

'Hey, Hae-jin!' I called. 'I'm in Mother's room.'

His footsteps continued upwards. Maybe my voice was too soft.

'Hae-jin!' I yelled, feeling panicked. 'In Mother's room!' I was shouting loud enough for the whole neighbourhood to hear me.

Hae-jin stopped. 'Huh? What?'

I yelled even louder. 'Mother's room, I said!'

'With Mother?'

Shit. I hadn't thought about how to explain Mother's absence.

'By myself!' No answer. No movement, either. The soles of my feet itched. I wanted to run up, grab him by the scruff of the neck and drag him back downstairs. 'Come quick!'

I wasn't worried that he'd go into my room or onto the roof. He wouldn't do that. Hae-jin would never invade someone else's privacy. Whether physically or verbally, he only moved within the limits granted by the other person. Even if he saw a girl drowning, he'd ask her if he could please grab her by the hand to save her – not that that would ever happen, because he sank like a brick in water, and was afraid of it, too. What concerned me was where he was standing. The door to my bedroom was closed, walls enclosed either side of the stairs, and there was no window on the landing. He was in a passageway with no air circulation. It must reek of blood and bleach. I had to get him off that staircase.

I screamed as though I needed his immediate assistance. 'I'm cleaning, hurry up!'

Finally, he moved. One step, then another, then a smattering of steps. When he neared the door to Mother's room, I realised it wasn't locked. Shit. I reached over and locked it at the same time as Hae-jin tried to open it. I must have been a tenth of a second faster. The lock clicked.

'What the hell?' Hae-jin's voice shot up. 'What are you doing?'

'I'll be right out,' I said. 'You go do your thing for a bit.'

82

'What the fuck? First you scream at me to get down here, and now you want me to wait outside?'

'I just took off my clothes. I'm hopping in the shower.'

'So?'

I didn't answer. It was best not to say anything at all, since there was no explanation for my behaviour.

'Why are you taking a shower down here anyway?'

'Mine's broken.'

'Oh. Where's Mother?'

'She's gone on a church retreat.' It would be so nice if that really were the case; then I wouldn't need to worry about anything or stress out about how Hae-jin was going to react to what had happened.

'That's so last-minute. She didn't say anything about it when she called,' he mumbled.

I was completely over this. I hated having to carefully choose every single word that left my mouth. 'I only found out when I came downstairs this morning. There was a note on the fridge.'

'Oh,' Hae-jin said, sounding suddenly reassured. Did he know something I didn't? 'Why are all the windows open?'

'I cleaned the whole place. Mum left a note saying I should have everything sparkling by the time she came back.'

He banged on the door. 'Open up. It's ridiculous, trying to talk through this.'

There was a key to every room in the house in the key cabinet in the hall. Hae-jin could fetch the key to Mother's room if he wanted to. I just hoped he wouldn't. 'Give me a second, will you?' To cover up my audible irritation, I quickly added, 'Don't close the windows. Otherwise the place'll stink of bleach.'

'Then why the hell did you *use* bleach? There are a ton of cleaning products in the laundry room. I guess you have no idea, since you've never cleaned anything.'

I nibbled on the inside of my lip. *Just give me a break.*

'By the way, I couldn't find your mobile at Kkosil's.'

Damn. He wouldn't let up.

'Maybe you left it somewhere else. Did you stop at Yongi's on your way home?'

I didn't know what to say. 'Oh ... actually, I found it in my room.'

A brief silence. I could practically hear the lecture about to erupt from his mouth.

'I literally just saw that it had fallen between my bed and the bedside table.'

Hae-jin finally snapped. 'Seriously? Why didn't you call me, then?'

I didn't answer. Keeping him mad was easier than trying to explain. Hae-jin didn't fight or argue; if he was really angry, he gave the other person the cold shoulder until he was ready to forgive them. What I needed right now was for him to refuse to speak to me. I needed to avoid a confrontation until I finished taking care of everything.

I stood behind the door, my ear plastered against it, waiting for him to move away. Thankfully it didn't take long. I heard him closing the windows. Had he forgotten that I'd asked him to keep them open? Or was he just doing it to show me how pissed off he was?

A few minutes later, I heard the door of his room open,

84

then close. Finally! He would place his bag on his desk, change into comfortable clothes, then come back out into the living room. It wouldn't take him more than a minute, but that was enough time for me to dash upstairs. I opened the door. All I needed was half an hour to clean my room and have a shower. I could grab the key from the cabinet, lock Mother's room, and clean that when I had a chance.

I hadn't expected Hae-jin to come out of his room without changing. His door was flung open as soon as I slid a foot out, and I was forced to retreat. I heard him head towards the kitchen. Something rattled, maybe a dish or a cup. Was he making coffee? Was he making himself another ramen? Either way, it didn't look like he was going back into his room any time soon. I had to change my plans.

I relocked the door quietly and took off the pad from under the steam cleaner. I erased my footprints and fingerprints methodically, going from the bedroom door to the bathroom. It was deathly quiet outside. It was making me nervous. But there was nothing I could do. I turned on the shower and stepped inside. I used half the shampoo in the bottle to wash my hair, soaped and rinsed my body four or five times and used Mother's toothbrush to scrub the blood from under my fingernails. From time to time I turned off the water to listen for Hae-jin's movements. Still no sound. I was so nervous that I wanted to rip my ears off my head.

After I'd finished showering, I lifted my left arm in front of the mirror and discovered Mother's parting gift. A large dark bruise stretched from under my arm, past my armpit, to my chest. Small teeth marks were printed in my armpit. Pain suddenly crashed over me, the nightmare of last night vivid again. I shuddered and lowered my arm.

With the damp towel hanging around my shoulders, I went to the writing desk. The clock indicated 11.40. Hae-jin had been home for forty-five minutes. He could have made another ramen, eaten it, finished the remaining broth with a bowl of rice, done the laundry and drunk a cup of coffee in that time. There was still no sound from outside. I went to the door and put my ear to it. I finally heard something. Not words, really, but staccato sounds. Hae-jin must be channel-surfing. He must have been waiting for me all this time, lying on the couch.

Did he have something to say to me? Did he detect that something was off? Had he seen something I'd neglected to scrub away? Suddenly, laughter rang out from the TV. Hae-jin snickered along. Maybe he wasn't waiting for me to come out after all.

I returned to the writing desk. Before I left Mother's room, I needed to find something to wrap the cleaning pad in; it had turned dark brown with blood. I opened the first drawer and dug around. Writing implements and stationery. The second drawer held Mother's red wallet and a thick black journal, the kind with rings so you could insert additional pages. I'd never seen it before. I glanced at the pen on the edge of the desk. Perhaps Mother was writing in the journal at her desk, then stood up in a rush and shoved it into the drawer. I lifted the cover, curious to see if I was right.

The first page was labelled 'December'. Underneath were three entries.

Tuesday 6 December

He's not in his room. He's started going out through the roof again. It's the first time in a month.

Wednesday 7 December

Second day in a row. I was waiting but I missed him.

Friday 9 December

I don't know where he went. I looked for him until 2 a.m. but I couldn't find him. I know I saw him. I'm cold and scared and terrified. Now

The line cut off there. Below was a completely different sentence: *Hello is barking. He's back.*

The 'he' she was referring to must be the same 'he' she had caught outside the front door last night. If she'd gone around looking for me until two in the morning, that meant she'd called Auntie and Hae-jin while she was out. She would have got drenched in the rain. That would explain why her shoes had been wet. But was she really roaming the neighbourhood, in the rain, in the middle of the night?

She wouldn't have done that. At least not on foot. Much of Gundo was still under construction, and more than half of the existing flats in our district remained empty. The road along Dongjin River, which marked the boundary between Districts One and Two, was always deserted and dreary, like the road into a cemetery. People didn't like to walk down there by themselves. Most residents didn't come out of their homes after nightfall.

I didn't believe Mother had been out wandering alone until two in the morning last night. She could have been driving around, but then why would her shoes have been wet? And why would she go searching for me anyway? Why not wait for me at home?

Hae-jin was whistling off-key. It sounded like he was going towards his room. I heard his door open, then close. This was my chance. I slipped Mother's journal under my arm, pushed the chair in and wrapped the steam cleaner pad in my wet towel. Before opening the bedroom door, I listened again for any noise outside. Still quiet. I poked my head out. Nothing.

I stepped out quickly, and closed the door. I lunged towards the stairs, taking several steps at a time. Was Mother's bathroom clean? Had I left any trace or object that would draw suspicion if Hae-jin were to enter her room? I was convinced I had cleaned up as much as I could, but I got the key and locked the door just in case.

I picked up Mother's mobile phone from under my bed. I must have dropped it at some point. The screen was dark. The battery was dead. Damn. I should have checked her texts, in case she had a conversation with Auntie or Hae-jin I didn't know about. But I didn't want to charge it now. Mother was supposed to be at a religious retreat; it would be safer to leave it like this, so it wouldn't ring or buzz, and in case someone overzealous decided to track its location.

The clock chimed downstairs – it was noon. Whatever else was going on in this flat, the clock continued to do its job. I placed Mother's mobile on my desk and laid next to it the following: jacket, vest, iPod, earphones, roof key, disposable mask, razor, car key and Mother's notebook.

I was the investigator interrogating the criminal. But the two were one and the same, the criminal had a slippery relationship with the truth, and his memory was spotty. If I couldn't learn more, I would come to one obvious conclusion: for some unknown reason, Mother had tried to kill me. Therefore, the murder was self-defence. Maybe excessive self-defence, but self-defence nonetheless.

I put on trousers and took out a T-shirt. I heard footsteps. Hae-jin was coming upstairs. I looked at the door. I hadn't locked it. The tussle that had happened an hour before by Mother's bedroom door would be reprised here. The murderer's and victim's belongings were strewn on my desk, bloodstained cleaning tools and a bin bag were in front of the door, the floor was streaked with blood, and my bed was a tangle of bloodied sheets and blankets.

Damn it. Why was he coming up here? I lunged towards the door, my arm outstretched like a goalkeeper diving for the ball. I opened it and stepped out into the hallway, closing it just as Hae-jin arrived in front of me. We stood facing each other, only a foot apart. My T-shirt was in my hand.

'Dude. Why didn't you come and talk to me before you came up here? I was banging on Mother's door ... ' He stopped short, his eyes widening. 'What's going on here?' He grabbed my left arm and lifted it.

I hadn't expected this. 'Oh. I bumped into the mop handle.' I tugged my arm away.

He studied the bruise on my chest. 'Doesn't look like it's from bumping into something.' He reached over and grabbed my arm again. 'Let me see.'

'Stop it!' I yanked it away violently.

Hae-jin gaped at me. A red flush began creeping up from below his collar.

'I bumped into the mop, okay?' I put on my shirt and hardened my expression so he would stop asking.

'What the hell, man.'

'What's up?' I said.

'Did you see it?'

It? Did I leave something in the living room? The kitchen? By the front door? 'What?' I studied his expression.

He looked like he was trying to be casual, but his large brown eyes were sparkling; I could swear he was about to burst out laughing. 'Isn't that why you just ran out like that?'

Half my mind was on Hae-jin, and the other half was on what I had just seen in my room. The objects on my desk skittered past my eyes. None of that could have anything to do with his grin.

'No?' He cocked his head.

I crossed my arms. *Stop fishing. Just spit it out.*

'Then why did you run out so fast?'

It took me a few moments to dig up a normal-sounding excuse. 'I'm starving. I have to eat something.'

'Oh, you haven't eaten anything yet?' Hae-jin looked sympathetic.

I didn't like this expression either; maybe he was trying to wait me out. 'So why did you come up, then?'

'Well . . . ' he said, then stopped.

My fingertips twitched. I wanted to throttle him and yank out what he was hiding.

'I was waiting and counting down,' he finally admitted. 'It was posted at exactly noon. Congratulations!'

I blinked stupidly.

'What the hell, you bastard? I said congratulations! You got in!'

My arms fell limply to either side. My cheeks crumpled and my mouth stiffened. Oh, that. Law school admission.

'Han Yu-jin,' Hae-jin said, waving his hand in front of my face. He must have thought I was in disbelief, or so happy that I was dazed. That might have been the case if nothing had happened last night; after all, my college years had been focused solely on getting into law school.

'How . . . how did you find out?' I managed.

'What are you talking about? With your test ID number, of course!'

I stared at him. *How do you know my ID number?*

'Don't you remember? I took a picture of your ID number when you registered for the exam.'

Of course. Hae-jin always celebrated by taking pictures, and that day he had made me stand against the living room wall with the piece of paper under my face as he took pictures from every angle, as though he were taking a mug shot.

'This is awesome news, man. Congrats!' He grabbed my hand and pumped it up and down.

Images of Mother appeared with each upward motion, then disappeared. She lunged at me, brandishing the razor; she lay in a puddle of blood with her throat cut; she was headed to the roof in my arms, wrapped in an old blanket; she rested on the swing; she was locked inside the table.

'Good job, man.' He let go and swung his arm around my shoulder. 'I'm so proud of you.'

My body grew stiff. I couldn't open my mouth. I was horrified to realise I was on the verge of tears. The fact that my life was over was being confirmed in a dramatic fashion. It felt as though a fist-sized lump of ice was sliding down my throat.

'Wait, are you crying?' Hae-jin stepped back and lowered his head to check. 'That thrilled, huh?'

I looked down. *Yeah, sure. Thrilled. So thrilled I want to cry. I want to cry until I fall over dead.*

'Now I get how you must have been feeling. Suddenly cleaning? I mean, you, the toughest guy in the world, getting nervous? You weren't like this even when you were swimming! No matter how big the competition was, no matter who you were up against, you were always so calm. Like it was just another practice.'

He was right about that. I used to be ballsy. I was never nervous or anxious. In the water, I was strong. After I left swimming behind, I became a dedicated student. Any mother would be proud of a good son like me. Mother had taught me that if you pushed, you got pushed right back; the easiest thing to do was never to push or get pushed, and I hadn't strayed from her advice until now; I'd lived according to that edict. I couldn't think of anything I'd done to deserve what she'd said to me last night.

'You should tell Mother,' Hae-jin said.

I nodded, still rooted in place.

'Go on, call her! She must be so nervous right now, just praying for this.' Hae-jin stood there casually, his hands in his pockets, eager to share his joy. I wanted that too; we were family. It was too bad that I couldn't join him.

'I'll call her when you go downstairs,' I blurted out.

'Okay,' he said, but he didn't move. He studied me carefully. 'Are you okay? Have you … Did you not take your pills?' He said the last part cautiously, as though he was worried that his words would anger me.

It had been four days since I'd stopped taking the pills. A week ago, I had experienced the worst and longest headache of my life, a common side effect of the medication. For several days my pulse surged and my ears rang, and I felt as though a metal skewer was stabbing my brain. Nothing worked. I tried lying still; I fell over with my head in my hands; I moaned with my head stuck between my knees; I pressed the back of my head with my fingers laced together. I waited endlessly. It felt like my tongue was swelling up and blocking my throat. After three days of that, I decided I didn't care if I had a seizure or not. I was enraged at Auntie for prescribing the pills, and at Mother, who was always watching to make sure I took them. I didn't want to take these stupid pills for the rest of my life.

'Hey, Yu-jin,' Hae-jin said, interrupting my reverie.

'Yeah?' I glanced up at him.

He looked beyond my shoulder. 'Phone's ringing.'

I nodded. It was my mobile, which was in my desk drawer, in my room, of all places. Who could it be?

'Aren't you going to answer?'

The phone rang on. I looked down at my feet. 'It's probably a cold caller.'

'How would you know that from here? It could be Mother.'

If only. I would have loved for Mother to call me from

the retreat. It would have been amazing if the call revealed it was all a terrible nightmare. The ringing stopped, then started once more.

Hae-jin glanced at my door again. 'She would know what time the results went live.' His logic had gone from 'It could be Mother' to 'It *is* Mother'. 'She must be so nervous. Go and answer.' He looked like he wanted to go in and answer it himself.

I just stared at him. If there was one thing I was better at, it was being patient. 'I will, in a sec.'

We stood there for another ten seconds or so. It felt like an eternity. His eyes were probing. *Why aren't you going into your room? Why are you making me stand outside like this? What's inside that you don't want me to see? Is that why you've been acting so strangely this morning?* I pulled the shutters over my eyes and emptied my head of thoughts. Finally the phone stopped ringing.

'Okay then,' Hae-jin said, breaking into a grin. 'Take your time. I'll make us some lunch.'

I nodded. He turned around and disappeared down the stairs, and I went into my room. I pulled my mobile out of my desk and checked to see who had been calling. *Aunt Hag*, it said on my screen. That overeager witch was as annoying as the yappy dog three floors down. She'd been calling since seven in the morning.

I didn't have to wrestle with whether I should call Auntie back or not, because the cordless phone began to ring insistently. I didn't hesitate; I picked up so that Hae-jin wouldn't. If she asked for me, he would obviously come back up to bang on my door. 'Hello.'

'Are you busy?' Auntie asked. Her dignified question masked her true thoughts: *What the fuck are you doing that you're only answering now?*

I, too, spoke politely. 'Have you had lunch?' when I really meant: *If you have nothing to do, fucking eat something instead of calling me.*

'Where's your mother?'

I was expecting that. In as casual a tone as possible, I told her the same thing I'd said to Hae-jin. 'She's gone on a religious retreat.'

'Retreat? What retreat? That's out of nowhere.'

I didn't answer, so she moved on to the next question. 'Where exactly has she gone?'

'I didn't ask.'

'You didn't ask?' Auntie repeated.

I looked for him until 2 a.m. but I couldn't find him, Mother had written. If she had called Auntie while she was out, Auntie would have asked her where she was, since it would have been obvious from the ambient noise that she wasn't at home. Did Mother answer truthfully? That I'd snuck out through the roof door in the middle of the night, that she'd come after me but couldn't find me? Did she ask her sister what she should do? What would Auntie have said? Would she have told her to go straight back home? Maybe she would have said, get in the car and look for him more thoroughly. Why did Mother call Hae-jin before calling Auntie, anyway?

'When did she say she was coming home?' Auntie asked.

I looked down at Mother's mobile on my desk. Hae-jin was next to Hye-won – my auntie's name – in the list of contacts. Did she press the wrong name? That was possible: Mother's eyes were getting worse. If she was outside, on some dark street corner, it might have been easier to find the wrong name than the right one. Everything seemed to click into place. If Mother had listened to her sister and come home, changed out of her wet clothes and taken the car to search for me, then some of last night made sense: her soaked trainers, the car key in the pocket of her nightgown.

'Yu-jin, what are you doing?' It was a criticism, not a question. She meant: *Answer my questions properly.* She had been calling from the crack of dawn, probably wondering if Mother had found me or not. She likely knew about my habit of sneaking out when I stopped taking my pills. She and Mother shared all kinds of information about me, probably down to how much toilet paper I used when I took a dump.

'I don't know when she'll be back,' I finally answered. 'I didn't ask.'

'Are you guys not talking?' She was probably trying to figure out if we'd fought last night.

I quickly calculated how long it would take for her to come barging into the flat if she couldn't get hold of Mother. Maybe one day, two if I was lucky. 'She wasn't home when I woke up.'

'Then how do you know she's gone on a retreat?'

'She left a note on the fridge.'

'Your mother?' Auntie said, disbelieving.

'Yes,' I said confidently.

'You're saying that she left the house quietly, without telling anyone, at dawn?'

'I slept in, so I don't know if it was at dawn or later.'

'You slept in?' Auntie zeroed in on that piece of information. 'Did you get to bed late?'

What was it she wanted to know? What time Mother left the house? Or how late I went to bed? I had to be careful. This hag always hung on every word I said. I pivoted. 'If you're so curious, why are you asking me? Why don't you just call her?'

'Maybe I called you because she isn't picking up.' Auntie put on this air when she was pissed off. It was a warning for me not to answer her questions with my own.

I tried a suggestion instead. 'Then maybe you should try again. Maybe she didn't hear it.'

'I just did. It's off. So what time *did* you go to bed?' she asked.

I didn't need to answer her every question; after all, she hadn't told me why she was calling. 'Do you need to talk to her urgently?'

'It's not urgent, but it's a little strange . . . ' Auntie paused.

I waited patiently.

'She had a nine o'clock appointment, but she's suddenly on a retreat. It's just odd.'

Could that be true? If Mother had a nine o'clock appointment, why would Auntie begin calling from seven in the morning? And why would she call so frenetically, trying the home phone and her mobile over and over? She was lying. I offered a banal but safe answer. 'Then I'm sure she'll call you soon.'

'Probably . . . ' Auntie didn't hang up. She hesitated, as though she was trying to find something to say.

I was so annoyed, I wanted to scream into the phone.

Only when someone said, 'Doctor?' behind her did she reluctantly wrap up the call. 'If you talk to her, ask her to ring me, okay?'

'Sure.'

'And you're still taking your pills, right?' she asked.

'Of course,' I said, pulling out the medicine bag I'd shoved in the bottom of the drawer to check. There was still ten days' worth in there.

'Isn't it about time for another prescription?'

'No, I have about a week left.'

'Are you sure you're taking the right amount? I think you should have three days' worth at most.'

'Well, maybe you can check my charts,' I suggested.

'I will,' she said, and hung up.

I threw the phone onto my desk and flung the medicine bag down. Mother and Auntie had unleashed the medicine into the centre of my existence, even though the pills had made me feel numb at every single important moment of my life. I'd started taking medication when I began swimming competitively, the spring I turned nine, when I won the junior Seoul City Children's Swimming Competition.

I suffered from severe side effects at the beginning. Once, I had to be hauled off to hospital because I began to slur my words, my body was covered in a rash and I was burning with fever. After switching medications several times, I was put on Remotrol, which was what I still took now. Auntie hadn't chosen badly; at least I didn't have to be carted off to hospital at regular intervals. The only thing was that Remotrol slung a metal ring around my head and shackled my hands and feet, taming me. I was flattened by horrible headaches, and a constant ringing in my ears made it impossible to find quiet. Sometimes I'd find that there were gaps in my memory. I became sluggish and less fit. I'd come home from training practically a corpse. But Mother and Auntie didn't give up on the regimen, saying that the side effects weren't fatal. The same way I didn't give up on swimming.

I'd learned to swim in second grade, in the spring. I'd joined an extracurricular programme at school to keep up with Yu-min. He was better than me at everything – school work, drawing, piano – but he was awful at swimming. He hated it and ended up giving up only a term later, while I learned and mastered all the different strokes in the same time frame. The following spring, I won a schools competition, and the year after that, I represented my school and won us a gold medal.

It was my coach who suggested that I swim competitively. Mother wasn't keen on the idea, but she didn't stop me either. Later, she admitted that she'd thought I would quit soon enough, either because I got bored of practice or because I realised that I wasn't all that good at it after all.

Unfortunately for Mother, I didn't get tired of it. I began to distinguish myself in national youth competitions. When I look back, I can see that I was fully myself, the way I was created, during those two years. It was before I was sent to Auntie for treatment and before I had to start taking medication – these two things happened in May of 2000, a month after Father and Yu-min died.

In October of that year, Mother and I moved from Bangbae-dong to Incheon. My new school didn't have a swimming team. Mother suggested that I give it up. But I liked water more than anything. I liked every moment of reaching out with my arms, slicing through the liquid, embracing and pushing it away. I liked the moment I shot forward like a shark. I liked competing with everything I had against someone else or even myself. I liked that moment every night, just before I fell asleep, when I saw myself standing in an Olympic stadium, on the tallest podium. I was free underwater, unlike on the ground, and I felt more comfortable in the pool than at school or at home. It was the only place Mother couldn't barge into; it was exclusively my world. I could do anything underwater. Anything, the way I wanted to.

So I insisted, and Mother acquiesced on the condition that I'd have to give up if I couldn't fight off the side effects of the drugs. She enrolled me in a swimming club called KIM, and began to stick close to me to watch over my condition. The coach probably thought she was dedicated to making her son the best athlete possible. My teammates figured I was coddled and spoiled, judging from my comfortable family situation, my devoted mother, and my natural talent. Nobody knew that my insides were rotting.

Since I wasn't on the professional athlete programme, I had to combine studying and training. On top of that, I had to deal with the side effects of my medication, of course. Things didn't improve in middle school or high school. In fact, the side effects grew worse. I nearly forgot what I'd been like when I first started swimming, when I had more energy than I knew what to do with. That was until I entered a national swimming competition on Jeju Island in March of my tenth-grade year.

I lost my bag on the first day. I'd left it on a chair to go to the bathroom and it was gone by the time I came out. In it were my pills, my iPod and headphones, games console and wallet. It was annoying not to have the other things, but the pills qualified as a real problem. The correct solution would have been to call Mother and ask her to bring me some more. She was in a nearby hotel; it wouldn't have been impossible, although she would have had to get on a boat or a plane to go all the way home to Incheon.

One doesn't always choose the right path, as it turns out. I saw a simple solution to my problem: I didn't have to take the pills. What could go wrong in a few days? What Mother was always worrying about had never happened, and I would be able to avoid the unjust situation of being berated over something that wasn't technically my fault. I didn't tell the coach about it either; if I told him I'd lost my pills, I'd have to tell him why I was taking them in the first place. They didn't screen for Remotrol in the sport, so there had been no reason to disclose it. He also didn't know I was seeing a psychiatrist. Mother had decided that he didn't have to know about it. He was led to believe that I was receiving sports psychology consultations at Auntie's clinic.

That night, I slept more deeply than I ever had. In the morning, my head was free and clear of headaches. I felt light and joyous. I was confident and ambitious. The day was peaceful for once. Thanks to my renewed joy, I beat my personal best by an astounding seven seconds in the

1,500-metre preliminaries and set a new record. Honestly, I wasn't sure even at that point: was I flying high because I hadn't taken the pills, or was it a coincidence? Although I wasn't fully able to shake off my worries about having a seizure, I enjoyed that dangerous edge I had throughout the competition, taking gold in both the 800-metre and the 1,500-metre freestyle. Even the coach was stunned. I was hailed as a rising star who'd arrived like a comet.

When I got home, I became certain that it was my medication that was making me feel so awful. My body returned to its sluggish self when I started popping the pills again. I stopped them once more to test my theory out, and by the second day I was back in an energetic, manic state. I felt the same as I had during the swimming competition. I remembered what I'd been like when I was in the junior division, before I started the medication. I soon grew confident that being off the meds for a couple of days wouldn't cause a seizure.

A month later, Mother and I went down to Ulsan for the Dong-A swimming competition and the trials for the Doha Asian Games. Everyone was interested in Han Yu-jin; would this boy who'd broken all records in the preliminaries prove his worth here too? Would he end up qualifying for Doha at the tender age of fifteen?

I was ready. I had trained intensively. I was physically at the top of my game, as I'd stopped taking my meds a few days earlier. I knew I'd go to Doha. I came in first in the 800-metre qualifiers. The stadium murmured: I hadn't appeared in the rankings. Instead, 'DSQ' flashed next to my name. Disqualified. Apparently my leg had moved before the pistol went off; it was a false start. I didn't realise I'd been disqualified until after the race was over. I didn't even realise that I'd moved my leg.

The next day, as I waited for the 1,500-metre qualifiers to begin, I broke out in a cold sweat and a heavy weight sloshed in my belly. But I couldn't have an upset stomach; I hadn't eaten a thing. I figured I was in shock at being disqualified the day before. I tried to forget the nightmare of the 800 metres. I counted, listened to music, focused on the race ahead. The stadium was filled with a metallic smell, but I attributed it to the sweaty crowd in the stands rather than an oncoming seizure.

A short whistle. I took a deep breath. A long whistle. I stepped onto the starting block. 'On your marks.' I crouched and bent over. I hooked my hands over the edge of the starting block and raised my eyes to look at the water. There was a hole there. It was like a sink drain. Black water was swirling violently around it, spinning like a storm, the hole widening. The drain became a sewer, then it grew to a manhole, and then a sinkhole big enough to swallow a car. The lane dividers twisted and writhed like enormous pythons; my lane grew wider. A metallic smell surged up from the water.

This isn't real, my mind reassured me. *You're seeing things because you're not feeling great. Don't be scared.* I turned to look behind me to find that the entire stadium had become a huge maelstrom: the people in the stands had vanished, and spinning black shapes swirled around the outer edges. Maybe this was what it would feel like if you were in a racing car whizzing around an arena. My gut flipped and surged up my throat, just as the starter pistol went off.

I threw myself into the middle of the black whirl of water. I surfaced and began to swim, but my body refused to go forward. I was circling the edge of the swirling water, as though I were going down a plughole. I began gasping. My body careened from left to right, and I thought I would flip over and be sucked in. I couldn't rip my eyes away from the giant dark void at the bottom of the whirlpool. I flailed for something to grab on to. I couldn't breathe.

I realised what was happening. I'd understood its possibility intellectually but I'd never experienced it before. This was the precursor to a seizure. I'd brought this disaster on myself. Fate always lurked; there might be times when it looked the other way, but that couldn't happen more than once or twice. Things that were supposed to happen did happen and things that were supposed to come around did come around. Fate had sent an assassin, deciding at this very moment to carry out my sentence. It was only the most important moment of my life, and it was about to end in the cruellest way possible.

I could either resist to the end and fall into the enormous void, or get out now and run away. I chose the latter. My hand grazed the touchpad. I grabbed it and came to an abrupt stop. I leapt out of the water, threw off my cap and goggles and left the pool. My coach was yelling at me, but I didn't look back. Honestly, I didn't have the energy or the time. Everything started to get darker. I could imagine myself with my eyes rolled back in my head, foaming at the mouth, twisting and curling. I had to go somewhere before that happened in front of all these people. I didn't think. I didn't know where I was going. My feet led the way and I managed to cover some distance. When the moment arrived, it was as if a bomb had gone off inside me. Everything turned white, like a snowy field, and the circuits in my brain stopped firing.

Mother told me later that she found me asleep in a corner of the underground car park, snoring and covered in sweat. She put me in the car as soon as I woke up, and slipped out of that place without telling anyone. Five hours later, I arrived at Auntie's clinic. Instead of explaining to my coach what had happened and trying to figure out what to do, I sat in front of Auntie as she interrogated me about the reason I had stopped taking my meds.

Nobody found out that I was an epileptic who'd had an episode during the race. I was disqualified and wasn't eligible to enter the next race. And of course, I was out of the running for Doha. My coaches were pissed off. My name was plastered all over the local media; the cameras that were circling the pool had nationally televised the insane kid who'd run away in the middle of a race. The fact that he had been a rising star who'd come out of nowhere made it even more newsworthy.

None of this meant I would have to give up swimming; if I had talked frankly with my coaches, they would have been compassionate and given me another chance. That was what I wanted to do. I wasn't afraid of telling them about my epilepsy; any embarrassment would last merely a moment, and swimming was everything. I wanted to speed through the water again. I was ready to be honest. Even if I had to live for the rest of my life shackled and restrained by Remotrol, I was confident that I would never complain.

I was sure that Mother would agree. She had dedicated herself to supporting my ambitions. She knew how rigorously I'd trained. She knew more than anyone else the importance of swimming in my life. But I had overestimated her. She dredged up the promise I'd made when I first began swimming, and told me I was done. She said she'd made her decision when she drove me out of the car park. She acted as though she'd been waiting for something like this all along.

Nothing worked. No excuses, no pleas; I knelt in front of her, weeping, protesting, asking if she was that embarrassed that I was epileptic. I threatened to leave school. I staged a hunger strike until I collapsed. My coach came over after he received notice from Mother that I was quitting, but he was sent away at the door. She didn't budge, not even when her beloved Hae-jin spoke up for me. She was a woman of steel, unmoved by anything, resolute and constant.

I even went to see Auntie on my own for the first time ever. All I had was epilepsy; I wasn't going to keel over and die if I swam past the age of fifteen. This was beyond unfair. Auntie listened to me with a smile on her face. I know, she said. So why did you stop taking your meds?

There are some people you just can't love. Even when they smile, they make you want to pull on either side of that smile and rip their mouth off. I scratched at my knees, my forefinger twitching, and pulled out my ace card. I asked her not to tell Mother, and confessed to it all. It was the first time I'd told anyone why I had stopped taking my pills. For the first time ever, I spoke honestly about myself, my dreams, why I had to swim, my desire not to be defined by my epilepsy. I beseeched her to talk to Mother for me.

The following morning, Mother called me to the living room. I'd never felt so nervous. I sat in front of her, my eyelids trembling as I looked down at my palms, which were damp with sweat.

'As long as you keep swimming, there's always the possibility that you might have a seizure in the water.' Her voice was gentle but firm.

The world spun around me. That won't happen, I wanted to say, but my mouth was glued shut.

'Someone who's already crossed a line will cross it again. You know what's on the other side, so you'll stop taking your pills again and again. You know that you'll feel so much more agile and that you can set records.'

I looked up at her. I realised that Mother would never change her mind. I also realised that Auntie had not kept her promise.

'I'm scared,' Mother said, her voice shaking. 'I'm so scared I don't know what to do. Your brother and father drowned in the ocean, in front of my eyes. That day in Ulsan, in the pool … I thought I was going to lose you too. My only surviving son.' Her eyes filled up.

I gritted my teeth. I couldn't feel her fear, but I could understand it. Of course she would be scared. But why did I have to be sacrificed for that fear? I took my meds in spite of horrible side effects. Couldn't she just watch me swim in spite of her fear? Didn't that make us even?

'So let's stop,' she said. 'Let's stop all of this now.'

Mother deregistered me from competitions. I gave up.

I shoved everything related to swimming in a big box – medals, scrapbooks of newspaper clippings, photographs, my training suit, my competition suit, even towels. I dragged it up to the roof and burned it all. I wanted to ask: *Are you happy now?*

It wasn't that hard to return to being a normal high-school student. I'd always studied alongside swimming, so I just went to school as usual. I didn't put in any special effort. My plans then were to laze around for the rest of my life, leeching off Mother forever. That was how I would get my revenge.

I changed my mind the following spring. I was in Hae-jin's room, flipping through a book, and I started to get excited as I read it more closely. It had been written by a defence lawyer whose clients included a young man who'd got drunk and hacked his father to death, a woman who'd killed her husband for insurance money, a man who'd strangled his family and tried to hang himself, an unmarried woman who'd killed her newborn baby and left the body in a bathroom. I was more captivated by the trial procedures than the incidents that preceded them. According to this attorney, criminal cases fell into two categories: those where you fought for acquittal and others where you entered a guilty plea and then fought over sentencing. The latter were harder to defend, as sentencing required considera-tion of the defendant's age, intelligence and environment; his relationship with the victim; the reason he committed the crime; the method and result of his acts; and what he did afterwards, in addition to ethics. What was important at this point, the lawyer wrote, was to find out what kind of life the defendant had led. I understood that passage to mean that morality was all about painting a picture to help your case. I found other similar books to read. I was drawn to conjuring stories. Perhaps I was disappointed that I couldn't defend myself properly when Mother laid down the law. Or maybe I liked this new idea of morality. Who knew? What was important was that I'd found something else intriguing. Any time a heinous crime became the target of the nation's outrage, I would appoint myself the invisible defence attorney and think how I would change various parts of the picture. After all, being true to life wasn't the only way to tell a story.

Of course, I knew that to do it for real, I had to become a lawyer. To do that, I had to go to law school; to get into law school, it was advantageous to enrol in an undergraduate law programme; and to do that, I had to study hard. I wouldn't even have attempted it if it hadn't been for Hae-jin. He helped me every step of the way, encouraging me when I was denied admission the first time I applied before finally getting into my choice of college the following year.

Ever since then, I'd remained devoted to my goals. I'd given it my all, the way I did when I was swimming. Maybe even more than that. Yet today, when I could finally see the results of all that work, I was sitting again with my neck bared in front of the assassin sent by fate. Of course, it was entirely my own fault: I'd made the same mistake that had torpedoed my life at fifteen. But as my own defence lawyer, I wanted to ask fate: wouldn't you too want to have just a few clear sunny days after living through sixteen years with a pounding head, a permanent screech in your ears, and limp muscles?

I picked up my medicine and threw it in the bin. I had to find the real reason why my life had been burned to the ground. I had to paint my own picture, and I had to do it fast, since Hae-jin was waiting for me downstairs. Who knew when Auntie would burst through the front door? I couldn't figure anything out if my skull was pounding and my ears were ringing. My body and mind had to be in that clear sunny space, even if it was dangerous.

I started cleaning my room. I swept all the things on my desk into the drawer. I hung up the jacket and vest in the wardrobe and folded away my self-pity while I was at it. I tossed my clothes, underwear and bedlinen into the bath-tub. I flipped the bloody mattress over to hide the stain. I'd have to deal with these things later. If I could, I'd discard or burn or bury them. At the very least, I'd try to wash them.

I wiped the blood off the floor, door and door handle with the dirty steam cleaner pad I'd brought up. I rinsed the broom and bucket in the bathroom, and took them out to the roof deck with the bin bag. I threw the bag in the round lidded bin next to the tap; Mother used that bin to make winter kimchi or store water. I leant the broom and bucket against the tap, then screwed the hose that was lying nearby onto the tap and washed the blood off the roof deck, the pergola, the swing and the table.

By the time I was done, the winter sun had poked its pale face out from the middle of the grey sky. The air was still chilly. The strong ocean wind was sharp and cutting. I cupped my frozen hands as I headed back to my room.

'Yu-jin!' Mother's scream stabbed me in the back of my neck.

I froze. I heard the rush of a river bubbling up from the depths of my memory. I closed my eyes and saw the yellow light of the street lamp. I saw myself running through the rain as Mother's scream echoed in the fog and disappeared into the darkness. A tarpaulin covering a construction site flapped loudly in the dark.

I opened my eyes. The images dissipated. I went back to my room, keeping the sliding door open. It would take a while for the smell of blood to go away completely. My mobile notified me of an incoming text. Hae-jin.

Lunch is ready.

Irritation flared up before simmering down. I checked the time. 1.01 p.m.

Coming, I tapped out, figuring he'd come back up if I didn't reply immediately. I looked around. Other than the stench of blood and the stripped bed, everything was the same as usual. I washed my feet and stood in front of the bathroom mirror to make sure my face was clean. I was met with thick, stiff hair, the round forehead I'd inherited from Father, and the black eyes and protruding ears from Mother. My reflection was the person I'd thought of all along as 'me', but who now looked wild and frazzled and anxious.

I washed my face and every bit of it hurt. My life had dis-integrated. I took out a towel and dried my face, then threw it by the bathroom door. I stepped on it carefully to dry the soles of my feet. The rough sensation of the towel underfoot brought me back to the present. Hae-jin was waiting for me.

*

When I got downstairs, Hae-jin was at the stove, checking the seasoning of the soup with a ladle. 'What were you doing all this time? I thought you said you were starving.'

The table was set with a few side dishes, steamed egg in an earthenware pot, and a spoon.

I sat down and he placed a bowl of seaweed soup and rice in front of me. 'What about you?' I asked.

'I just had ramen. I can't eat right now.'

I looked down at my soup bowl, chock full of seaweed and beef with barely any broth. That was the way Mother served me soup; I was on a low-sodium diet per her sister's direction.

'You should be moved to tears,' Hae-jin joked. 'I made it all myself, just for you. With beef and seaweed that was already here, I mean.' He sat in front of me with a cup of coffee. He was wearing a white shirt, a navy cashmere sweater Mother had bought him and a pair of jeans – dressed to go out.

I picked up a strand of seaweed and stuffed it into my parched mouth. It was hot and slippery but didn't taste much like anything. He really should have seasoned it some more; what was he doing all this time with that ladle?

'What did Mother say?' Hae-jin asked.

I shrugged. 'Her phone's turned off. Maybe she's praying.'

'Yeah?' Hae-jin cocked his head. 'Or maybe she doesn't realise her battery died.'

I nodded.

'Then how are we going to reach her? We can call the retreat centre. Did she say where she was going?'

'Don't worry. I'll handle it. Let me eat first.'

Hae-jin opened his mouth, then closed it without a word.

I shoved another strand of seaweed into my mouth.

'Eat some rice too,' he said. 'Don't just eat the seaweed.'

'Are you going somewhere?'

Hae-jin looked down at his sweater. 'Yeah, to see someone from school.'

'Where?'

'Gimpo. He's headed to Tokyo this afternoon. I have to bring him something.'

'You should probably get going then,' I said, taking care not to appear too eager.

'I have time.'

Ah. I shoved more seaweed into my mouth.

'Oh, did you hear?'

'Hear what?' I asked.

'There was a murder around here.'

I looked up. The seaweed snaked down my throat. I swallowed it whole, my eyes watering. Murder? 'Where?'

'At the dock.'

'The rest area by the sea wall?'

Hae-jin nodded. 'On my way home I saw people up top, staring down. It was mobbed with police cars. So I stopped to take a look. You know how I am, I can't help myself!'

Suppressing the urge to say, *And?* I spooned some rice into my mouth.

'There was police tape by the dock. Apparently the person working the ticket booth found a body caught on the anchoring rope of the ferry this morning.' Hae-jin paused. 'They were saying it's a young woman.'

I chewed before replying. 'Just because they found a body doesn't mean she was killed, does it? Could be suicide, or an accident.'

'Yeah, but why would the police come out in full force if that was the case?' Hae-jin paused. His mobile was ringing from his room. He practically threw his cup down to run and answer it.

I picked up a strand of seaweed, listening to him saying, 'Yes, Auntie. Yes, yes. One second.'

He closed the door and I couldn't hear anything else. Whatever was left of my appetite vanished. Auntie? Hae-jin was taking her call with the door closed. Had that ever happened before? I couldn't remember. Probably not. Hae-jin wasn't the type to talk secretively on the phone; he answered calls loudly and publicly as he thought it was the polite thing to do. That meant Auntie had demanded this behaviour, but what did she have to tell him?

I placed my chopsticks down. I thought back to my conversation with Auntie, in case there was anything I had said to her that was different from what I'd told Hae-jin.

Hae-jin came out of his room ten minutes later. He had his camera bag on one shoulder and was holding his parka.

'Sorry for not keeping you company while you were having lunch.' He said this apologetically, as though he watched me eat every meal every single day.

I shoved my hands into my pockets casually. 'So what did Auntie say?'

'Hmm? Auntie?' His mouth tightened. He averted his eyes.

'Weren't you just talking to Auntie?'

'No . . . ' Hae-jin turned around to open the door to the porch. The back of his neck above his collar was turning red, which then spread to his ears. 'It's a woman who was one of the crew when we were shooting *Private Lesson*,' he said, belatedly remembering which 'auntie' he had been speaking to. 'We caught up a bit. It's been a while, and we were on that island for three months.'

I leant against the door frame, wondering why he had given me so much detail.

Hae-jin slid his feet into his shoes and bent down to lace them up. He paused, then straightened up, holding something in his hand. 'What's this?' He turned and handed it over.

I took it without realising what it was. An earring. A single pearl earring.

'What's that doing here?' he murmured, looking over at my palm. 'It's not Mother's, is it?'

It wasn't Mother's. Her ears weren't pierced and she rarely wore earrings. She didn't really go in for jewellery at all, in fact. The only thing she wore was the anklet she had had on last night. It went without saying that the earring wasn't mine, either. Hae-jin had found it closer to the interior than to the front door; it couldn't have rolled inside accidentally. Someone must have dropped it here.

Regardless of who or when, the earring didn't look all that special. But the sensation of the smooth, round surface bothered me. More precisely, the déjà vu I felt when I touched it bothered me. It made my heart race. Where had I touched something like this before? When? I rubbed the round part with my thumb and looked at Hae-jin. 'I'll put it in Mum's room. She'll know what to do with it.'

Nodding, Hae-jin headed towards the front door. I put on slippers and followed him out. 'When will you be back?'

'Soon.' He opened the door. 'We should pop some non-alcoholic champagne or something. Even if we do the real celebration when Mother gets home.'

I stood in the doorway. The lift was already on its way down to the ground floor from the eighth floor. It would take a few minutes for it to come back up to our floor. It would be an awkward few minutes for Hae-jin, who wasn't a good liar. He began to run down the stairs, raising a hand as he disappeared. It could have meant anything: I'll be back soon, see you later, go back in, I have to run because I'm incredibly busy right now.

Hello started barking on the seventh floor. I looked down again at the earring in my hand. The tip of the post had dug into my palm. I picked it up between two fingers like a gemmologist and peered at it. It couldn't have fallen off someone's ear lobe, because the back was still attached to the post. It had to have been in a bag or a pocket before falling out, which meant that this someone would have to meet two conditions: she had come to our flat, and she wore earrings.

Could it be Auntie's? I wasn't sure if she had pierced ears, but she wore different earrings each time I saw her. I remembered a red gem that dangled like a teardrop, a crown stud against her ear lobe, a star that twinkled blue. Why wouldn't there be a pearl among them?

Hello finally stopped barking. I closed the front door. I

took my slippers off in the foyer and stepped back into the flat. I heard something strange, like a small pebble falling to the ground and rolling away. I remembered taking my hands out of the *Private Lesson* jacket. Right here. Last night. I'd looked down for the sound and I hadn't been able to pick up whatever it was that fell because Mother was right behind me. I opened my palm again and looked down at the earring. The back of my neck prickled. It couldn't have been this . . .

The clock chimed. Two o'clock. I shoved the earring into my pocket. I felt jittery. My imagination was running away with itself again.

I went out to the balcony off the living room. I opened all the windows Hae-jin had closed. It still smelled like bleach everywhere. Blood and handprints were possibly still visible on the walls along the corridor upstairs, the walls of the stairwell and landing and parts of the living room, the top of the door frame to Mother's room, the leg of the key cabinet in the corner, even on the family portrait. I glared suspiciously at the speck of blood that had splattered on the clock face. Had Hae-jin not noticed this? The guy who could see a fly hovering over the key cabinet from the doorway to his room?

I concluded that he hadn't. If he had, he would have said something, something like 'What did you do, slaughter a pig in here?'

I rummaged around in the emergency kit and found the hydrogen peroxide. The half-litre container was about two thirds full. I emptied the air freshener out of its spray bottle and poured the hydrogen peroxide inside, then began to methodically spray everything, starting with the doorway of Mother's bedroom. White foam grew like mould every-where that had been splattered with blood. I wiped those spots with toilet paper, then flushed the used bits of paper down the toilet. I moved on to the key cabinet, table, stairs and upstairs hallway, checking carefully for blood.

I dragged my mattress downstairs and swapped it with Mother's. The bloodstains weren't going anywhere, but I thought it made sense for Mother's traces to be returned to her room. Who knew if it would be one night or more, but it didn't feel right to sleep on her blood. Thankfully the mattresses were the same size. As I spread the cover out on her bed, I stiffened.

I don't know where he went.

Mother's voice. She sounded calm and refined, as though she were reading out loud from a book – her journal. That was where I'd seen that sentence. It was also something I'd been asking myself all day. Where had I gone? What had I done for two and a half hours?

I know I saw him.

What came after that? I couldn't remember. Was it *I'm cold* or *I'm scared*, or maybe *I'm terrified*? It was definitely one of the three.

I began to shiver when I stepped out of Mother's bed-room. It was freezing in the living room. I closed all the windows and cast a final glance around the room to see if I had missed anything. Everything was clean. I ran upstairs. I settled in front of my desk and took out the journal. I hadn't been entirely correct, but I hadn't been completely wrong, either. It wasn't one of the three; it was all of them.

I'm cold and scared and terrified.

It made sense that she would be cold. Last night was rainy and it was the middle of winter; it would be strange if she *wasn't* cold. But scared and terrified? Those weren't the kind of feelings she would have had without reason. She wouldn't be scared of her own son, would she? Sure, she might have been disapproving of whatever I'd been doing, but she wouldn't have been terrified. So that had to mean that the 'him' she had seen wasn't me.

'There was a murder around here.' That's what Hae-jin had said. 'They were saying it's a young woman.'

Was that it? Did she witness the young woman being killed? Where could that have been? The docks? The sea wall? On the footpath along the river? It wasn't beyond the realms of possibility that the body would reach the dock. Dongjin River flowed between the two districts of the city, and the floodgates opened at the mouth of the harbour from midnight to one in the morning. The woman could have been killed and pushed in the water at just the right time, when the water that had been trapped all day surged into the ocean, following the enormous current sweeping downriver.

I heard something behind me, like a stick scraping the wooden floor. It sounded like the swing creaking in the wind. I got up and opened the blinds. Somehow it had become evening. The pergola light was still on and Mother was sitting on the swing. Her hands were laced together and propped on her stomach, her head was tilted up, as though looking at the dark sky. She looked like she was just taking a little break. Her white dress fluttered as the wind rocked

119

the swing. Her bare feet dragged on the deck floor. The wound across her neck gaped open like a red mouth, like the Joker.

You really don't remember? the Joker asked.

I knew I was seeing things, but I found myself speaking out loud. 'Remember what?'

You saw it too, the Joker said.

'Saw what? When? Where?'

The conversation ended the way it always did, with the delusion not responding. But I remembered the odd images that had danced past my eyes. The yellow light of the street lamp, the dark shadows of the river that rushed and swirled below my feet, the crimson umbrella bowling along the road, the tarpaulin flapping in the wind.

The back of my neck prickled. These images didn't have anything to do with the ferry dock or the crossing by the sea wall. The lamps along the sea wall had LEDs that gave off crisp white light, and there was no building site covered by tarpaulin. The ocean was on one side of the wall, and on the other side was the road by the riverbank, lined with blocks of flats and buildings. So the only place where water could be swirling below my feet would be the road along the river. I didn't know exactly where on that street, but it probably wouldn't mean much even if I could figure it out. These images must have been what I'd seen right before my seizure; I'd had similar experiences before.

I'd settled on a conclusion but it didn't feel great. I felt as though I'd had a glimpse of the road to hell. A hunch, something ominous, was closing in on me. My mind yammered on like a woodpecker. *That can't be right! Why would you remember meaningless scenes? There has to be something in those images.* Something cold and scary and terrifying. Did I see something last night? I suddenly remembered a man singing in the darkness. The song about a girl he couldn't forget; about her walking in the rain.

I was growing more and more confused. Instead of answers, thousands of questions were piling on top of one another like scrap metal. I closed the blinds and threw myself down in the chair. Something sharp stabbed in my inner groin. The pearl earring. I pulled it out from my pocket and grabbed my mobile. I opened a browser and typed in some key words: *Gundo young woman body.*

There were a few hits. I opened the first link, a *Yonhap News* item.

Young Woman's Body Discovered by Gundo Sea Wall Dock

Today, around 8 a.m., a woman's body was discovered at the ferry dock by the sea wall in Gundo, Incheon. Police said that a ticket office employee discovered the body caught on a mooring rope. The deceased was determined to be B- (age 28) of Flat A in District Two. Police sources said that the possibility of homicide was high; the body had been damaged by a sharp object. The National Institute of Scientific Investigation will conduct an autopsy and the police are questioning potential witnesses.

The other articles were along the same lines, as though they had been written from the same news release, with similar words and sentence structures. They consistently reported the identity of the dead woman, her address, that her body had been damaged somehow, and where she had been found. I suddenly thought of Yongi's, the stand selling sugar pancakes near the crossing by the sea wall. Maybe the owner of the stand knew what had really happened.

A few metres from Yongi's was a spiral staircase that went down to the docks, where there was a rest area. There was only a single snack stand down there, but quite a number of people came by during the day on their way to the ferry. The popular oar ferry transported tourists from the sea wall and the marine park, and at weekends the queue went all the way up to the wall. Yongi's was in the prime commercial area, where you could see all the people on the dock and along the bicycle path, and all the comings and goings from District Two. The gossipy owner would be more useful than the CCTV installed at the traffic lights, since he greeted passers-by and knew the area like the back of his hand. He would have enjoyed a surge in popularity today, what with the police and curious bystanders visiting his stand.

I took a pair of sweatpants and a blue parka from the wardrobe and slung a towel around my neck to complete the look. I put my mobile, the entry card for the building's front door, a single 5,000-won bill and the pearl earring in my pockets, then ran downstairs. It was 6.07 p.m. If I was lucky, I would be back before Hae-jin returned. I had to confirm something before putting the earring on Mother's desk: whether the clattering and rolling sound had had anything to do with it, and if it was related to what Mother had seen last night. There was no guarantee that Mr Yongi would give me what I wanted, but he was the one person who might have information. If my luck held, I might even be able to make it down to the dock to look for further evidence.

I put on my usual running shoes, still covered in mud, and took the lift down. Outside, I began to walk quickly. There were three ways to leave the complex of flats: the main gate, which faced the majority of the buildings in the neighbourhood, most of which were still under construction; the rear gate, which was closest to our building; or a side gate that brought you out by the walking path on the road behind Gundo Elementary School. Just like last night, I began to run once I got to that road.

About five hundred metres from the side gate was where you met up with the road along Dongjin River. Further on took you to the crossing by the sea wall, then came the entrance to the marine park, and just on from that, the bridge and the observatory. It was the perfect route for a run. There was even a bicycle path between the sea wall and the observatory, used by runners or walkers, usually in the early morning or early evening.

Of course I had been running regularly since we moved here. It reminded me of swimming: you sprinted forward as fast as you could towards the end. It wasn't bad: you could look at the river and then the ocean. I liked how my heart would leap and buck like an angry lion when I didn't have many opportunities to feel that way, or even to feel excited, tense, nervous or angry.

I didn't always run at the same time of day. Sometimes I went out at dawn, sometimes in the late morning, and other times in the late afternoon. But at night I could run freely without anyone getting in my way, without bumping into someone gazing at the scenery. If I fell over, I wouldn't be embarrassed. Today was the first time I'd gone out at this time, right after sunset.

Police cars sped by, maybe because of the murder. I noticed taxis from other cities. People were walking in pairs or groups. The first was a man and a woman, followed by three women and two men. They were all holding bags of sugar pancakes from Yongi's.

Near the First Dongjin Bridge, a bright light shone from behind me. I glanced back. A police car was following me. The way it was slowly moving forward made me think that the officers were going to stop to ask me some questions – where do you live, maybe, or where are you going, or why are you out running at night? Did you know someone has been murdered?

Aware of the officers inside the car, I made an exaggerated gesture of wiping my face with the towel around my neck. I ran so that it would look like I was a professional athlete going about my usual business. When I got to the pedestrian crossing, the police car turned on its siren, made a left, and disappeared toward the marine park. As I waited for the light to turn green, I tried to peer into Yongi's across the road to see if he was in.

'Yu-jin,' Mr Yongi called out from his shack as soon as I crossed over.

I tried to pretend that I was on my way to somewhere else.

'Come here for a second,' Mr Yongi said, waving. 'I have something to tell you.'

I stepped inside the shack, still acting like I had somewhere else to be.

'Are you out for a run?'

I nodded and looked down at the grill. On the edge was a stack of sugar pancakes.

'You've been out late for the last few days, haven't you?' Mr Yongi picked up a pancake with a pair of tongs and handed it over.

I accepted the hot delicacy. 'No.'

'No? I haven't seen you around in the afternoons.'

'I've been coming out at dawn.'

'I see.' He nodded. 'So did you come out at dawn yesterday, too?'

'No, not yesterday. I didn't go for a run.'

'I see.'

I waited patiently.

'Going to the observatory again?' He rubbed his hands on his trousers and picked up a paper bag.

I stared at his clothes and raised my eyes to his woollen winter hat. Behind him a change of clothes hung inside a transparent zip-up bag – a grey coat and a hunting cap. A clean shirt, necktie and suit were probably tucked inside the coat. Below the hanger stood a large suitcase.

I'd seen him in that hat, coat and suit, wearing his polished shoes, dragging his suitcase onto the 11.30 p.m. Ansan-bound intercity bus after closing his shop. His outfit made him look like a middle-aged office worker going home after a long trip, not a man selling sugar pancakes in a small shack. I'd also seen him get off the bus at nine in the morning wearing the same things. He would open up his shack, change into his work clothes and get down to business as the town gossip and pancake maker.

'I wouldn't go today,' he finally said, unable to wait for me to respond. 'I don't know if you heard the news. They found a body at the dock this morning.'

'What does that have to do with the observatory?' I asked.

'What are you talking about? The police are all over this place! Don't you see those two cars over there? They've been patrolling at ten-minute intervals, but they haven't found a single clue yet! So only the residents are being inconvenienced. I haven't done any business today. The police come and go, the plain-clothes guys come and go. They ask the same things. What time did you close up shop yesterday? Did you see anyone suspicious hanging around? Do you know the people who frequent this road at night?'

I looked down and took a bite of the pancake, barely able to contain my curiosity about his answers to those questions.

'And I tell them I haven't seen anyone other than the same people who always stop by late at night, and they grill me and want to know who those people are.'

The hot sugar slid straight down, burning my throat and making my eyes water. My throat felt tight.

Mr Yongi quickly handed me a cup of cold water. 'Hey, hey, take it easy!'

I poured the whole cup down and managed to prise my eyes open again.

'Oh, you can just give me three thousand won,' Mr Yongi said, shoving the nine remaining pancakes in a bag. 'I'm giving you a huge discount! I haven't seen you in a while.'

I would have to take the bag without protest if I wanted to hear what else he had to say. I held out my 5,000-won bill.

'So you know how you come out late at night to run sometimes?' Mr Yongi flattened the bill and slid it into his money belt. 'If they discover that, they'll really get up your ass. Don't worry, I didn't say anything. How would I know everything about every person I see? Right? All I know is that you live in Moon Torch.'

How did he know that? Moon Torch wasn't near the sea wall. I'd never told him where I lived. I stuffed the rest of the pancake in my mouth just to keep up the act of doing something normal.

'Remember that girl I introduced you to over the summer? The one who was wearing sunglasses in the middle of the night when it was raining? Her hair was long, all the way down her back. She sat there.' Mr Yongi pointed at the white plastic stool in the corner. 'You remember?'

I did remember.

'So yesterday she gets off the bus by herself. It wasn't that late, maybe it was right after nine, maybe just before. Anyway, she comes in and sits down on that stool like it's hers, crosses her legs, and asks if you've been out today. I say no and she looks so disappointed. So I figure she likes you or something. She tells me you live across the road from her, and she lives in ePurun, so you must be in Moon Torch.'

I suddenly remembered the crimson umbrella rolling along the road. And the woman I'd seen at the crossing last night. Was her umbrella crimson?

Mr Yongi continued. 'So she sits here for close to an hour but she doesn't eat a single pancake! She says she's allergic to flour or whatever. I mean, if you stay that long, shouldn't you buy a bag? Just to be polite? I don't care if you throw it on the street on your way home. Anyway, finally a man walks in and they leave together.'

'So she's the one who died?' I asked, swallowing the pancake down. I sure hoped so. If she was the victim, then I was clearly irrelevant to the incident. Another man had left with her last night.

Mr Yongi, who was holding out my change, tapped the bills on the back of his hand. 'What? Are you listening? When did I say that?'

'Oh . . . no?' My voice crawled into my throat.

'The plain-clothes police officers who came showed me the dead girl's picture and asked if I'd ever seen her, had she come into the shop . . . I looked at it, and honestly, I nearly had a heart attack!' He stopped and put the change back into his money belt.

It was clear that if I wanted to hear why he had nearly had a heart attack, I'd have to forgo my change to make up for the pancakes the girl didn't buy last night. I blinked in agreement so he would go on.

'I remembered her. She'd come in a few times. She wasn't a regular, but I remembered her instantly. Because she wore an earring on the outer rim of her ear, but only on one side. I asked her about it once – I couldn't help myself,

128

I was so curious – and she said it was her late mother's and she'd lost the other one. I told the police, and they asked me what the earring looked like.'

Without realising it, I put my hand in my pocket. The sharp end of the earring grazed the tip of my finger, and I flinched.

'No point in describing it really,' continued Mr Yongi. 'It was just a simple earring with a single pearl on it.'

The world spun. Mr Yongi's voice faded and returned. 'Man, those dirty flies are back.' He was looking behind me.

I looked back too. A black car had stopped in front of the shack. Two men got out and strode inside. The first had short hair and eyes that were set far apart. The other was older, middle-aged, and wearing a dark coat. They both looked at me.

'We're closing,' Mr Yongi said.

The one with the goat eyes looked at his watch. 'It's still early.'

'I'm all out of batter,' Mr Yongi said, throwing his tongs into a plastic bowl with a clatter.

'Are you a regular customer?' the one in the dark coat asked. It was clear they were detectives.

'He's a student who lives around here,' Mr Yongi answered for me.

This was the perfect time for me to leave. 'See you later,' I said to Mr Yongi, and walked out before the detective could start asking questions. It was only a few steps to the crossing, but I nearly fell over several times, my knees were shaking so hard.

It was just a simple earring with a single pearl on it.

I looked back at the shack. Mr Yongi was gesturing and

making grimaces as he delivered some sort of fiery speech to the two men. I took out the earring. It had a single pearl on it. I closed my fist quickly. It couldn't be. I shook my head. My mind started babbling. *Don't worry about it. It's just a coincidence. Any woman would have at least one pair of pearl earrings.*

Bright light shone from the bus stop. I turned and saw a bus drawing up. It wasn't raining hard, but the windscreen wipers were on. A woman and a man got off the bus, and the woman opened a red umbrella and walked towards the crossing. The man followed, his hands in his coat pockets and his shoulders hunched, heavy. They weren't together. He looked like he was drunk.

I started to cross the street and passed them. Behind me, the man, slurring, began singing loudly, something about a girl in the rain who he couldn't forget. He must have had at least four or five bottles of *soju*.

Something felt off. The man's bellowing song was all around me, but I didn't hear any footsteps. In the centre of the road, I looked back. There was nobody there. Not the woman or the man. Not even the bus. Only the song rang out in the fog.

I looked over at the shack again. The detectives were standing side by side, facing Mr Yongi. Had they not heard the singing? I broke into a run. Everything was spinning; dozens of crimson umbrellas flapped like a colony of bats. The singing followed me all the way home. I must be slowly going crazy.

I got a text from Hae-jin as I stepped inside the flat.

On my way to Muan on the KTX. Just got asked to fill in

to film a wedding. I'll be back tomorrow night. Did you talk to Mother? Her mobile's still off. Text me when you do. Sorry I can't celebrate with you tonight.

I sent my reply. *No worries. Take your time.* I had so much to do too.

I trudged up the stairs. Nothing made sense. I still couldn't remember what had happened. But now I was starting to realise something. The things that had seemed unrelated to one another and the clues I'd shrugged off or ignored were beginning to come together. I just had to figure out what had happened during the two and a half hours between midnight and 2.30 in the morning.

I took off my jacket and hung it on the back of my chair. I sat down. I put the bag of pancakes and the pearl earring on my desk. *It was just a simple earring with a single pearl on it.* I thought of the sentence in the news article that had made me go to Yongi's in the first place. *Police sources said that the possibility of homicide was high; the body had been damaged by a sharp object.*

I took out the razor from my desk drawer. I unfolded it. *You, Yu-jin . . . You don't deserve to live.* What should I do? Where should I begin? Even the thought of doing something frightened me. It seemed that anything I could do would result in putting shackles on myself. I was just falling further into the hell I'd glimpsed earlier. Wouldn't it be better to sit still and not do anything at all?

Exhaustion rushed at me. I wanted to crawl into my bed and sleep, even if it was just for a moment, until I reached the catastrophic end. I closed my eyes and pressed my hands to my forehead. There were things you couldn't avoid in life – being born, becoming someone's child, and for me, the events that had already transpired. Still, I didn't want to speculate; I wanted to take control of my destiny. No matter how this fucking situation was going to end, I would make the decisions in my life. That meant I had to do what I could and uncover the two hours and thirty minutes shrouded in darkness.

I put the razor down next to the earring. I took my iPod, earphones, key to the roof and car key out of the drawer. I touched each one. I opened Mother's journal. It was the best place to start.

I flipped through it from beginning to end. It was longer than I'd thought; blue tabs separated the years from 2016 to 2000 in reverse chronological order. The records were separated into months, also in reverse order, from December. The notations on each page were in chronological order, though. Some months she had written nearly every day, while in others she'd written only a few times. Sometimes she'd skipped entire months. The entries ranged from a single line to long ones that ran to two or three pages. Nothing was standard. That was probably why she kept it in a binder, so that she could add pages easily. There was another benefit to this: I could check for specific months in a particular year, like a library catalogue.

The notations had started sixteen years ago, on 30 April 2000: *Yu-jin is sleeping peacefully, deeply.*

I flipped forward and looked at the most recent records again, from December 2016. She had written on the 6th, 7th, and 9th. They were all about me. Was the whole binder like this? If so, it would be fair to call it a record of my every movement. I shuddered. Why did she take these notes? Was it so that she could report to Auntie everything I did and said without forgetting anything? Why did she have to keep it all written down?

Tuesday 6 December
   He's not in his room. He's started going out through the roof again. It's the first time in a month.

Wednesday 7 December
   Second day in a row. I was waiting but I missed him.

Friday 9 December
   I don't know where he went. I looked for him until 2 a.m. but I couldn't find him. I know I saw him. I'm cold and scared and terrified. Now
   Hello is barking. He's back.

Three things were true. Mother had followed me. She and I had met somewhere. The thing that had made her cold and scared and terrified had occurred between 12.30 and 2 a.m. Ominous and incomprehensible blank spaces loomed between the sentences. I couldn't work them out, at least not right now.
   I turned to November.

Monday 14 November
   He went out through the roof. I didn't expect it – everything was fine the last few months. If I'd gone out when Hello started barking I would have caught him.
   Something made me open his drawer and check on

133

his pills. There are exactly eleven days' worth left. Does that mean he's taking them like he's supposed to?

I picked up my desk calendar and flipped the page forward to check the date. I had placed small dots on the days from 11 to 15 November. That was when I stopped taking the pills for the oral exams; it was the second time since August. Instead of popping a pill in my mouth at each meal, I flushed it down the toilet. That was the best way to keep everything straight and not get caught. But it was clear that she suspected I wasn't taking them, and she'd drawn that conclusion from the fact that I'd gone to the roof – another action out of my usual pattern of behaviour. That meant that she knew those two actions were linked. Maybe there had been a precedent that led her to that conclusion.

I thought carefully about possible precedents. Nothing remotely plausible came to mind.

Tuesday 15 November
I feel like I'm playing hide-and-seek with the wind.
I ran out when Hello started barking but I didn't see him. The security guard by the back gate said nobody had gone by in the last thirty minutes. Same thing at the main gate. I tried the side gate and bumped into Hae-jin, coming home from work. No Yu-jin.

So Mother followed me all the time. Why? Sure, she retained absolute command over my life, but it still didn't seem normal. Most mothers didn't tail their sons just because they left the house in the middle of the night, unless they were insane or they had a good reason to. The security guard at the back gate must have known about her abnormal obsession. Maybe everyone who lived in our building knew about the widow who wandered around the neighbourhood looking for her son. But unlike last night, on 15 November she probably didn't go all over the place, since she had bumped into Hae-jin.

I wasn't sure if the dates matched up, but I did remember seeing Hae-jin in the street a few weeks ago, probably around then. It was late, and I was running towards the sea wall along the footpath by the river. Near the First Dongjin Bridge, I heard a phone ringing in front of me.

'Yes, I'm on my way home,' said a voice.

I could pick that voice out in a street filled with a hundred people talking in a hundred different voices. Hae-jin. Should I say hello? Then he'd ask what I was doing out at this hour. If I told him I was going for a run, Mother would hear about it and I'd be giving her a new reason to nag me.

'No, no, that's okay,' Hae-jin said, about ten metres in front of me. His dark shadow appeared out of the fog.

I swiftly hid behind a street lamp, in the tight gap between the lamp post and the railing along the riverbank. It wasn't a bad place to hide; it was dark back there with the neck of the lamp stretching out toward the road, and I imagined I had some cover from the fog coming off the river. He was far away enough not to see me.

'Yes, I'll be in Sangam-dong by two tomorrow.'

I stood facing the river as I listened to Hae-jin's voice pass behind me. I watched the water sluicing towards the flood-gates and had a sudden urge to pee. There was no way he could see my face; it was dark, my back was towards him, and I was wearing a mask and a hood, my head ducked low. I did worry that he would catch the words *Private Lesson* stitched on the back of my jacket, though.

I didn't like the fact that I was hiding in the shade of a lamp post, hunched over in case he recognised me. I wasn't a criminal on the run. Why was I so worried? God. Why couldn't he leave? Just leave already, please?

Eventually he did. When I couldn't hear his footsteps any longer, I continued on my way. What would have happened if I'd said hello to him that night? Would Mother have stopped following me? But what had she been worried about specifically? Why was she so anxious?

The next page wasn't October. She had skipped two months.

Tuesday 30 August
    The boys came back from Imja Island close to midnight. They weren't planning to come back until tomorrow. Yu-jin was sweating in a Gore-Tex jacket in this heat. Just looking at him was suffocating. There was a cut on the back of his hand and I thought I saw a bruise on his head. His hair was plastered with sweat.
    Could he have stopped taking his meds again? He couldn't have ... could he? Did he have a seizure?

She must have written 'could he' as a safeguard against being wrong. Because when we stepped inside the house, I knew she'd figured it all out the moment her gaze landed on my forehead. Her question, 'What happened

136

to your face?' made it clear she'd had her suspicions confirmed.

But I didn't want to do all the work for her. 'I banged into the ferry as I was getting on.'

She looked at me flatly. 'And why are you wearing a jacket? It's so hot.'

I looked down at myself. Why was I wearing this again? My mind scrambled for an answer. *To cover the scratches and bruises I got when I had my episode.* 'Hae-jin gave it to me. You always say it's good manners to use a gift right away.'

Hae-jin was sitting on the couch, taking his socks off, pretending to concentrate so hard on that very important task that he couldn't possibly pay attention to our conversation. He was uncomfortable with my lie, and also how a memento from his very first shoot had somehow become a gift for me. He was also uneasy with Mother's mood.

Mother didn't dig further. After I retreated upstairs, she probably asked Hae-jin: was that really what happened? Hae-jin would have said yes. I trusted that he would have remained firm even when she asked a few more times, even if his expression betrayed him. The unconfirmed truth would have floated around Mother's mind: ten years ago his whole life was turned upside down because he arbitrarily stopped taking his meds. There was no way he could have done it again. Or could he have?

Was that why she attacked me last night? Maybe she couldn't keep looking the other way when I went out through the roof. Or maybe there was some other issue. I guess I could understand her exploding like that. Goodness knows how she was able to keep it under wraps until yesterday. Mother being who she was, it made more sense for her to stop me at the very beginning rather than follow me around secretly and observe me for four months.

Wednesday 31 August

Around 10 p.m. I was getting into bed when I heard a strange bang upstairs. It wasn't strange in that I didn't know what it was, but in that I knew exactly what it was. It was the wind closing a heavy steel door. And there's only one door that could possibly make a sound like that.

Why did he go out through the roof? Where did he get a key? I never gave it to him.

She was right about all of it. The steel door fitted too snugly into the frame, making it impossible to close it gently in a single motion. The only way to shut it quietly was to use both hands, carefully, in a certain way. It had banged against the frame that night by accident, and possibly twice more after that. I placed a finger in between the two paragraphs in the journal. There was a big space between them. I borrowed Hae-jin's favourite conditional phrase and applied it to the gap. If I had been Mother, I would have gone straight up to the roof as soon as I heard the noise.

That door was a problem from the very first day we moved in. It was constructed shoddily, so it didn't fit very well into the frame, and therefore it didn't lock properly. She first tried to get it repaired several times by the construction company that had built the flats, but they went bankrupt and it never got fixed. Someone came from the building management and installed a hook-and-eye closure, but it was like putting disinfectant on a broken leg: when a typhoon came through, that door crashed open a couple of times a day, pulling out the hook and eye. Mother ended up hiring someone to repair the frame, replace the door and install a lock and a deadbolt. The repairman swore that there was no way the door would open on its own again unless the rooftop blew away.

Mother would have wanted to go and check to see if the repairman had been exaggerating. She would have seen the pergola light on, and at the steel door, she would have realised that it was locked but the bolt was undone. Would she have opened the door and looked out? Would she have heard my feet clattering down the stairs? Would she have come into my room to check on me? Did she count my pills that day too? There would have been the correct number. Maybe she went outside to look for me, going to the back gate to ask if anyone had gone by. Did she meet Hae-jin near the side gate that day too? Why didn't she confront me about it? They weren't difficult questions. Why did you go out via the roof? Why did you take the key?

Why did Mother not say anything to me while she kept worrying? Why would you do that? It wasn't such a big deal.

I'd made a copy of the roof key for a reason, but it wasn't some grand reason that required Mother to roam the cold, dark streets. The thirty-first of August was, I think, the first time I used that key, the first day I went out through the roof. It was the day after I came home from Imja Island, and I still hadn't taken my pills. Didn't I deserve to be gentle with myself? I'd had a huge public seizure after unshackling myself from my medication for the first time in a decade. I wanted to remain in a magical state for one more day. Just one more.

I'd spent that precious day in my room, wearing a long-sleeved shirt and long trousers to hide the scratches and bruises on my limbs. I'd blasted the air conditioning and lounged around on my bed. Hae-jin had gone to Sangam-dong early in the morning, so I didn't have anyone to talk to. Rather, I didn't have anyone I *wanted* to talk to; after all, Mother was there and she had a mouth with which she could speak.

That morning, Mother had come up to the roof and bobbed around in my eyesight. She didn't seem to be doing anything in particular. She crouched by the garden bed and pretended to weed, even though she had already pulled out all the weeds. She pottered around by the pepper plants, constantly glancing over her shoulder at my room. If I closed the blinds, she would come and rap on the sliding door. Of course, there was a new reason she needed to talk to me each time. Isn't it getting stuffy in there? You'll catch a cold if you're in the air conditioning for too long. The sun feels so nice; do you want to come out and have some tea with me?

I didn't want to drink any damn tea; that was what you did when you were sick. I didn't have to ask what she wanted either. I could figure out what she was thinking. I could see through her the way she could see through me. 'Want to have some tea?' meant 'Confess to everything that happened at Imja Island.' 'The sun's so nice' was an offer to discuss my weakness.

By sunset, she had given up and I was bouncing off the walls. I'd realised something so obvious that I'd never even thought about before. Whether young or old, humans needed a place to go to and something to do. I didn't have anywhere to go or anything to do. I didn't know how to laze away a day; I had always needed to train or study. I didn't have anyone I wanted to see; I didn't have any films I wanted to watch. There was nothing I wanted to do. I couldn't even go out at night, since I couldn't drink and my curfew was 9 p.m. That was why I felt destroyed when Mother sometimes asked me, 'Are you seeing anyone?' Everyone knew that you couldn't gain something if you were allowed nothing, but Mother, who knew everything about everything, didn't seem to know that.

At 10 p.m., I had got up from my bed. I couldn't stay put any longer. My insane urge was raising its head and my muscles were twitching. I slipped on the *Private Lesson* jacket and took out the trainers I'd hidden in the bathroom ceiling for just such a day. I opened the steel door. I'd made a copy of the key to prepare for this very day. Even when I took my meds faithfully, I had dreamed of a door I could run through behind Mother's back. The door slammed behind me because it was a tricky door, of course, but really it was because I was impatient. If I had been a little calmer, I wouldn't have stirred Mother's hunting-dog instincts.

Once on the other side of the door, I ran downstairs without glancing back. My feet were restless and my head felt hot. I thought Mother would call my name at any moment. That shitty feeling disappeared only after I'd run out through the side gate and along the river and crossed the street in front of the sea wall. I stopped and took a moment to breathe. I leant against the railing and looked down at the dark ocean. Darkness and fog hid everything – the waves, the gulls, the marine park, the observatory, and at the halfway point of my run, the horizon. Only the searchlight cast a beam as it circled around slowly. I thought I could hear it saying, *Come here, let's play.*

Yongi's was closed, even though it wasn't yet 11 p.m. Something must be up. Only when something happened in Mr Yongi's personal life did the stand close early. The following were types of events that qualified for closing early, according to Mr Yongi: he felt physically or mentally unwell; his batter wasn't perfect; for some reason he got the sense that it was an unlucky day; it was windy and he was feeling lonely; it was raining and he was feeling sad; there was a full moon and he was hating humanity; the weather was bad and he was feeling bad too.

It must be the last reason; it had been hot that day. Now, damp fog lay low and grey clouds were amassing in the dark sky. I wasn't affected by weather when I was under the power of the insane urge. I practically flew all the way to the observatory and soared back to Yongi's. Along the footpath by the river, I heard someone laughing up ahead of me. I couldn't see who it was through the fog.

'No, that's not what I mean.' It was a low voice, but clearly a woman's. I didn't hear anyone else; she must be talking on the phone.

I was a little annoyed. If I didn't want to be seen as suspicious by this woman walking alone at night, I had to either run ahead past her or cross the street and take the path by the neighbourhood park.

'Are you deaf? Why don't you understand what I'm saying?'

Are you deaf... I remembered a woman I'd encountered on my way home from a morning run in May. Mother was okay with me running in the morning. I was crossing the street in front of Gundo Elementary School when I stopped short. I'd had a headache since the night before, but it flared up intensely right then and there as though I was about to have a seizure. I couldn't see anything. It was as if I'd been hit in the eye socket with a hammer. I couldn't move another step. I might have dropped to the ground with my head in my hands if a horn hadn't sounded right next to me. A car whizzed by, and through a window, a woman's voice called out, 'Prick! Are you deaf?'

This was on a road in front of a school, designated as a pedestrian protection zone. Even if it hadn't been, a driver should really wait if someone was staggering on the crossing, holding his head, not insult him by shouting 'Prick!' before zooming off. I wanted to write down the licence plate or at least the make of the car, but the early-morning fog was waist-deep, my headache was making everything bleary and the car was already turning left onto the road along the river. For a moment, I forgot about the headache; I was so incensed that I crossed the last few metres quickly. Once I was on the other side of the street, I looked around. I wasn't sure what to do. The car was gone. There was no

CCTV on that stretch of road yet. There was nothing I could do. I started to cool down a bit. My biggest flaw was that I stopped seeing clearly when I got angry; on the other hand, I gave up easily when there was no point in being angry. I gave up on getting revenge.

But that night in August when I first slipped out through the roof, I was certain that the woman I'd encountered in May was the same woman who was ahead of me now. Her voice sounded identical. I didn't need to think about it any longer. I ducked behind the street lamps along the river and walked quickly to get closer. I finally detected a dark shadow moving slowly in the fog. I saw her long, wind-blown hair. I slowed down and followed, giving her some distance. I swear I had no other plan. I just wanted to know where she lived. She chattered on for another five minutes.

'It just broke down in front of Kyobo Bookstore in Gwanghwamun ... What do you mean, what did I do? I called the tow truck, of course, and took it to the garage! ... No, I took the bus. I can't take a taxi, it's so far to get here ... No, no, I'm not scared. It's only midnight, it's practically early evening! And the moon's really bright tonight, too.' She'd begun to walk past First Dongjin Bridge when she suddenly fell silent. It was as if she'd just realised that midnight in Seoul and midnight in Gundo were completely different. The streets here were dark and quiet. Nobody was around, not even cars. All you could hear was the seagulls crying behind the thick fog. She whipped around and looked towards where I was standing. She seemed most uneasy about what was behind her.

From behind the street lamp, I watched her standing under the yellow light. What caught my eye was one of the fingers gripping her phone. More specifically, it was a gold ring on her pinky. I don't know if the moonlight bewitched me or if the lamplight gave it an aura. Even through the fog, the ring twinkled mysteriously in the dark, like a star crossing the galaxy. The voice in my head decided to quiz me. *What's the easiest way to take the ring off her hand?* I knew the answer instantly. *Cut off her finger, of course.*

'No, no, it's nothing,' she said into the phone. 'I just thought I heard something behind me.' She turned around and began to walk again.

I followed, matching her pace.

About ten metres later, she stopped and looked behind her again. 'Look, let me call you when I get home.'

I stopped too, grinning. She should have done that at the very beginning.

She put her phone in her other hand, turned around once more, and then started to walk ahead quickly. I could sense her nervousness. Her sixth sense, drilled into her through the history of humanity, was probably whispering to her: *Doesn't that sound like someone's behind you?* Or maybe she heard the whispers in my mind: *Can you feel me behind you?*

I sped up too. My thighs tensed. My gums tingled, as though I was about to sprout new teeth. Small goose bumps dotted the skin below my ears. It wasn't exactly excitement or tension; it was similar to what Hae-jin had told me about once.

It was four years ago, maybe in the late spring or early summer. Hae-jin had gone out to see a slightly older girl in his department he'd had a crush on for a long time, and hadn't come home until the next morning. It was probably the only time in his life he stayed out all night without letting Mother know beforehand. It was one of the very few times Mother had scolded him. While she nagged him, I stood by the kitchen island, watching. Even though he kept saying, 'I'm really sorry,' he wasn't paying much attention. Stars were twinkling in his brown eyes; he was probably floating somewhere far away in space. I became curious. Who was she, this girl who'd sent him into space?

As soon as Mother walked away, I asked, 'Was it that good?'

Hae-jin's neck reddened and he gave an evasive answer, as if I were Mother. 'I don't really remember. We were drunk.' He wanted to keep it to himself.

I didn't want to respect his privacy; he'd clearly experienced something important that was a complete mystery to me. 'But how did you feel about it?'

'Well . . . ' He hesitated for a long time before sharing his rambling literary thoughts. I don't remember exactly what he said, but the gist was this: if God comes to take me on my deathbed when I'm ninety and asks, where in your life would you want to return to before you leave this world, I would answer that I want to go back to that moment last night when I felt the whole world slide away.

What was it like for the world to slide away? I hadn't experienced intimacy or love but I had slept with two women. What I'd experienced both times was worlds apart from what he was talking about. The first woman had had small, perky breasts just the way I liked, but I couldn't get into it. In fact, my pulse slowed. Even the moment of release wasn't electrifying. It was the same the second time around. It was so boring to kiss her that I found myself tracing her teeth with the tip of my tongue. But I wasn't attracted to guys, either. Hae-jin's dreamy expression was incomprehensible to me. It seemed to signal feelings that I would never be able to understand.

That night, when I started to follow the woman with the sparkling ring, I finally found a clue to unravelling that mystery. I suddenly realised what I was attracted to. I was attracted to someone feeling afraid.

The moon slipped behind dark clouds. The fog spread out, growing thicker. I stopped when she turned around and followed when she went on so that she would sense someone behind her. The closer I got, the clearer I heard the sounds she was making; they fired up my senses. The clanking of coins or keys in her backpack. Her footsteps, falling faster and more unevenly. Her bare thighs rubbing together with each step. Her hair being whipped around by the rough wind. Her ragged, wet breathing. I thought I could even hear the flow of blood under her jaw.

I imagined all the things I would do to take off the gold ring. I would grab the hair that danced above her shoulders. I would cover her mouth with my other hand. I would drag her to the river. I would rip off the ring with my canines and shove her into the water.

As we approached the crossing, she broke into a run. She kept looking back, almost twisting her ankle in her heels. She was a wuss. But even for a wuss she had some nerve.

When she got to the crossing, she whipped around and screamed, 'Who are you?'

I didn't answer. How dare she speak to me that way? What the hell had I done? I hadn't spoken to her, I hadn't bothered her; I hadn't even appeared in her sights. All I was doing was going where I had to go.

Right then, her phone began ringing. She screamed and flapped about. The phone flew into the middle of the road as she dashed across and screamed again. A car that had rounded the corner in front of the primary school had to screech to a stop. All the sounds mixed in the fog: the tyres skidding, the screaming that echoed and grew fainter, the sound of the phone ringing in the middle of the street.

Quiet returned. The car and the woman were both gone. I strode towards the crossing. I stood under the light for a moment, my arms limp. The joy was gone. I was so hungry. I was drained and my head felt muffled. What had I done? What was I yearning for that made me so famished? I picked up her phone. The name of the caller was on the smashed screen. *Mimi.* I walked over to the water and tossed it in.

And that was the last time I'd seen the woman. Maybe she'd made sure not to be out alone in the dark again. As for me, I developed a habit of going out in the middle of the night to see if the electric feeling the woman had given me had been real. After several test runs, I confirmed that I liked following women more than men. Their sense of what was behind them was better attuned, and they were much more afraid. There was nothing more thrilling, honestly. When I reached the crossing by the sea wall after

rounding the observatory, it was fifty-fifty whether someone would get off the last bus. And the possibility that it
would be a woman was half of that. The road by Dongjin
River was my playground. But the baseline for getting that
jolt went up each time. Each time I went out, I'd need to
take a new object with me, something to set the mood and
get my imagination going. Like heavy metal in my headphones, a disposable mask, or latex gloves.

I didn't go out every night. I went out when I was off
my meds, and only if I had the urge. If I encountered a
woman and got my fix, I could start taking my pills again,
and I wouldn't feel like going out for a while, as though
I were in remission. But if I didn't see a woman, the urge
continued unabated. Since that August day, I'd felt it a total
of six times. Two of those times, I'd seen a woman. The
first was on 15 November, and the second was last night,
the only time I'd run away when I was following someone.

I thought she'd got off the bus alone, but now a question popped into my head: had she really been alone? I
remembered waking up this morning with the vision of the
crimson umbrella rolling along the road. I'd remembered
something else when I left Yongi's – a woman opening the
crimson umbrella as she got off the bus, and the drunken
man who followed her, his singing reverberating through
the streets.

Another question occurred to me. Had I really been
standing in front of the crossing last night? A chill began
creeping up my legs. No. I had been behind Yongi's. I
hadn't even been standing; I was sitting on the railing,
looking down at the ocean, waiting for the last bus to

arrive. That made the most sense. Mr Yongi usually closed his shack at 11.20 and was on the bus ten minutes later. I arrived at Yongi's after rounding the observatory around 11.50. The last bus got in around midnight. That had been the schedule every night I've been out via the roof; last night would have been the same.

Had I really run away from her? Or maybe the question was: had I really been feeling the symptoms of a seizure all day today? It wasn't like I'd had an episode every time I stopped taking the pills. Did I think I was about to have one just because that was the easy explanation for why I couldn't remember anything? Perhaps the confusion and memory loss I'd been experiencing today was actually due to something else entirely.

A bright light blinded me. A screech behind the curtain of light; the sound of a car braking suddenly, skidding on the wet road. The sound of a car door opening, and Mother screaming, 'Yu-jin!'

The man's singing had stopped a while ago. It was deadly quiet. Only the wind was screaming past.

I know I saw him. I'm cold and scared and terrified.

Please stop! I wanted to scream. The voices and images flashing in front of me were jumbled; I couldn't thread them together into chronological order. I lay down on the journal, my cheek resting on the page. The things on my desk rotated across my visual field as though they were on a conveyer belt. The razor, the pearl earring, the key to the roof. I raised my head. I stared at the iPod and earphones, feeling unsettled. I thought back to the very beginning, right before I left my room last night. I picked the iPod up and pressed the power button; my playlist was stopped at Vangelis's 'Conquest of Paradise'. If I listened to this playlist from the beginning, this was the song that came on exactly one hour and fifty-two minutes later. So I was right. I'd left the house at 10.10 p.m., rounded the observatory, and turned off the music when I arrived at the crossing by the sea wall around midnight.

I slid the earphones into my ears. I closed my eyes and thought back to last night, when the clock in the living room had chimed ten times. I tapped the first song on the playlist and hit play. The song, 'Mass', began. Boom, boom, boom, boom, boom boom, boom, boom boom, boom . . .

The clock in the living room chimed ten times.

Mother had gone into her room thirty minutes ago and closed the door. Hae-jin wasn't home yet. For the last half-hour I'd been lying on my bed with my head in my hands, not because of a headache but because of my insane urge. It had been four days since I stopped taking the pills. I'd been roaming the neighbourhood like a wild dog for the last three nights. A part of my mind was coaxing me, trying to convince me to go out and play just once more. The faint buzz I was still feeling from last night fervently supported that. *Don't be such a wimp. You're not hurting anyone, you're just enjoying yourself. How is it different from masturbating? And you didn't land anything the last two days. Just do it, unless you plan to stop altogether. You're not one to do things halfway.*

I flipped onto my back. I laced my fingers under my neck and calculated the date. I'd stopped taking my pills in

August, before the exam, then two months later before the oral exams in November, and now, not even a month later, for no particular reason. Maybe I'd stop taking them completely. Then either I'd have another seizure, or Mother would figure it out before it got to that point.

So the only solution was to go out tonight. If I didn't, it was likely that I wouldn't take the pill tomorrow either. The danger would grow. Today was the last day. Tomorrow, or maybe the day after that, I'd become the best person I could be.

I got up. I opened my wardrobe and took out some clothes and put them on quickly. A black turtleneck sweater, sweatpants, socks, the padded vest and the *Private Lesson* jacket. I stuffed a pair of latex gloves, the roof key and the building entry card in my left jacket pocket. I put on a disposable mask, slid my iPod into my right pocket and secured the earphones with a clip under my ears. I pulled the hood onto my head and cinched it with the cord. I took my shoes from the panel in the bathroom ceiling and picked up the razor. I'd never gone out with the razor. I'd saved it for the end. Since tonight was probably – definitely – the last time, I put it in my pocket. My heart was already pounding from that simple act.

I locked my bedroom door from the inside, listening for any noise downstairs. It was quiet. Mother was probably already asleep. Please sleep through, I thought. I checked my clock: 10.10. I put on my shoes and left the sliding door slightly ajar, putting an earphone in one ear. 'Mass' started. Boom, boom, boom, boom, boom boom, boom, boom boom, boom . . .

It was raining hard. It was dark and the fog was thicker than usual. I moved like a blind man, feeling the ground with the tips of my toes. I inched over to the pergola and turned on the light.

I ran down the stairs, the music booming in one ear and Hello's barking ringing in the other. When I reached the ground floor, I could see someone opening the main door to leave the building. This late at night? Whoever it was, I didn't want to see them. I ducked my head down and darted out so that the CCTV camera by the front entrance would catch only the back of my head. Outside, I began sprinting.

When I got to Yongi's, the fourth song on my playlist, 'Cry for the Moon', began. The waves were crashing loudly beyond the sea wall. The roads were quiet, almost eerie. Other than infrequent headlights, nothing moved. Yongi's was already dark. He must have closed early. I crouched in front of the shack to tighten my shoelaces, and then I flew like Usain Bolt until I stopped in front of the observatory, my engine overheated. I was panting, my head was hot, my ribs were sore. I had a stitch in my side and my thighs felt stiff. I hobbled down below the observatory and sat on the safety fence along the cliff, one of my favourite spots. If it was a clear night, I would be able to see the lights of District Two straight ahead. On those nights, I'd look back in the direction of Yongi's shack, as though searching for constellations. Right now, though, I couldn't see a thing other than the glaring searchlight.

The rain pounded down on me. The wind threw jabs. I stayed there despite that, listening to the six-minute song, because a police car, which appeared at infrequent intervals in the area, had started circling. I sat there, hunched, waiting for it to go; there would be nothing good about being spotted by the police. As soon as the patrol car left, another pair of headlights appeared. The vehicle drove all around the park with its full beams on, as though it were looking for a runaway wife. I took out my iPod and checked the time: 11.21 p.m.

When the car's lights finally disappeared over the other side of the bridge, I stood up. I tightened the cord of my hood and took the path back. I ran lightly this time, as though I were a boxer doing road work, to the beat of the music. By the time I got to the sea wall, the fifteenth song, 'Conquest of Paradise', had begun. It was already two minutes past midnight, but the last bus wasn't here yet. At least I hadn't seen it as I was running up.

I went behind Yongi's. Between the wood-framed shack covered in plastic and the sea wall, there was a narrow space where one person could sit. It was similar to the area behind the street lamps along the side of the river – it was dark back there and the fog provided another layer of concealment. Behind the lamps was a good place to play in, and back here was a good place to wait for a playmate.

I sat on the railing with the ocean behind me, the wind slapping me on the back. The rain was coming down at a slant. I heard squeaks below the railing: the shrieks of the boats moored at the dock as they rode the waves up and down. The searchlight danced through the fog with its beam of light. The music soared towards its climax and I tapped my foot along with the beat. I felt more excited than usual for some reason. Maybe it was the leftover dopamine from running or the primitive pounding of the music or because I was looking forward to meeting my final playmate.

The bus appeared as 'Conquest of Paradise' came to an end. It was nearly five minutes later than usual. I turned off the music and stuffed the earphones in my pocket. The bus halted and blood began to course through the vessels in my ears. Someone must be getting off, otherwise it wouldn't have stopped. I felt a chill when I saw a figure standing by the door in the bright bus. Attraction and nervousness collided. Was it a woman or a man?

It was actually both, a woman and a man. I couldn't really see, but I was able to tell that much. I felt deflated. It was the perfect night – rainy and foggy – to play with someone for the two kilometres home along the empty streets; even after running fourteen kilometres, I was bursting with energy.

The bus disappeared into the darkness. The woman, holding a crimson umbrella, had long straight hair and was wearing a purple coat, short skirt, and high-heeled boots. She kept glancing back at the man as she walked quickly down the footpath. They didn't seem to know each other and she didn't look too happy about her companion.

Even from far away, I could tell that something was wrong with him. He was huge, his stomach the size of an oil tanker. Each time he took a step, his body, clad in a thin disposable plastic rain poncho, wobbled about. His knees gave way every other step. He weaved from left to right. He was wrestling with a hanky-sized plastic umbrella, trying to open it with his giant hands. The umbrella would open halfway before folding; the one moment it seemed the man would succeed, it flipped inside out from the wind. Rain was pouring down on his bald head. The giant ranted, 'Fucking umbrella!' and 'Fuck this fucking rain!' He wiped the water off his head and pulled down the hood of his poncho. As soon as he'd solved the problem, he seemed to become content and began singing at the top of his lungs, some song about an unforgettable girl in the rain.

By that time, the girl had crossed the street. The crimson umbrella stood stiffly above her shoulders, like a warning. There was no way the giant man understood that warning. He followed her. They disappeared into the fog.

I came out from behind Yongi's. The light was red but I crossed the street anyway. Time was ticking. I was worn out and disappointed. My stomach roiled. The giant had taken what was rightfully mine. It wouldn't be my fault if I didn't take my pill today and had to run out again in the middle of the night tomorrow. It was all *his* fault.

At the start of the road along the river, I crossed to the other side, adjacent to the park. I could hear the giant still singing. His voice was louder than before. I spotted him weaving in and out of the fog. The girl was walking in the street, only stepping up onto the kerb when a car appeared. She was clearly afraid of being near the man, but I sensed she was even more afraid of being completely alone.

I stopped paying attention to them. I took the razor out of my pocket and fiddled with it. Should I come out tomorrow? One last time? Or should I take a pill as soon as I got home?

I was close enough to make out First Dongjin Bridge when the girl let out a shriek. She spun around and started running towards my side of the street. The giant was standing in the middle of the lane she'd been walking along, pissing with his pants pulled all the way down, brandishing his dick like a fire hose, continuing his slurred singing. Swinging her umbrella, she leapt onto the footpath about five metres from me. I was already hidden behind the street lamps. She stood there, panting. She was so afraid that any small movement would make her freak out and run away screaming.

This changed everything. Blood surged under my jaw. A car began honking in the opposite lane; it was flashing its lights, trying to turn left onto the seashore road. The giant hoisted his pants up and slowly withdrew into the fog. But after the car had passed by, he appeared in the middle of the lane again. This time he began swinging his umbrella, zigzagging between the two lanes of the road. He was singing even more loudly, as if he were a dying elephant.

The girl started walking again, her eyes glued to the giant. Her breathing was shallow and uneven, her heels skittered sharply and nervously. I put on the latex gloves and began to move like her shadow, running and stopping when she did. The giant got out of the road at last, trying to avoid a car that had come out of a side street next to the park.

The car pulled over to the kerb, inching forward as though looking for a parking spot. I couldn't see the make or the licence plate; all I could tell was that it was a white saloon. The giant stumbled towards the other side of the road in his search for the girl in the rain. She stopped, then unexpectedly ran behind the street lamp. The giant continued to follow her. We were about ten metres before the bridge, and the river flowed right next to the footpath on which I stood.

Blood rushed to my face. She was right in front of me. She was so close that if I reached out I could touch her. I heard her breathing. I could even hear her ribs move. I smelled adrenalin, as sour as sweat and as clear as perfume. It was the first time I'd smelled something so provocative so close up. My chest tightened. My stomach hardened. All of my fantasies spun in a loop in my head – following someone, her noticing, catching up with her, her running away, pursuing, hiding, finding, coming face to face . . .

The razor was open in my right hand.

The car on the other side was headed towards the junction. The giant man arrived at the entrance to the bridge and stopped still. He turned a full three hundred and sixty degrees, perhaps looking for the girl. He gave up and walked onto the bridge. I could hear him singing as he crossed the river. If that was his route home, that meant he wasn't even a resident of District Two. He'd come up this road only to follow the girl. What a piece of shit.

When he'd gone more than halfway across the bridge, the girl let out a deep sigh. She didn't detect the piece of shit behind her, maybe because she was exhausted at being followed by the drunk man. She hoisted her bag up on her shoulder. She was still close enough for me to reach out and touch her.

She stood still in the light of the lamp, suddenly stiff. The umbrella held slightly to the side, she hesitantly looked back at me. Her eyes met mine. My eyes were drawn to the pearl earring in her outer cartilage. Everything in this world vanished, one by one – the man singing, the rain, the wind, the river rushing by. It was the kind of quiet that made my fingertips tingle, a silence that made my heart leap.

She turned abruptly, her long ponytail slapping my face, and lurched towards the road with a sharp, ripping scream.

I took a big step out and reached out. My hand grabbed her hair, twisted it roughly, pulled her into the shadows and angled her head to expose her neck. The razor dug into her flesh. The screaming stopped after a short time.

Her eyes were wide open but unseeing. The communication with her brain had been severed. I watched, still holding onto her hair, as blood gushed with force. In her eyes was the desperate look of life trying to cling on.

A thrill ran down through my entire body. I was out of breath and dizzy. It was as if the razor had gripped my hand and pulled it into her, so powerfully that it was impossible to resist. Everything in sight began to shake. My hand holding the razor tingled. Shock crashed over me. Something thudded shut inside my head, the passageway that had been cracked open to this present world. I was at the border of another universe. I had no way of going back, nor did I have the willpower.

I'd imagined this very moment countless times. I was always confident that I'd be able to control myself. Now that it had actually happened, I realised that I'd been deluding myself. I had reacted to the orders of my sympathetic nervous system and crossed over the boundary to fantasy. It had been too easy and too quick. The flames that had been burning me up inside let loose in my lower abdomen, like sexual desire. This was the moment of ignition, the magical moment where the possibility of sensation expanded infinitely. I could read, see and hear everything about her in that moment. I felt omnipotent. Everything was possible.

She slumped onto my chest, and I heard a car braking and skidding. Headlights covered everything in sight. I dragged the woman back a few feet and pushed her over the railing into the water below. I heard the splash. The crimson umbrella bounced and rolled along the dark wet road. I couldn't hear the giant singing any more. I heard a sharp scream. 'Yu-jin!'

My heart instantly returned to its regular beat. Still standing in the shadows, I looked out at Mother, who was holding the driver's door open.

She was shaking in the pouring rain. It was as if she didn't want to believe that the murderer standing a few metres from her was her son. 'Yu-jin . . .' Her voice was low and pained.

I glanced down. Under the lamplight, rain was washing away the splattered blood into the sewer. I didn't regret it. I wasn't afraid, either. I just wanted to get out of this situation. I took my latex gloves off and threw them in the river, then turned and ran as fast as I could towards the interior of the neighbourhood, filled with large-scale construction sites, where Mother couldn't follow me by car.

I finally stopped at a building that was half finished. A dim light hung on the entrance and the plastic tarpaulin shrouding the site flapped loudly in the wind. I stood there a long time. I was doing the most important task in the cold, quiet, deserted darkness: I was reflecting on that moment where I could sense that girl and her entire being. I fantasised about her body as it passed through the river and was swept out to sea. A cold breeze hit me. I hadn't realised that I was completely exhausted; I hadn't even realised I was holding something small and round in my hand. When I came back to myself, I couldn't feel my fingers and toes. Only my instincts were awake. *Get a grip*, they whispered. *It's time to go home.*

Somehow I got back to the flat. I didn't bump into Mother. I didn't see any police cars either. I remembered the giant, but dismissed that thought. He wouldn't have seen much of anything. I tried to ignore the fact that he could have heard Mother scream. He might have even heard my name. But there had to be tons of people named Yu-jin; I couldn't possibly be the only one in the entire nation with that name.

And Mother couldn't have been certain that it was me. The footpath, three metres wide, had been between us. Mother was under the street lamp but I was in the darkness. It wasn't as if I answered her, and we hadn't exactly come face to face, either. I didn't want to think about how she knew it was me; I was too tired to think.

I entered the building, my head ducked. I ran up the main stairwell to the sound of Hello barking and got to the roof door. That was when I realised again that I was holding something in my fist. A small white thing. The pearl earring I'd yanked out of her ear immediately before I pushed her in the water. I didn't know why I'd done that and I couldn't begin to guess. It was just something my hand had done. I shoved it in my pocket and reached for the roof door.

The front door opened downstairs. 'Yu-jin,' Mother called, as if she had been waiting for that very moment.

Oblivion was the ultimate lie, the complete falsehood. Last night I had done something I couldn't deal with. As a solution, my mind had selected oblivion, and I'd spent an entire day struggling with fragments of images and sounds that swam around in my consciousness.

Only now did I realise that I'd known I would kill some day. Why else did I keep warning myself to stop the dangerous game along that road? I'd continued it, confident that I would never cross the boundary of fantasy; that was how much I'd believed in the solidity of my socialised ego. I'd had no idea I didn't have the power to stop myself from exchanging my life for a pleasurable pastime. I had overestimated myself. My reckless belief that I was in control had made me offer myself up to fate last night.

Maybe Mother had known this all along. Maybe that was why she kept tailing me. How had she planned to fix this? I thought about her voice last night, when she called me from downstairs. It wasn't that different from usual; it sounded like a teacher calling a student instead of a mother calling a son, cool-headed and calm. I probably would have been suspicious if she'd sounded nicer than that; I was exhausted but I hadn't lost my mind. And if she'd called me angrily, I would have fled, despite not having anywhere to go. Nothing was scarier than an angry mother, at least to me. That was obvious; that was why I'd ended up killing her last night.

She'd called me again. I didn't move, but I sensed this in her tone: *I didn't see anything. Even if I did, I'm going to pretend that I didn't.*

I had gone downstairs, thinking about the day ten years ago when I'd had the seizure during the swimming competition. She had taken me out of the car park without telling anyone. I thought she had decided to do the same thing with what she had seen by the river, just as she had hidden my epilepsy for so many years.

But now I was curious. Why didn't she report me? Why did she wait for me at home? Did she want me to confess? But she hadn't even brought it up.

I remembered what she'd said when she had pushed me into the corner of the landing and tried to shove the razor back into my hand. 'Don't worry. When you're gone, I'll go too.' That wasn't a threat. It was a plan. She was going to cover everything up by making me kill myself and then taking her own life. Maybe that was why, as soon as we stepped inside, her demeanour changed and she forced me to take my jacket off, rifling through my pockets. She probably became aggressive because she was so angry that she wasn't thinking straight. She could never have imagined that Father's razor would emerge from my pocket. Maybe she took it as an insult to his memory.

How was she planning to kill me? She wouldn't have been able to make me surrender; I wasn't five, I was twenty-five and a former athlete. Even if she'd got Hae-jin to help, it would have been hard for them to get the upper hand. If I refused to go along, there was no way Mother could have done it. Maybe she was going to poison my food. I mean, even a raging wild animal had to eat.

The landline had been ringing for a while now. Who was it? Hae-jin? Auntie? I picked up the phone and looked at the screen before pressing the talk button. The number started with 032. I didn't know who that was. I didn't feel like speaking to someone I didn't know. I put the phone back down and went to my chair. I ignored the ringing and looked over at Mother's things on my desk. The journal, the car key . . .

But last night, when I saw her in the street, she hadn't been wearing a white dress. I couldn't remember what she was wearing, but it wasn't a skirt or a dress. Maybe she had changed once she got home. Mother always put things back where they belonged, so that meant that the key in her pocket hadn't been used yet. She was planning to use it. She was going to drive me somewhere. Maybe to the ocean or the river, where we could both die in seclusion. She would have had to lock the doors and windows, so that I wouldn't end up surviving on my own.

Finally it all made sense. Mother didn't have to be stronger than me, and I wouldn't be able to resist. All the problems would get sorted out in one act. If we died in a car accident, I wouldn't be arrested for murder. She wouldn't be known as the mother of a killer. What she had seen would remain a secret among the dead, and the murder would remain unsolved. Or maybe the giant, who would have been caught on camera by the bus stop, would be falsely accused. He'd argue that there had been a third person on the street, but nobody would believe him. That road didn't have any cameras, and there were no witnesses. It would be hard for the giant to prove that he followed the woman but didn't do anything.

So I'd killed someone in front of Mother's eyes and she had planned to die with me instead of giving me over to the police. But because she was so incensed over the razor, she had ended up dying alone.

Yet there were still some loose ends, like Mother's mysterious attire. Why was she wearing the white nightgown I'd given her, of all things? Did she want to be wearing what her son had bought her when she died next to him? That was an overwrought sentiment but I supposed it made sense. She'd worn Father's gift, the anklet, for sixteen years. And why had she left this journal? If she was planning to die with me, she should have got rid of it too. Maybe it was for Hae-jin, so that he would know that we'd had to go out of necessity. But it was not very useful for that purpose; it was only a record of facts, with no context. What would he be able to figure out from this? For him to be able to read between the lines, it meant that he knew what she knew. Were they that close? I suddenly recalled the spring of 2003, when Hae-jin and Mother first met.

It was one of the two days a month that I had to go and see Auntie. I ran out to the front gates of school as soon as the bell rang. Mother was supposed to pick me up at one for my two o'clock appointment, but she didn't arrive till two. She didn't tell me why she was late, but drove so quickly that she didn't see that an old man with a trolley full of recycling paper had stepped out from behind a bus. She braked, but it was too late. The tyres screeched, there was a smash, and the old man was slumped under our car. The trolley, flipped upside down, slid all the way to the bus stop across the street. Recycling paper and cardboard boxes scattered like birds. Buses stopped and people rushed over and circled the old man. Mother glared out through the front window, gripping the wheel as though she wanted to rip it out.

'Mum. Mum!'

She blinked, as if awoken from a dream.

'Hurry, see what's happened.'

Mother unfastened her seat belt and got out. I followed. The old man was tall and skinny. His leg, clad in worn trousers, was bent at an awkward angle. It didn't seem like he was breathing or moving. I thought he was dead, but I crouched down next to him and shook his shoulder gently. 'Grandfather, are you okay?'

The old man peeled his eyes open. From his toothless, sunken mouth, a scream erupted like thunder. 'Hae-jin!' He couldn't move. But he held his left leg, gasping and yelling, 'Hae-jin! Oh, Hae-jin! Grandpa is dying!' He kept yelling throughout the journey to hospital by ambulance.

Thankfully he hadn't suffered a life-threatening injury; his leg was broken. Every time the nurse asked him a question, he screamed, 'Hae-jin!' He reeked of alcohol. He needed surgery since it was a compound fracture and his muscles had ruptured. Neither his head nor his hip had been injured. He seemed to have his faculties about him, too. He unfailingly gave a clear, instant answer when asked about the accident: 'I'm telling you, it's all that woman's fault.'

Mother interjected, saying, 'He suddenly appeared in front of me . . . ' and then had to endure thirty minutes of ranting: 'Why would a woman drive around without any purpose and run over someone who's busy trying to make a living? I'm the only one supporting the family; now what will we do?' Then the old man began to wave and yell towards the door. 'Oh, Hae-jin! Here! I'm here!'

A boy wearing the same school uniform as me ran over. 'Grandpa!'

It couldn't be. Was it the same Hae-jin as that day? The same old man? Was it really them?

'Are you okay?' Hae-jin asked, looking at the old man's splinted leg.

'Ask them,' the old man said, stabbing his long, skinny finger towards me and Mother. 'Ask them what they did to me.'

Hae-jin turned to look at Mother. Mother, who had been continuously and anxiously sweeping her hair to the side, froze. Her mouth dropped open. She stopped herself from speaking. I watched her with interest, knowing what she'd almost said. Mother, who was normally so calm, was clearly shaken, completely taken aback. She looked like she had forgotten that the old man was there, that I was there, that people were coming and going, or even that we were in a hospital. I knew what she was feeling, since I'd felt the same thing when I saw this kid on the first day of middle school.

That day, Hae-jin had become the star of the school.

Right when the welcome ceremony was about to start, a strong, high-pitched voice rang out. 'Hae-jin! Hey, Hae-jin! I'm here! Grandpa's here!'

The auditorium hushed in an instant. Hundreds of pairs of eyes looked over at the old man who was rising in his seat, waving his rake-like hand, and the boy turning beet red.

'Here! Right here!' the old man continued to yell, finally standing all the way up. He was in a suit he must have worn fifty years ago on his wedding day. He was so thin that it looked like a feather duster was poking out of his sleeve, not an arm.

The boy waved back, but his hand didn't go side to side; it went up and down, indicating, *I know, I know, sit down.*

I was sitting right behind him. I couldn't take my eyes off his face. I nearly called out, 'Yu-min!' It wasn't a passing resemblance; he looked exactly like my brother. The same gentle brown eyes, the same wavy hair, the same neat demeanour of a star student. My eyes slid down to find his name pin. Kim Hae-jin.

Our names even shared the same last syllable. If we had the same surname, people would think we were siblings. I felt as if I had just found out about a brother Mother had kept hidden from me.

Mother was probably feeling all of this here in the hospital; she would be thinking she was meeting a son she hadn't known she had. 'Are you Hae-jin?' she managed to say, her voice trembling.

'Yes.' Hae-jin looked at me standing next to her. We stared at each other for a long time.

'Do you know each other?' Mother cut through the awkward silence. 'Same school, I see ... '

My eyes still on Hae-jin, I didn't answer. Hae-jin didn't have the chance to say anything, as his grandfather called him and he immediately turned towards him.

'What are you doing just standing there? Go and get the nurse. It hurts so much! I think I'm going to die!'

That day, I didn't end up going to Auntie's office. The old man was admitted at 8 p.m., and Mother volunteered to handle the paperwork normally done by the insurance company. She requested a good room, lobbied for an earlier date for surgery, and pushed the old man's gurney from the X-ray room to the examination room to the ward. It was obvious what she was doing. She didn't want to say goodbye to Hae-jin. She would have wanted to show him what kind of person she was: I did break your grandfather's leg but I'm not so bad.

On our way home, she asked, 'Yu-jin, you know that boy, right?'

'Yes.'

I could tell she wanted details. I was strangely annoyed by all of this, so I didn't offer anything else.

'Are you in the same class?' she asked.

'Yes.'

'Are you not friends?'

'No.'

'He's pretty tall, too. Does he sit at the back with you?'

'Yes.'

'But you're not friends?'

Honestly, what did that have to do with anything? Was

169

it constitutionally mandated that people who sat near each other had to be friends? I didn't answer.

'Does he not talk to you?'

'No.'

'And you don't talk to him?'

'No.'

Mother nodded dreamily and didn't say anything else.

Looking back now, I could see that Hae-jin hadn't been Hae-jin to Mother over the last ten years. To her, he was Yu-min, which meant that she could have told him her secrets. The only question was whether it was possible for Hae-jin to keep those secrets. He was so transparent. It was impossible for him to hide what he was thinking or feeling; anything she told him couldn't be kept quiet. I was an expert when it came to him, and from how he'd acted today I was sure he didn't know a thing.

So then the journal wasn't for Hae-jin. But it wasn't as though she didn't have time or a way to get rid of it; all she had to do was burn it in the barbecue on the roof and it would disappear into a pile of ash. I thought about the second person Mother had called last night. Was it Auntie who knew everything about me?

I thought carefully about each word I had heard from Auntie on the phone earlier today. I didn't get the sense that she knew anything in particular; she'd asked questions that poked around every which way. It was 1.31 a.m. when Mother and Auntie had spoken. Mother would have just returned home. What did they talk about for those three minutes? Did she tell Auntie everything she'd seen? Did she ask her for advice? It couldn't be. If that had happened, there was no way Auntie wouldn't have taken action. She would have reported it immediately and she would have turned up at the flat herself with the police.

My head pounded. My thoughts were so tangled that I couldn't even remember what I was trying to figure out. But a feeling of regret pressed down on my chest. Why had I come home? If I'd stayed out, Mother wouldn't have died. If I'd come home just a little later, everything would have turned out differently.

I let go of the journal. I looked down at my hands, which appeared so alien to me all of a sudden. Twenty-seven bones, twenty-seven joints, one hundred and twenty-three ligaments, thirty-four muscles, ten fingerprints. My hands, which had held food, washed themselves, picked up objects and touched the things I loved the most, had become murder weapons overnight. I tried to focus my thoughts. I thought about my twenty-five-year-old life that had become wrecked, the rest of my life that was looming outside, the things I could and could no longer do. Nothing could save me now. Hope slipped out of my grasp. Cold, heavy fear tightened its grip around me. There was no way back. I couldn't fix any of it.

Just a few hours ago, I'd believed that I had to know. I had wanted to hear it from myself. I'd thought I had to see the real me. I was human, after all; Hello could live happily without knowing that he was Hello, but I couldn't keep on living without knowing who I was or what I had done. Now that I knew all of it, I realised it was a pointless exercise. No matter what I knew, I didn't have a way forward.

I turned my despair on Mother. Why hadn't she kept calm even when she got angry? Why hadn't she followed her original plan? Why hadn't she just shoved me in the passenger seat and driven into the ocean? Then I could have left these secrets where they were. I wouldn't be looking at myself with such hatred and misery. I wouldn't have had to face the enemy inside that had pushed my life to ruin.

I laid my head on my desk. My body went limp. I closed my eyes and listened to the creaking swing outside. Wait! My eyes flew open. The sound wasn't coming from outside. It wasn't the swing. It was downstairs, the intercom from the entrance of the building. I looked up at the clock: 9 p.m. Who would ring the bell at this hour? It wasn't Hae-jin. Was it Auntie? The security guard? Maybe Hello's owner? Sometimes she forgot to bring her entry card and rang us when nobody else was home. I'd rung her myself twice.

The buzz was persistent. I swept the things on my desk into the drawer and went downstairs. It *was* the intercom. But it wasn't Hello's owner. When I turned on the screen, a man in a black cap and black jacket appeared.

'Who is it?' I asked, pressing the speaker button.

The man moved away from the screen and straightened up. 'I'm responding to a call. Open the door, please.' Another man in the same outfit was next to him. Police. Goose bumps spread on my cheeks. The giant man flashed in front of my eyes. I heard Mother say, *Now what will you do?*

I took my finger off the speaker button and took a step back. Now what will I do? Should I run, Mother? Should I confess? Should I kill myself?

III

A DANGER TO OTHERS

'We're here from the Gundo Patrol Division. Can we come in?' The police officer stood outside the doorway. He was young, at most in his mid thirties. His partner looked to be around the same age. Their question sounded rhetorical and so I nodded as they entered and walked past me.

'Do you live here?' asked the first officer.

If I didn't live here, why would I be here to open the door for them? 'Yes.'

'Is anyone else at home?'

'No.'

'What is your relationship to the homeowner?'

'I'm her son.'

'What's her name?'

Where was this going? If their purpose was to arrest me, they should have checked my identity, but they were focusing on the flat and the homeowner. 'Kim Ji-won.'

The two police officers glanced at each other. They both

looked me up and down. I was wearing a T-shirt and jogging bottoms, nothing on my feet.

I looked them over too. If the giant man had witnessed last night's events and reported them to the police from a belated sense of justice, and if they had evidence that pointed to me, they wouldn't send just these two. An entire investigative team would have descended on me.

'So you're saying you're Ms Kim Ji-won's son?' the first officer asked.

I nodded. 'What's going on?'

'I'd like to see your ID. We need to take a statement from you.'

I quickly guessed that they hadn't come at the giant's urging. They were here to see Ms Kim Ji-won, so it couldn't have much to do with what had happened last night. But no one knew Mother was missing, so what was going on? I stood in front of the interior door. 'What's this about?'

The first officer craned his neck to look behind me. 'About an hour ago, your mother called to say that there was a burglar in the house. She said she was afraid to go inside and asked us to come out immediately.'

'My mother called?' I didn't have to try to look surprised; I was genuinely shocked. What was this ridiculous story? 'She's gone to a retreat. She's praying.'

'She's praying? When did she go?'

'This morning. Is this a false alarm?'

'We confirmed the caller was her.'

True, they wouldn't have come blindly. They would have confirmed the caller's identity first.

'What was the number of the person claiming to be my mother? I can tell you if that's her number or not.'

'She called from a pay phone. Let me see your ID.'

I didn't want to leave them here and go upstairs. Who knew what they'd do? 'It's upstairs. I'll give you my ID number.'

'Go and get it,' the first officer said, crossing his arms and squinting at me, clearly annoyed that I was dragging it out.

'Wait here, please,' I said, and went into the living room. I put my foot on the first step and glanced back. Just as I'd thought he would, one of them poked his head in and looked around. I ran up the stairs three at a time. Mother was inside the table on the roof, Auntie was at her office and Hae-jin would have arrived at Muan station. Mother couldn't call and Hae-jin wasn't a woman. Auntie. She knew Mother's citizen ID number, she was around the same age, and she could easily pretend to be her. I'd have to figure out why she called them.

It didn't take me more than a minute to return downstairs. I handed over my ID to the first officer. He glanced at it, and then at me, before handing it over to his partner, who took it outside. I could hear him talking on his radio, asking someone to look me up. The first officer and I stood there, staring at each other.

'All clear,' the partner said, coming back in and handing my card to the first officer.

The first officer slowly gave it back to me. 'So, your family ...?'

'It's the three of us. My mother, my brother and me.'

'Nobody else living here?'

'No.'

'By the way, how long have you been home?

'Since yesterday.'

'Then why didn't you pick up the phone earlier?'

'The phone?' The unknown number I'd ignored earlier must have been the police calling to check before coming over. Maybe the fake Ms Kim Ji-won who'd called from a pay phone had given the home number as her contact information. It had to be Auntie. 'I didn't hear it. Maybe I was in the bathroom.'

The first policeman's radio went off. They were being called back to the station for an emergency meeting. The second officer held out his business card. Gundo Patrol Division. 'When your mother comes home, please ask her to call us right away. If it turns out that she made a false report, she'll be required to come down to the station.'

I nodded and watched as they left, closing the front door behind them. I heard the lift whirr. I ran over to the living room balcony and opened the window to look down. The light on their patrol car flashed under the white fog. They soon disappeared towards the back gate.

Considering that it hadn't even been a day since Auntie had spoken to me, this was too risky a move. She knew she could get in trouble for making a false report. She must have had her reasons for doing it. I mulled over the possibilities: 1. She knew something. Or she knew something that could lead to the truth; 2. She wanted to check if what she knew was true but was too scared to come over herself; 3. She wanted the police to see if there was anything going on here.

*

She would have chosen robbery from a list of possible incidents she could have made up to get the police to come over. She would have had to reveal her true identity to report a missing person, and it hadn't even been twenty-four hours since Mother had disappeared.

I thought back to when Hae-jin had gone into his room and closed the door to talk to someone. That had to have been Auntie. What had she said to him? What had she said about Mother? About me? She must have been concerned about Mother's safety, since she'd got the police to come. And since she'd called Hae-jin, the source of her worries must have been me. I needed to work out what she knew.

I sat back down at my desk. I took out the journal and flipped to 2015. Only a few entries that year. The same with 2014, 2013, 2012 and earlier.

He says he wants to go to law school.

He's back in school.

He's working in public service instead of going into the military.

He took a break from school.

He got into an undergraduate law programme.

He, he, he ... It was all about me. There wasn't a word about Hae-jin, the one she loved so much. Nothing about Yu-min, whom she missed so much. Nothing at all about Father. These records, for whatever reason, were focused entirely on me. But I didn't see anything special. Most of the entries were only a sentence. The longer entries didn't reveal much. But then I flipped to late April 2006.

Thursday 20 April

His eyes beg me every moment of every day. Please let me get back in the water. How can I ignore eyes like that, coming from my child? Just now, I called Hye-won to see if there's any way we can let him keep swimming. She said the same thing: 'No, it will happen again.'

I know this. Of course I know this. I know my son. I'd basically asked her, Can't we stop the drug regimen? She told me not to forget: the important thing was not whether Yu-jin became a champion swimmer but whether he could lead a harmless life.

I have to accept that. That's my life's goal, after all, and the purpose of her treatment. For him to live as an average person, unscathed and harmless.

I felt dizzy. Was I reading this correctly? I read it again, my finger tracing each word.

I'd stopped swimming at the end of April 2006. That was when I'd approached Auntie, asking for her help to convince Mother to let me carry on. I'd told her everything because I'd so desperately wanted someone to help me. My hopes were crushed and my world was flipped upside down when she'd responded coldly, but I didn't blame her; I just vowed never to trust her again. But I'd had no idea that the situation had been the exact opposite of what I had believed. Mother had been the one who'd wanted to let me swim and stop the medication. And Auntie was the one to disagree. The most important decision in my life had been made not by my mother but by her younger sister, a woman who hadn't given birth to me, brought me up, or even loved me.

I remembered how I felt on the day I was deregistered as an athlete. I remembered the anger burning in my heart and the sobs I had pushed deep down my throat. I remembered how Hae-jin had stood at the entrance to the roof, feeling awful for me and not knowing what to do, as though it was all his fault that this was happening. Mother hadn't even come up to the roof. When I came down to the living room, she'd just asked flatly, 'Have you had something to eat?' And it was Auntie who made her do that.

I pushed down the hot rage that bubbled up. I tried to keep a level head. I struggled to sift the truth from the confusing sentences. Did 'live as an average person, unscathed and harmless' mean 'live without seizures'? But that didn't make sense in my gut. I turned it and flipped it around in my mind, but I kept coming to the same con-clusion. You didn't become an unscathed, harmless being just because you stopped having seizures. That meant that the millions of people who went about their lives without having seizures were unscathed and harmless. The world wasn't like that.

So this was what that meant: *for him to live without being dangerous, he has to take the medication.* Which meant: *with medication, he won't be a dangerous person.* Why would I be dangerous? And why did I need to be medicated? Was it to suppress the seizures, or was it to achieve Mother and Auntie's goal? I had to figure out what the pills did to me.

I typed in 'Remotrol' in the search bar on my phone. I already knew most of what I found. The medication was to treat epilepsy, manic depression and behavioural disorders.

Nobody had said I had manic depression or behavioural disorders. But epilepsy . . . I could only remember having suffered two seizures. Then I found something that might contradict that diagnosis. *Seizures in the temporal lobe have been reported for long-term patients who did not slowly wean themselves off the medication.* Was this what had happened to me? Did the seizures come back when I stopped taking the pills, or were they mere side effects of stopping cold turkey? The answer had to be in the journal. I didn't skim even a single sentence as I flipped back through the pages. The previous time Mother had mentioned medication was 2002.

Thursday 11 April

He was practically dead all week. The side effects are at their peak. He complains of headaches, tinnitus, lethargy. He competed yesterday, but feeling the way he was feeling, he came in 0.45 seconds too late to be considered for a medal. I can still see him looking up at the scoreboard after he hit the touchpad. His eyes were angry.

He didn't sleep all night. I could hear him in bed, groaning and moaning like his teeth were being pulled without an anaesthetic. Pure rage. He didn't let me try to help. He is so angry at his situation. He probably hates me for making him take the medication.

I paced in front of his room. I'm not sure I can live with this decision.

She was wrong about something, though. The most painful thing for me wasn't the side effects or losing; it was the punishment of not being able to go to the pool any time I broke Mother's rules. I couldn't go for two days if I broke one, four days if I broke two. Sometimes, if I broke three or more or a really critical rule, I was banned indefinitely until Mother felt like letting me go back.

I swear I tried my best to follow her rules. But sometimes I couldn't understand what constituted conforming to them. I couldn't understand which behaviours were in the same category as a rule. Like how borrowing something in secret and forgetting to return it was the same as stealing, or how not acknowledging the truth was the same as lying, or how getting back at someone was the same as being violent.

The autumn of my fourth-grade year, one month before we moved to Incheon, was when I was indefinitely banned from the pool for the first time. I got home after practice and Mother's voice flew over from the living room. 'Han Yu-jin. Come here and sit down.'

She was sitting on the sofa with a box in front of her on the table. I knew that box. I knew what was in it, too – a butterfly hairpin, a sparkling headband, a plastic figurine, a key chain, a coin purse, a mirror, a sanitary pad, an eraser, a pencil case, a black one-piece bathing suit, a swimming cap that looked like a penguin . . .

I put down my bag and sat next to her.

'What is this?' she asked, pointing at the box.

I glanced at the name Han Yu-min written on the corner of the box with a marker.

'Don't disappoint me. Don't lie to me. I found this behind your bookcase.'

I wasn't planning on lying. It was Yu-min's box, given to him by Mother so he could keep small objects in one place, like blocks or screws or BB gun pellets. Mother would know that better than anyone: she was the one who'd written his name on it. All I did was put in random things I'd secretly borrowed from other people. Usually girls. A girl I liked or didn't like or one I just knew or someone I didn't know or a sloppy one who liked to toss her things around everywhere. At first I did it for fun. Then it became a game. I began raising the stakes, trying to grab things that were harder to get. Like that sanitary pad.

'Yu-min gave it to me,' I said, meeting Mother's eyes.

'When?'

'When I was in third grade.'

We stared at each other.

'So you're saying you started this last year.'

I should have told her that I didn't know how the box ended up in my room. 'No, this is all his stuff. I'm sorry I didn't tell you about it. I forgot about it after Yu-min died.'

Mother didn't question me any further or tell me a story from the Bible about not stealing or lying. Instead, she told me I was barred from the pool. I had to miss practice. The sentence was indefinite. All because I'd broken important rules: I'd stolen, lied and insulted my brother. Until we moved to Incheon, I wasn't even allowed to go near a pool. Every night, I tried to quench my desire to be in the water by pretending to swim face-down on my bed.

Mother knew exactly how to get under my skin, what

to take away from me in order to get me to submit. The guilt coming from one part of her heart would have been offset by confessing in her journal just how painful it was to bully me. I turned the page.

Monday 4 February

I am realising how desire can make someone superhuman. He no longer complains about the side effects. He takes the pills willingly and doesn't spit them out in secret. At 5.30 every morning he wakes himself up and gets ready. After morning practice he eats his breakfast in the car on his way to school. I thought he'd get exhausted and give up if I forced him to train and study at the same time, but he doesn't even show how hard it is. It's been like that since December, when he asked me if epilepsy was the disease where you foam at the mouth and have seizures.

I understood what he was really asking me. Had he discovered what the medication is supposed to treat? Who knows? Maybe he walked into a pharmacy and asked someone. Maybe he looked it up online. All I knew was that he was afraid. He was afraid of foaming at the mouth and flailing in the pool. He was afraid he wouldn't be able to keep swimming.

I didn't correct him. It's better to let him think that. I know what he was hoping I would say. I thought maybe he'd give up swimming, but he's accepted the medication and the side effects as part of his life. He seems to believe that if he just takes the medicine he can continue to swim.

I feel so guilty every time I see him completely spent. Hye-won says that now that it's come to this, I should use his misunderstanding for our purposes. She says I should think of it as something that will keep him under control, like a braking system against the possibility of him stopping the medication. I asked her if that's really the right thing to do, and she told me it was too late to talk about right or wrong.

I looked up. The words were swimming in front of my eyes. I felt as if Mother were swinging a shovel against the back of my head. Did I understand what I'd just read? I read it over a few more times to see if I'd got it wrong. But I hadn't. The barrier that had blocked my life had never existed to begin with. My mother had conspired with Auntie to rob me of my life.

Confusion scattered inside my head. I really was a son of a bitch. What a cruel thing this was. It had made my life a ruse. It had made me an idiot.

The way Mother and Auntie had treated me flashed before my eyes. I thought of all the things I'd given up, the things I'd had to accept, the awful nights I'd trembled in despair. All of those things had been because I thought I had epilepsy. Rage coursed through my veins; my body burned up like a piece of coal on fire. I felt as if I were breathing inside a blaze. I wanted to run out onto the roof and scream into her face: *Why? Why did you do this to me?*

'Don't throw a tantrum,' I heard Mother say behind me. The swing was squeaking again. I stood up and opened the blinds. She was sitting there looking up at the sky. Her long dark hair floated in the wind, her small pale feet scratched at the floor, and she whispered, 'Can't you see there was a reason for all of that?'

Of course. Of course there had to be a reason. There had to be a good reason to ruin my life. It would be in her journal. Yes, Mum, okay, I'll calm down and find out the reason. But it'd better be convincing, convincing enough to make me understand. You know it takes me a while to get things sometimes, right? And you know I hold grudges for a long time. So you'd better help me understand this properly.

My mobile began to ring. I picked it up. A beautiful name decorated the screen. *Aunt Hag.*

It was 5.30 a.m. The longest day and night of my life had ended. A new day was finally arriving. For the last few hours I had wrestled with all the evidence. I had soaked the bloody wool blanket, sheets and clothes in the bathtub. These were impossible to get rid of; I couldn't burn them or throw them out. There was no way to hide them; I would just have to try and wash them.

I began with the simplest method, filling the bath with cold water and detergent and stepping on them to work the blood out, changing the water frequently until it ran clear. When I couldn't feel my feet, I got out of the tub and warmed them with hot water before starting again. The results weren't that satisfactory, given how much effort had gone into it. The bloodstains had turned dark brown, but that was it. But the act of doing something calmed me down. My emotions had burned out and my head had cooled. I'd recovered the will to make it through all this confusion. I needed to know.

I didn't feel like going straight back to the journal, though. I was scared. I was afraid that Mother would enrage me from the grave, that my body and mind would instruct me to punish somebody. And to make matters worse, the person I would need to punish was testing the limits of my patience by calling me incessantly. She'd called at midnight, then again ten minutes later. I didn't pick up, as I was angry and it was too much of a risk – I was ready to explode.

I'd remembered Google only five minutes earlier. It was as if my brain had stopped working. I looked up how to get rid of bloodstains. Expert tips popped up. Rub with toothpaste, rub lightly with face wash, cover the stain with grated radish, dab with a towel doused in hydrogen peroxide. These were clever ideas, but they wouldn't work on the heavy blanket or the sheets – I wasn't dealing with a speck of blood. I decided to remain loyal to the bleach. I shoved the blanket, sheets and clothes into the bucket and took the *Private Lesson* jacket out of the closet. I might as well wash everything that had to do with that night.

I went downstairs to the laundry room and put the clothes in the washer-dryer. I picked the 'normal' cycle and pressed the 'quiet' button as I didn't want to risk Hello barking from below.

The phone started ringing again as soon as I'd loaded the machine. Auntie. 5.56. I couldn't ignore this one. She would know I was up by now. I pressed the talk button.

'Did you go to bed early last night?' she asked, sounding annoyed.

I hadn't wanted to talk to my mother's younger sister on the phone at midnight. I'd wanted to sleep. She too should have been in bed by midnight, whether she was sleeping with a man or a woman or an animal or by herself, I thought.

'Yu-jin?'

'Yes, I did.'

'Oh, I see. I was going to go to bed too, but then I got so curious I had to call. Didn't you get your exam results?'

I was curious too. Why of all times would she think about that at midnight? 'I passed.'

'Really?' She sounded shocked, as if she were saying, *You, of all people?*

That just annoyed me; I knew she had already heard from Hae-jin. Then again, everything that came out of her mouth annoyed me.

'Your mother doesn't know yet, right?' Finally, the point of her call. She sounded blindly certain. *I know you know where your mum is.*

'Her phone's still turned off, so I sent her a text.'

'She hasn't called? It's been twenty-four hours. Shouldn't you go and look for her?'

Did she really think I wouldn't know that she'd called the police? Maybe she knew that I knew but was trying to get me to react. 'Well, you're getting me worried now.'

'So what are you going to do? Do you have a plan?'

'I'll talk to Hae-jin when he gets home.'

'Oh, he's not home?' asked Auntie innocently.

'He's in Muan.'

'Why?' she asked, feigning curiosity.

189

'For work.'

'Oh, work. So what will you do now?'

A long sigh escaped my lips. When would she hang up, at the end of next year? 'I was about to go for a run.'

'But the sun's not up yet. Do you always go at this time?'

'Yes.'

'Yesterday too?'

I prayed that someone would yank the phone out of this woman's hand. 'I said I slept in yesterday,' I snapped loudly. 'I told you that.'

'Okay, Yu-jin. No need to be angry.' She sounded taken aback.

This was what always happened. The sisters would fill me with rage, and then act surprised when I fought back.

I promised to call her when Hae-jin was back, and hung up. Then I went back to my room and opened the journal. It took me two hours to read the entries from 2002 to 2000. The entries from 2000 were numerous.

Friday 21 July

Yesterday Yu-jin went to summer camp in Mount Jiri with the swimming team. I was worried as soon as they left. I worry about his safety more than anything else. He was suffering side effects from the initial medication, so we've switched to another brand, and we're pushing back the new regimen until after his liver function returns to normal. Hye-won was against this trip because of that, but I ended up letting him go.

I couldn't keep ignoring his pleading eyes. The coach is there, the other kids are there. What could possibly happen? I sent him without telling her about it. I couldn't sit still all day. I just stared at my phone. I knew the coach would call me straight away if anything happened.

The phone rang around dawn. I knew it was the coach before I even opened my eyes. He said Yu-jin was missing. He said he found out when he made the rounds. Nobody saw him leave the camp. He said the police and emergency workers were searching nearby but they hadn't found any trace of him.

I got in the car and the coach called me again as I drove through Inwol Tollgate. They had found him. He'd been at a bed-and-breakfast eight kilometres away. He had come pounding on the door at dawn. My hands were shaking.

He was asleep when I got there. He looked okay; he had scratches and he was bruised in places, but he was fine. I sat down next to him, and a policeman asked whether anything like this had happened before. Did he have a habit of wandering at night? Did he have a chronic illness, like somnambulism or narcolepsy or epilepsy? No, no, no, I kept saying.

Yu-jin said he'd got up to use the bathroom and had heard someone calling for help. He said he went to take a look and saw a white thing fluttering and dancing. He followed it away from the camp but then realised he didn't know where he was. He realised he'd come too far but he was already lost. There was a full moon that night so it wasn't dark, and that's when he saw a yellow ribbon hanging on a branch. He said he remembered

191

how his dad had told him that the ribbons were trail
markers. So he followed the ribbons and ended up at the
bed-and-breakfast.

It didn't make any sense, and the coach and the
police agreed I should take him home. He slept the
whole way back to Seoul. I wanted to wake him up and
ask him, What happened? Tell me the truth.

I remembered exactly what had happened, even though
it was a long time ago and the events before and after the
incident were a little faint. That afternoon, on my way
back from playing in the creek, I had found some strange
metal contraptions in the potato fields. I asked Coach what
they were, and he said they were traps to stop rabbits from
eating the crops. He told me not to go near them. Which
was the easiest way to send a nine-year-old boy straight to
them. At night, when everyone else was asleep, I left the
camp with a flashlight. I was curious; could you really catch
a rabbit with these traps?

I crouched under an acacia tree where I could see the
traps, turned off my flashlight, and waited for the rabbits to
appear. I wasn't scared; it wasn't dark at all. With the full
moon in the sky, the forest glittered, and gold stars hung
low above my head. I don't remember how long I waited.
I started drifting off at some point, listening to the sounds
of the night as I rested my head. An owl hooting, a frog
croaking, a cricket chirping, water trickling . . .

Suddenly, a strange sound. Under the bright moon, I
saw a dark leaping shadow. I stood up. A rabbit. An ash-
coloured wild rabbit was leaping up and down, its hind

leg caught in the trap. I stepped closer, and a sweet smell washed over me. Its back leg, with the tight loop digging into it, was drenched in blood. Its frightened eyes glistened, wet and black in the moonlight. My heart thumped. 'Hold on,' I said. 'I'll untangle you.'

I began to unwind the wire from the stake. It was wrapped around it several times, but it wasn't hard to undo it. It just took some time. The rabbit writhed and bucked, and as soon as the wire loosened it bolted away. I followed it. I wasn't trying to catch it to do anything to it; I was just curious about what was going to happen, where it was going, how far it could go with that long wire still on its leg, whether it could survive the blood loss.

It darted through a bush, across a creek, up a hill and under a tree. I didn't use my eyes; I followed the scent of blood. It smelled as strong as meat being cooked. I could see it as clearly as a flame. The rabbit slowed. At first, I had to run to keep up, but soon I was just walking. Then it stopped completely. It was hiding under a thorny bush. It didn't run away when I approached. I stuck my hand in and grabbed it, but it didn't move. I picked it up by the ears. It was limp. It was dead. I lost interest and threw it into the bushes. I don't remember much after that. It wasn't important.

A question occurred to me now. Had that been a coincidence or inevitable? The rabbit sixteen years ago and the woman two nights ago; the two situations were identical in that I'd smelled blood, I'd stalked a frightened creature in the middle of the night, I'd ended up with a corpse in my hands, and both had happened while I was off my meds. The night sixteen years ago was the seed of the flower that bloomed two nights ago. The only difference was that the girl hadn't been injured when I spotted her.

Maybe she was on her period. It wasn't rare for me to smell menstrual blood in an enclosed space like a lecture hall or a classroom; it was easy to identify the person who was bleeding since it had a clear, unique smell. But in a forest or on a wide-open road? How was that possible unless you were a hunting dog?

Looking back, I realised that I had been attacked by smells every time I stopped my meds. Usually they were pungent – blood, fish, sewage, dirt, water, trees, grass. Even perfume or scented oil was strong and unpleasant. This whole time I had believed it foreshadowed a seizure. Now that I apparently did not have epilepsy, I didn't know what my strong sense of smell meant.

Every time I stopped taking the pills, I'd returned to myself. So my sense of smell must be part of my true nature. If that made me see the world a certain way, which affected my life in a certain way, which in turn took my life down a certain path, then I could see how it might become a problem. Maybe that was why Auntie had pre-scribed the drugs.

Friday 28 July
    Hye-won was angry, saying that a mere nine-year-old was toying with her. Smirking all the while. He apparently hasn't been cooperating in his sessions after returning from camp and going on the new regimen. He exhausts her with crafty wordplay, and in group therapy

he sets a bad example by being rude to the other kids
and egging them on. During hypnosis, he pretends
he's hypnotised and unspools lie after lie. She says that
yesterday he acted like he had become unconscious
from being so deeply hypnotised and made her panic.

What do I do? I knelt by the Virgin Mary and asked,
Mother, wise Mother, what do I do?

I remembered fighting for years with Auntie. I was
resistant to her treatments for a few months after being
banned from the pool for taking Yu-min's box. After we
moved to Incheon, Mother offered me a deal. If I under-
went treatment sincerely and honestly, she would let me
swim again. I accepted. Auntie had won.

I went downstairs. The wash cycle had finished a long
time ago. I pressed the drying button and returned to my
room with a bottle of cold water. The next entries were
in June 2000.

Saturday 3 June
We marked the forty-ninth day of their deaths. After
Mass at dawn, we got in the car. Hye-won offered to
come with us, but I said no. I wanted it to be just the
two of us. For me to be able to continue with this, I have
to shake off the things that are hurting me. I wanted this
short trip to be a new beginning.

We stopped at the flower market in Seocho-dong and
went straight down to Mokpo. He was like a shadow
next to me. He didn't move or talk. He didn't even say
he was hungry or he had to go to the bathroom. He just

sat there, leaning back, looking out of the window or playing with his Rubik's cube.

I realised I'd rarely had Yu-jin next to me in the car like that. If I drove, either his father or his brother sat in the passenger seat. I preferred having Yu-min next to me. I could drive a long time without noticing how tired I was because he chatted so much. I never thought about Yu-jin as he sat in the back. Now that Yu-min isn't here, I realise how quiet Yu-jin is. I remembered my sister saying that it would take something special to make Yu-jin's pulse quicken, and how she was afraid because she didn't know what that might be.

It took five hours to get to the harbour at Mokpo. We caught the ferry that went to Tan Island. Summer had already arrived and hot, damp wind blew from the brown ocean that had swallowed my family. Thunderstorms were forming along the horizon and the forest was turning greener. The trees were growing apples from the places where the flowers had fallen. Everything looked so peaceful that it made me want to weep.

I pulled up to the lodge and the manager came out. He showed us to the cabin we'd stayed in, the one with the two clean rooms, the long living room, the picture of the sunset hanging on the wall, and the terrace from which you could see the bell tower. It all looked the same but it was much quieter now. I couldn't hear the sound of the bell in the wind.

We unpacked and left the house. Yu-jin carried a

bouquet of chrysanthemums and I took a box of their clothes. We walked along the path lined with trees, which had felt so long before but now brought us to our destination quickly. We walked slowly but it didn't even take twenty minutes. When we arrived at the cliff, the sun was sinking behind the horizon.

I opened the box and took out my husband and son's clothes. I'd picked them out a few days ago. Yu-min's favourite red jacket and the navy suit Min-seok wore the most often. I lit them with a lighter. The flames blazed in the westward wind. I sat next to the fire, thinking about that summer day ten years ago, the day when I discovered I had a remarkable knack for making children. Exactly three months after I had Yu-min, I'd become pregnant with Yu-jin. So Yu-min was the child I conceived the first night I spent with Min-seok before we even married, and Yu-jin was the child that came from the first time we were together after I gave birth. I hadn't been careful enough.

It was awful. It was worse than that; I felt as though I'd become a raging beast. Min-seok was an only child so he was thrilled, but I didn't feel the same way. He'd begun his business importing furniture and I was working hard as an editor. I thought I might need to give up work. I didn't like what I saw when I imagined growing old and being responsible for two kids. For a few days, I even wondered whether to keep it or not.

This pregnancy was as different as the boys' personalities. Yu-min had been boisterous *in utero*, kicking, punching, making me jump. I was so nauseated that I couldn't eat much of anything until I was about to deliver. He was two weeks late and had to be induced; maybe he preferred being inside.

By contrast, Yu-jin was so calm. He was quiet and watchful, but he came into the world impatiently; prematurely by C-section due to placental abruption. I went into shock after losing a tremendous amount of blood, and they had to perform a hysterectomy to save my life. He had nearly killed me in the process of his own birth.

They grew up to be even more different. Other than their looks, everything about them was a contrast – their interests, their personalities, their behaviour. Yu-min was outgoing and charming, loved by everyone. Yu-jin was quiet and reserved, yet he was the one who drew the most attention. Quite a few people would stop suddenly in the street and stare, drawn by a strange magnetism that couldn't be put into words. Although he didn't mix with others or react, he made you aware of him.

Hye-won always said the biggest difference between Yu-min and Yu-jin was the way they interacted with other people. Yu-min was interested in relationships with everyone he met, while Yu-jin focused all of his attention on himself, assessing people through one method only – is that person useful or harmful to me?

There were only a few pages left, but I needed a break. I went downstairs and took the clothes out of the washer–dryer, then loaded the sheets and blankets in and set it going again. I went into the kitchen, suddenly hungry, and put the clothes on the counter. I'd only eaten a sugar pancake from Yongi's last night. Hae-jin's seaweed soup was still on the stove. While I waited for it to heat up, I set the table with chopsticks and rummaged in the fridge for side dishes. My head was ringing with the words Auntie had supposedly said sixteen years ago.

It would take something special to make Yu-jin's pulse quicken. I'm afraid because I don't know what that might be.

Auntie's words didn't leave my head even when I went into the shower, toothbrush in my mouth. Something special. How did she know that when even I hadn't known it until just now? Did she medicate me to suppress my nature, which craved that special something? Then that meant Mother knew before Auntie did, since she was the one who took me to her in the first place. Why did she take me there? Nothing I'd read so far had offered a clue.

I came out of my bathroom and sat at the desk without putting any clothes on. I felt hot and feverish, like I was burning up. I opened my phone and searched online for any additional news about the body that was discovered last night.

There it was. An article suggested that the killer was a young, strong, clean-cut man. What did clean-cut mean, anyway? That he looked innocent enough that women wouldn't be wary of him? Or did it mean good-looking? And what was the standard of 'young'? Forties was young relative to fifties, but thirties was younger than forties, while teens and twenties even more so. But it probably meant the killer was in his twenties. The strong part I understood, since he'd have to be strong to subdue the girl and kill her.

I searched 'population of Gundo, Incheon'. Twenty-four thousand three hundred and forty-three, combining Districts One and Two. How many of them were strong, clean-cut men in their twenties? Whether the number was a hundred or a thousand, I would likely become a focus of their investigation. The police might return tomorrow morning, since both Hae-jin and I fitted the profile and lived nearby. And I wouldn't be able to stop them. The only thing I could do was to wait for them while I did what I needed to. I turned to the next page of the journal.

Friday 12 May

I went to see my sister at the Future Paediatric Clinic in Incheon. It was larger than I expected. Six departments and six specialists. Of them, Hye-won is the most popular. When I asked to see her, I was told I would have to wait for a long time. I ignored the nurse, who recommended a different doctor, and waited.

I felt like I couldn't breathe. I couldn't stand that I would be facing her. Not because of pride, but fear. I was afraid that the warning she had given me three years ago was right.

That summer, I was still at the publishing company and Yu-jin was six. Hye-won was a resident specialising in youth behavioural disorders at Yonsei University Hospital. One Friday, we were supposed to meet up in the evening. Something came up at work right before I was going to leave, and I was running late. Then a downpour created a traffic jam. Hye-won got out on time for once. She picked the boys up from the art studio and they were waiting for me in the restaurant.

I rushed inside and saw Hye-won sitting at a table by herself, looking at something. The kids were in the playroom, Yu-min diving into a pool of balls with other kids and Yu-jin sitting against the wall, playing with his Rubik's cube. I sat across from Hye-won, and she showed me what she'd been looking at. A piece of paper ripped out of a notebook. It was crumpled, so I smoothed it out and saw what had been drawn with coloured pencil. A girl's head, topped with a crown, was pierced on the tip of an open umbrella. She had a dark grey face, the mouth drawn with an X, two circles for eyes and long black hair that trickled down onto the umbrella-like strands of seaweed. Water was dripping down the handle, and above the umbrella was a storm cloud.

Hye-won said Yu-jin had drawn it. She asked me if I'd seen him draw anything like this before. I'd never seen anything even remotely similar. In all honesty I hadn't looked very carefully at Yu-jin's sketchbook or picture diary, let alone his scribbles in a notebook; I wouldn't have been able to describe my six-year-old's artistic style. It might sound like an excuse, but I was so busy and Yu-jin wasn't a boy who needed a lot of attention. He did everything on his own as soon as he could.

What's the problem? I asked. I could hear how pointed my tone was. I wanted to tell her to stop psychoanalysing a six-year-old's scribbles or criticising

201

his morality. Maybe this was the first indication of a genius artist who would take the world by storm. Didn't Jean-Michel Basquiat make strange scribbles in the streets?

Hye-won explained that the children were just coming out when she pulled up to the art studio. Yu-min had run out calling, 'Auntie!' then Yu-jin and a girl wearing a white dress came out together under a plastic umbrella. She was a pretty little girl, and from the way the umbrella was tilted towards her and the way Yu-jin was smiling and looking into her eyes, they looked like they were good friends.

It had taken them a while to get to the restaurant because of traffic. Yu-jin was in the back seat, drawing with his coloured pencils and ignoring Yu-min, who was addressing him from the front seat. He stopped sketching only when Hye-won parked. He laid the notebook in his lap and put his pencils back in his bag. Yu-min stretched out towards the notebook, but Yu-jin snatched it away and Yu-min accidentally tore the piece of paper out. Yu-jin glared at his brother.

Hye-won confiscated the piece of paper so that she could give it back to Yu-jin. That was when she saw the picture. The girl in the picture was his little friend from earlier; she had also had long hair and a crown headband. Hye-won asked if that was indeed his friend, but neither boy answered. Yu-jin asked for his picture back and Yu-min was deflated and silent in the front seat. She said that even when they went inside, he kept looking apologetically at his younger brother.

Hye-won said she had spoken to Yu-min privately, and that he had told her it wasn't the first time Yu-jin had drawn a picture like that. When he liked a girl he drew her in similar ways and put the drawing in the girl's bag or desk. One girl who'd received this unwanted gift had cried and made a scene, but the teacher couldn't figure out who'd done it.

She suggested we run some tests, that there might be something seriously wrong with Yu-jin. My face burned. I felt like a stranger had slapped me in the middle of the street. I became argumentative. Had she asked Yu-jin about it? Had she given him a chance to explain? She nodded. When she asked him, Why did you draw this? he said, Because it's fun. He didn't elaborate on whether it was fun to draw the picture or scare the girl and make her cry.

What did that have to do with anything? A child could imagine something that could shock an adult, and he could draw from his imagination and play around. I reminded her of that. I reminded her that Yu-jin wasn't sixteen but only six. Hye-won retorted that if he was sixteen they wouldn't need to run any tests, that he would already be in a youth detention centre for sending threatening pictures. She said Yu-jin knew exactly what he was doing. She said the fact that I'd never seen him draw anything like this was proof that he knew it was something to hide. She pointed out that he'd never been caught even though he'd done something similar several times. She said he was meticulous.

I was so angry that I felt dizzy. I couldn't believe she

was saying he was a troubled child. But she didn't back down. She pointed at the girl's head in the drawing and said it wasn't about the girl. She said it was about me. That for boys his age, all girls were the embodiment of their mother. That if a child cut off his mother's head and speared it on an umbrella, it indicated a serious problem. She said she was just asking questions; why was I getting so angry?

I grabbed the boys and left the restaurant. I thought I'd get physical with her if I stayed any longer. We were never sisters so much as competitors. She was less than a year younger than me, so we always wore the same clothes and read the same books. She was always first in the class but she couldn't stand it if I won an award in a writing contest. Even though people told her all the time that she was smart, she couldn't handle it if someone occasionally complimented me on being intelligent. She wrote her name in large letters in my beloved collection of world literature and scribbled her name on an award I got. She even stole my book report once and submitted it as her own. Even after we became adults and lived our own lives, there was always tension between us. It wasn't that we weren't close. We were always engaged in a power struggle. That was why Min-seok sometimes complained that she looked down on him.

I stopped speaking to her after the incident in the restaurant. I heard she left the university and opened her own clinic, but I didn't get in touch. I tried my best to avoid her during holidays or at Dad's birthday. She never tried to reach out either. We met again a month ago, after they died.

As we left the funeral home, she told me to come by if I needed any help. She isn't someone to just say something to be polite. She would only say, Let's have lunch sometime if she definitely wanted to eat with that person. So telling me to come by was an indication that she wanted to help in some way. Maybe seeing her sister like this after three years of silence was so sad that it swept away all the previous emotions. Maybe she knew I'd have to bring Yu-jin in the near future. In either case, her assistance was a matter of urgency for me as time went on, my only hope.

When the nurse finally called me through, Hye-won didn't seem surprised to see me; she didn't ask what I was doing there or how I was. It would have been easier to bring it up if she'd said anything at all, but she just sat there staring at me. So I had to say it. I reminded her of a doctor's vow before I told her anything, the oath to keep a patient's secrets.

She didn't answer right away. I could tell she was annoyed that I was asking for help, but I could also sense that she was curious about what was going on. I waited. I needed her promise; I couldn't tell her without it. I sipped the water the nurse had given me. Hye-won finally opened her mouth when I was nearly done with the glass. *I promise.* I suddenly went mute. The speech I'd prepared over the last several days became a knot in my head. Where should I start? Should I start from the night before That Day?

I tried to move my tongue clearly, to speak calmly, to lay out the events in order. She didn't speak even when I finished. She didn't even change her expression. It seemed to me that she hadn't blinked once. What do you want from me? she asked coolly.

I wanted tests. I wanted those tests she'd suggested three years ago. I could forgive Yu-jin if there was no cause and effect between the 'serious problem' she was worried about then and That Day, if it had all just been a terrible accident. I could stop hating him. I could stop being frightened of him. I could live my life with him somehow.

Hye-won asked me the question I'd been dreading the most. What will you do if I'm right? Will you handle it with common sense? I sat there twisting my poor fingers. Please, Hye-won, I said, tears filling my eyes. I looked down at my lap as I cried, the way I'd always done since we were girls. She sighed, glared at me and said she would help.

She said the tests would be spread out over a few days. First there would be basic psychometric tests at her clinic, then she would refer us for a comprehensive test at the neuroscience lab at Yonsei University. I hesitated at the word 'refer' but I trusted she would keep her promise. She didn't make promises easily, but once she did, she always kept them.

My eyes stung. I leant back against my chair. I pressed my palms into my eyes and thought about the heads of little girls. I couldn't remember drawing anything like that. But

206

that wasn't why I was taken to Auntie; Mother had become afraid of me only three years after I had supposedly killed her in my artistic imagination. What was That Day she kept referring to?

I realised I had skipped an entry. I flipped forward, wondering if she had written about That Day.

Friday 19 May

The last week has been an eternity. I thought I was going to suffocate to death. This morning, when I saw myself in the mirror near the front door on my way out, I thought I looked like a corpse. My skin was sallow, and the circles under my eyes made me look like I had been punched. I looked insane. I wondered briefly if I should put some make-up on but went straight to the clinic. I didn't have the energy to care.

When I arrived, Hye-won glanced at me and shook her head. She looked at her chart. As I sat in front of her, she dragged out the inevitable, flipping through the test results. I felt like I was waiting for my own execution. I didn't know what exactly I wanted, but I kept talking to the Virgin Mary in my head.

Hye-won said the results weren't what she'd expected, not because she was wrong, but because they were so extreme. I balled my hands into fists then spread them out and put them in my lap. I was starting to sweat. This was the first time she and the specialists at the university had encountered a case like this. That might have been why the results were late; she said they'd talked it over and over, in case they'd misjudged or missed something.

Yu-jin didn't have any congenital brain deformities. He was stunningly intelligent and he was more self-possessed than other kids his age. He'd failed the tests that had been set to display emotional empathy and understanding of morality, and they had found it hard to get him engaged or excited about things – much more so than the average child. That meant that it would take something special to make his pulse quicken.

Hye-won said she was afraid because she didn't know what that might be. At first she thought he had a juvenile form of conduct disorder and ordered some tests for that, but that wasn't it. After discussing it with her colleagues, and doing some MRI scans, they'd determined a potential dysfunction to his amygdala, the core fear system in the human brain. I asked her what this meant in language I could understand.

She said this was off the record, and she wouldn't speak to an ordinary client like this, but he was essentially a danger to others. I couldn't believe it, but she repeated it again. 'Yu-jin is a danger to others. The worst kind of psychopath.'

Psychopath? This silly word was what had made my life what it had been over the last sixteen years? This was the absurd diagnosis that had been affecting me all these years? I felt frozen. All the thoughts that had been circling had stopped. I took my eyes off the journal. The entry continued but I didn't want to read any more of it. I felt as removed from it as though I was meeting a whole different set of characters, in a completely different world from my own. It was almost as if this was a serious problem only for another person and it had nothing to do with me.

'Do you really think so?' I heard Mother say from behind me. I stood and moved over to the sliding door. She was swaying back and forth on the swing. The sky was darkening over the pergola roof. 'Why don't you read the rest?'

I shook my head. 'I'm not interested.'

'You must be curious about That Day.'

I wasn't. I was curious about something else. Why had she continued to stand by me, even going to her estranged sister and begging her for help? If she was so afraid of me, why didn't she just tie a leash around my neck and lock me in a basement? Then I wouldn't have become a killer and she would still be alive.

'Yu-jin.' It wasn't Mother this time. This time it was coming from the hallway. I turned around. 'Are you in there?' Someone was knocking on my door. The handle turned. I glanced at the clock. 1.48 p.m. The journal was open on my desk. Of course the door wasn't locked. Why would I lock it when I was home alone? I realised I was naked when the door swung open to reveal Auntie standing there. 'What are you doing?' she said, almost smiling.

This was unexpected. I'd thought she would come over at some point, but I hadn't realised it would be now. I hadn't thought she'd burst into my room without being asked. Even Mother never came charging in like this. I looked down at my naked body. The skin across my stomach tightened and my thigh muscles hardened. All of my focus was on Auntie. My enemy was here.

'This is a surprise,' I said, stepping in front of the desk. I pressed my thigh against the edge of the desk and stood with my legs open.

Auntie's smile vanished. She spun around, making a guttural noise. The layers of necklaces around her neck spun with her, clattering. 'What do you think you're doing?' she asked. She didn't sound panicked, but she didn't sound ecstatic either. I wanted to tell her not to be embarrassed, as she'd held me and watched me since my dick was the size of a thumb. What could be so scary now that I'd grown a little and so had my manhood?

I looked at Auntie's round behind, clad in jeans. It was the only soft part on her bony body. It reminded me of a soccer ball in the middle of a field. I always wanted to kick it. How had she got in here anyway? I didn't have to think for very long. Hae-jin. When he left the house yesterday, he must have stopped at the clinic to give her the key card for the front door and the combination for the flat.

'That's what I'd like to ask you,' I retorted. 'What are you doing standing there like that?'

Auntie, still facing away, crossed her arms, relaxing her shoulders. 'Put on your clothes, would you? I can't talk to you when you're naked.' She sounded like she could wait a thousand years until I put my clothes on.

'That'll be a bit difficult, Auntie. You're standing in front of my wardrobe.'

She lifted her chin and glanced back, her eyes flicking over me. She seemed to decide that the current situation put her at a disadvantage, and so she uncrossed her arms and turned towards the door. 'Will you come downstairs, then?'

'Sure.'

She seemed to want to show me that she wasn't cowed, maintaining her dignity as my aunt. She lifted her chin and, with a ramrod-straight back, left my room and closed the door behind her. I was sure she hadn't seen the journal.

Yu-jin is a danger to others. The worst kind of psychopath.

I turned towards Mother. 'Mum, Auntie came here to devour me. What should I do? Do you think I should let her, or should I devour her first?'

Mother didn't answer. Do what you want, I thought she was saying. She grinned with her red Joker mouth.

I turned round and closed the journal. Even if I had been dying to know what That Day was, right now wasn't the time. I slid it into the drawer and put on some underwear, black sweatpants and a black T-shirt. I closed the blinds and padded downstairs.

Auntie wasn't in the living room or out on the balcony or in the kitchen. Mother's room was still locked. She didn't have any reason to enter Hae-jin's room. I wondered if she was in the bathroom, but I didn't hear a thing. Her grey coat and her blue handbag were on the island.

I remembered something I'd once read. Something about seeing into a woman's soul if you looked into her handbag. I'd never been curious about Auntie's soul the way I was now. What kind of soul saw an omen of matricide in a six-year-old's picture? What kind of soul sentenced her nine-year-old nephew to life as a psychopath? What kind of soul fucked up another person's life in the name of treatment? What kind of soul burst into the home of a so-called 'danger to others' all alone? Next to her bag was

211

a cake box. The cake, which I could see through the clear plastic, said 'CONGRATULATIONS' across it. I went through the kitchen toward the laundry room, not making a sound, not even breathing. My mind was chatting away: *Don't do anything rash; say nice things and send her on her way.*

Auntie was standing in front of the washer-dryer, craning her neck to look inside. The buttons on the machine were all unlit. It would have finished its cycle a long time ago. I stopped behind her, my hands resting behind my back. It was hard to watch as she opened the door and rummaged around inside. She grabbed a corner of the blanket and yanked it out of the machine, and my heels itched. I wanted to kick her in the back and shove her in the machine, then slam the door behind her.

'What are you doing?' I asked.

Auntie stopped and I thought I saw her shiver.

'You're washing blankets?' she said, turning around slowly, as though she'd known I was behind her all along. The corner of the blanket she'd dragged out fell limply to the ground like a dead person's arm. 'Did you wet your bed?' I could almost detect a merry smile spreading across her face.

I smiled too. 'Have you come to take care of us while Mum's away?'

'I heard the machine beep.' Her gaze went to the blanket and returned to me. 'Looks like it's done.'

'Don't worry about it. I can take care of it.' I turned and stood to the side, trying to usher her away. Hurry up and get out, you stupid bitch, I thought.

'Okay.' She went back into the kitchen.

We looked at each other in front of the balcony. Auntie glanced at my all-black outfit as I looked down at her wrinkled neck, remembering.

Last year, at New Year, we'd spent the holiday in Kusatsu, Japan, enjoying the hot springs. We had all gone: Mother, me, Hae-jin and Auntie. We'd bumped into a woman whose child was a patient of Auntie's. She was a little clueless about the rules of confidentiality; she went on and on even though Auntie looked visibly annoyed. She said they were on a family trip too; that her child was calmer thanks to Auntie, and all he needed to do now was study hard. She should have stopped there, but then she glanced at Mother and began to praise her dramatically. Oh, Doctor, your younger sister is so beautiful, she looks like a young actress! Mother corrected her in embarrassment, saying she was actually the older sister, and the woman kept saying, My goodness, I thought you were the baby! What do you do to look so young? Auntie's face had contorted, her forehead wrinkling deeply. I remembered how she'd muttered after the woman left, 'What a bitch.'

She broke the silence. 'When did Hae-jin say he was coming home?'

I answered by asking a question of my own. 'Didn't you ask him that yesterday, when you saw him?'

She cocked her head. 'What makes you think I saw him yesterday?'

'How else did you get in?'

'Oh, I know the code to your front door. And I followed someone into the building. Why, is something the matter?' Auntie flashed a smile, revealing her teeth and her gums, as though she'd just realised something. 'You're upset because I went into your room, huh?'

She was being fake; I should have rummaged through her bag when I had the chance. Then I could have shoved the evidence in her face.

'I even brought a cake to celebrate your exam results,' she said, going over to the island and showing me the cake box.

'You didn't have to. It's not like I passed the bar.'

Auntie raised her eyebrows. 'Getting into law school is a big deal. If your mother knew, she'd have thrown you a big party. Don't you think so?'

Would she have thrown me a party? Mother was pretty indifferent to my studying law; all she wanted was for me to follow the life she had laid out, in which I would graduate college, go to grad school, get a degree and spend my days in an office. Now I knew where that blueprint came from: this woman standing before me, this woman holding up that pathetic cake, asking, 'Don't you think so?'

The two of them had devised an invisible prison to contain this psychopath for the rest of his life, so that he could live unscathed and harmlessly, among people but not with them. The result of this plotting meant that I remained a child, having to return home by nine every night and not being allowed to travel by myself.

'So should we wait until Hae-jin comes home?' Auntie asked.

I didn't reply.

'It'll be more fun when he's here, right?' She answered herself, then took the cake box towards the fridge. She was going to stay here until Hae-jin got home. 'Your mother hasn't called yet, has she?' She put the cake in the fridge.

'No.' I sat on a chair by the island, from where I could see Auntie's movements without having to turn my head.

'Still nothing, huh?' She pretended to look in the fridge. She asked casually, 'Did she take her car?'

Mother's car would still be parked in the garage. Auntie would have seen that when she parked there herself. I decided to head her off. 'I checked yesterday and her car's still here.'

'Your mum left her car?' she said, sounding incredulous.

Mother rarely went anywhere without her car. I decided to continue along this track, now that I was committed to it. 'Maybe she went in someone else's car, someone she was going with.'

'Who?'

'If I knew that, wouldn't I have already called them?'

Auntie closed the fridge door and came towards me, a calm, gentle expression on her face. What kind of face would she make if I became angry or agitated? 'But Yu-jin,' she said kindly, 'why is her door locked? Does she lock it every time she goes out?

I was about to say yes but remembered arguing with Hae-jin through the door. I doubted Hae-jin would have told her that but I had to be consistent. 'I locked it.'

'You did?' She was watching me.

'The police came yesterday.'

'The police?' She pursed her mouth and her eyes grew wide, the way people typically conveyed surprise. She'd look more convincing if she tried a bit harder.

215

'Someone seems to have called in a false report that there was a burglar.'

'Really! Who would do that?' She would be interested in the conversation I'd had with the police. I decided to put some pressure on her.

'Apparently the caller used a pay phone near Inhang Street. The police said they'd be able to see who it was when they checked the CCTV footage. I asked them to let me know when they found out.'

Auntie was about to say something, but stopped herself.

'I wonder who it was,' I added for extra effect.

We stared at each other. It was clear that Auntie realised that I knew who'd called the police. The conversation was basically over.

'So what made you lock the door?'

'I went to get my ID and they barged into her room. I locked it so they couldn't do that again, just in case they returned when Hae-jin was here and I wasn't at home. You know what Mother is like about her things. She wouldn't want anyone touching them.'

Auntie squinted suspiciously at me. 'Do you have the key?'

I glanced over at the key cabinet in the corner. It was almost a reflex reaction. Auntie's gaze followed mine.

'Can you open it?' she asked.

'Why?'

'I want to have a wash. I came here as soon as I had a moment, and I didn't even have time to wash my face.'

But apparently she'd had enough time to put on a necklace and a pair of earrings. I gestured to the hallway bathroom. 'You can use that one.'

'That's Hae-jin's,' Auntie protested. 'Do I need your permission for every little thing? Aren't you being a little possessive just because your mother's not home?' Her tone was light but her eyes were steely.

I wanted to ask her what she was if not a guest in our house. She picked up her bag and coat and looked at me, silently ordering me to open the door. She seemed certain that there was something to see in the bedroom. 'Yu-jin,' she prodded.

I got up. I found the key and opened the door.

'Thanks,' she said as she walked inside. 'Don't mind me. I'll wash and take a little nap until Hae-jin comes home. I didn't sleep a wink last night.' She closed the door in my face. I heard the lock engage. I didn't hear her moving around. Maybe she was standing by the door, listening. I tossed the keys back in the cabinet and went into the living room. I didn't want to leave her alone downstairs in case she roamed around and found something I'd missed.

I lay on the sofa like Hae-jin had done yesterday morning and started flipping through the channels. Films, fishing . . . Auntie began moving around in my mind's eye. She would put her bag down on Mother's writing desk. She would hang her coat on the back of the chair. What next? She'd fulfil her purpose of coming to this house. I could see her entering the dressing room. She would look in the bathroom, open the door to the study, then come back to the wardrobe and open the doors. She would look over the neat vanity and the things on the shelves, the pots and creams and perfumes, the hair dryer, the make-up brushes, the hats and purses and luggage and backpacks. She wouldn't find anything

217

suspicious, since she wouldn't know what Mother would have taken with her. She would return to the desk and open the drawer. What was inside? I tried to remember. A notebook, pens and stapler, glasses case. My thoughts stopped at Mother's red wallet. I could practically hear Auntie, triumphant: *Your mother left for a trip and didn't even take her wallet?* Then I remembered that Mother's driver's licence and credit card were in her mobile phone case, and that was in my bedroom. Not bad. She'd have to ask me in order for me to answer, but still.

Next she would open the linen cupboard. She wouldn't find anything out of place there either, since I'd checked several times and wiped any surface I had touched. The only thing was the mattress. I'd put a white sheet on it, but if she wanted to, she could easily lift it up and take a look. How likely was it that she'd want to?

There was an action film on the TV featuring Kristen Stewart. I placed the remote on the table and lay back on the sofa. I aimlessly followed the story about a druggie convenience store clerk who was planning to marry his girlfriend. The clerk actually turned out to be some sort of a superhuman groomed by the CIA who had lost his memory. I looked up when the clock chimed four times.

I hadn't slept a wink since waking up at dawn yesterday. I hadn't even relaxed for a moment. But for some reason I wasn't tired. My eyes were dry but I felt pretty good otherwise. Even though I'd been watching the film for over an hour, I didn't feel sleepy. When I thought back to two nights ago, when I was on the verge of collapse, this level of alertness was inexplicable, as though my entire body had entered a state of emergency. Thoughts floated around my head without context and mixed with emotions of all kinds – despair that I wouldn't be able to lead a normal life, anger towards Auntie for branding me a latent killer, resentment at Mother, who hadn't given me any choice over my life, scenes from the killings that flickered like embers, the suspicion that I'd never be able to forget the feeling of fullness and pure joy I'd felt with that woman with the earring.

Someone once said that humans used a third of their lives dreaming, and that they led entirely different lives in their dreams. All kinds of foolish, violent and dirty desires came to life during this time. I was the kind of person who didn't fight against anyone or anything. I was the one who waited all by myself with a knife, along the back wall. Thousands of bastards were on my hit list: bastards I didn't like, bastards who sided with those bastards, bastards who were friendly with the bastards who sided with the bastards I didn't like, bastards who walked past the bastards who were friendly with the bastards who sided with the bastards I didn't like ... On nights when my mood was foul, I summoned each one into my dreams and cut their throats. Auntie might say that was psychopath porn.

I was in elementary school when I first dreamed something pornographic. The bastard who appeared was the one Mother mentioned in her journal, the guy who took the medal from me by 0.45 seconds. As the diary noted, I moaned all night long. I fell into a light sleep and woke up having had a wet dream.

I had countless wet dreams after that. I didn't feel guilt; my dreams only revealed the desires hidden within me. In dreams, everything you wanted came true, and unimaginable things happened all the time in the name of your desires. That was normal and I was entirely normal as well. There wasn't a hint of any desire that would elevate me to a special level, until last August, when I met the woman with the sparkling ring on the night her car had broken down.

She was the pilot light that made me step into the streets, tired of the same old porn in my dreams. And because of that, I was cornered. I only had a couple of choices. I had to craft a story that made sense in case I was arrested or decided to confess. Nobody would believe me if I said I'd acted out the images in my head without realising that it was real life; that Mother had discovered that and tried to kill me; and that in defending myself I'd ended up killing her but that I certainly wasn't a bad person. If I decided to flee . . . My heart began to beat faster. An intuitive thought flickered beneath my consciousness. I didn't grab it, but left it where I could fish it out any time.

I looked up. The phone was ringing. Hae-jin. I picked it up and pressed the talk button.

'What are you doing? You busy?' He sounded out of breath, like he was the busy one. I could hear people talking, something rattling by, cars honking.

'I'm watching a movie. Why?'

'I'm going to be on the 6.05 train. I got caught up in something.'

'So you won't be back until at least nine?'

'I'll be at Yongsan by 8.30, so it won't be until after ten,' he said apologetically. 'Can you do me a favour?'

What kind of favour was it that he was dragging it out like this? 'Go ahead.' I picked up the remote and started changing channels. All I saw were food-related shows. On one channel they were eating marinated grilled spare ribs, on another a man was cutting a slab of meat into pieces, and on a third two soldiers were grilling pork belly over charcoal. Every organism learns from the moment of its birth how to survive and how to wait, learning how to eat and how to forge on until it can eat again. But modern-day humans don't learn how to be hungry. We eat all kinds of things without regard to time and place, indulging ourselves in restaurants and never learning to delay gratification. This obsession over consuming food isn't any different from psychopath porn. From that perspective, it seemed that humans were the most impatient about their desires out of all living beings on earth.

'You know the DVD section in my room with Eastern European shorts?'

'Yeah.'

'There should be a movie in the middle called *Dual*. Can you find it and take it to Yongi's? Now?'

Now, of all times? I was annoyed and didn't say anything.

Hae-jin added a long explanation as though he could read my thoughts. 'So the director of *Private Lesson* needs it immediately, but since I'm in Muan I can't get it to him. But he and the people from the production company are going to be near the Gundo sea wall. You can leave it with Mr Yongi and they'll pick it up.'

'If they're coming all this way anyway, why not ask them to come to the flat to pick it up? I can take it down to the car park for them.' I glanced at Mother's door.

'Apparently it's not his car and he's with a group, so it might be tricky.'

'So if Yongi's isn't open, I have to stand there and wait?'

'It's almost always open at this time,' Hae-jin said, sounding a little deflated. I could hear him thinking, I went all the way to Yeongjong Island for you when you thought you'd lost your phone, and you can't do this one thing for me? 'It's okay if you're too busy.'

I managed to stuff the words 'I'm too busy' back into my mouth. It would take only twenty minutes if I ran. As Mother always said, if someone gives you something, the best thing to do is to return the favour. I didn't want to refuse this small favour and risk him getting suspicious. 'No, no. I'll run over. I don't have anything going on right now.'

Hae-jin's voice brightened instantly. 'You don't have to run. It just has to happen in the next half-hour. Just tell Mr Yongi about it.'

I hung up and approached the bedroom door to listen. I couldn't hear a thing. Maybe Auntie hadn't been rummaging around in the room all this time. Was she reading a book from the study? Had she in fact had a wash and fallen asleep like she'd said she was going to? Other than that, what was there to do in there for hours? It would be okay to leave for a little bit.

I left the TV on and went into Hae-jin's room. I found the DVD right away, where he had said it would be. I slid

222

the door to the foyer open and picked up the running shoes I'd worn to Yongi's last night. The front door lock would beep if I left that way, and Auntie would realise that she could roam around the house freely.

I went upstairs. I locked my door behind me and put on my padded vest. The entry card and my mobile phone went in my pocket. I left the glass sliding door open a crack, walked quickly across the roof deck, and stepped into the stairwell. Hello started barking as usual, so I went down to the ninth floor and took the lift in case the barking brought Auntie out. It went straight down to the ground floor.

Clouds covered the sky, and the air was cold and damp. It was going to start raining soon. As I walked slowly towards the side gate, something nagged at me. I felt as if I'd overlooked something important, or left something vital behind. I walked through the gate and my mind murmured, *If this is Auntie's plan . . .* I stopped in my tracks. I felt like I'd been punched in the gut with a realisation. How long would it take her to go through the entire house?

I looked back towards the building with unfocused eyes. Ten minutes.

The lift was still on the first floor. I got off at the ninth and walked up the last storey, the way I'd done on my way down in reverse. I heard Hello growling but I didn't rush. I wanted him to bark ferociously; I wanted Auntie to hear it. I wanted her to realise what that meant. But for once his growling grew quieter, and by the time I got to the door of the flat, he was silent. Fucking useless mutt.

I punched the code in and walked inside. I didn't detect any noise. I put the DVD on the kitchen island and went to

Mother's bedroom. I quietly pressed down on the handle. Locked. I put my ear to the door. Nothing. She must be asleep. For a moment, relief washed over me. I'd been overly suspicious and deluded, I decided. There was no way Hae-jin would join forces with Auntie, of all people.

I turned around to face Hae-jin's door and felt another nagging in my gut; something said, 'Are you sure?' The best way to confirm was to see it for myself.

I went inside his room and headed straight to the door that opened into Mother's dressing room. I opened the door to her bathroom. It didn't look like it had been used. There wasn't a single drop of water on the sink, in the bathtub, on the walls or floor. The toilet lid was up, the same way I'd left it yesterday. The only difference was that the bathroom slippers were squarely on the floor. I'd left them leaning against the wall, I knew I had. So Auntie had come in here, maybe to look around or to call someone.

I went back out and stood in front of the closed door to Mother's room. I paused for a moment. Auntie would either be in there or not. If she was, I needed a reason for why I was walking straight in: I needed something from Mother's desk but I thought I'd wake her if I knocked. That sounded like a lame excuse. Maybe it was better to just not care and not give a reason, just the way Auntie had acted when she came into my room.

I pushed the door open slowly, hoping: please be inside; whether you're sleeping or not, please be in the room. Didn't some famous novelist say that all of humanity's problems stemmed from the fact that a person couldn't just sit quietly in a room and do nothing?

I stepped inside. The room was empty. My heart speeded up a little. So she'd left, whatever the cost. I started to feel hot and my skin and muscles prickled. Noise rushed into my ears – cars driving along the road far away, the sharp laughter of kids ringing from somewhere in the building, the lift moving up and down, the fridge in the kitchen, my pulse pounding in my head. I knew now that this wasn't a precursor to a seizure; that it was what happened when I felt the urge, a reaction born from my excitement and my need to follow it.

I paused at the desk. As I'd imagined, Auntie's coat was on the back of the chair and her handbag was on the desk. I couldn't tell if she'd gone through the drawers or not. Everything, including Mother's wallet, seemed to be in its rightful place. I noticed that the curtains to the balcony had been pushed aside. The bed – the blanket I'd pulled tightly and neatly over it – was slightly disturbed. She hadn't used it. She'd lifted the covers to look.

I went over to the bed and threw the blanket back. The sheet underneath had come loose. Did that mean she'd seen the bloodstain? I had flipped the mattress over when I carried it downstairs, so she couldn't have stumbled upon it; she would have had to pull the blankets back and pick up the mattress to take a look underneath. She must have gone into the bathroom to quietly call Hae-jin. Did she tell him, I think Yu-jin killed your mother? I have to search the house so can you lure him out?

What are you doing? You busy? Hae-jin had sounded out of breath when he called. Maybe he was excited. His voice had been half an octave higher than usual, as if he were in a good mood. There was no way he would sound like that if he'd heard about Mother. And Hae-jin and Auntie weren't so close that he'd just believe her without seeing the bloodstains with his own eyes, unless they'd secretly communicated all along without my knowledge.

Maybe Auntie hadn't explained the exact reasons, and Hae-jin had followed without knowing the full truth. Still, that meant he had collaborated with her.

I closed the bedroom door behind me and went into the living room. I checked the key cabinet; all the keys were gone. She was doing exactly what I'd thought she'd do, heading down the path I'd hoped she wouldn't. I didn't want to rush upstairs and stop her, though. As long as she hadn't gone past the sliding door in my room, I'd be okay. She'd better not go beyond that, for both our sakes.

I heard a thud from above, a low, dull vibration. I quickly realised I was out of luck. The noise was her closing the sliding door to the roof deck carelessly. I instantly realised what events would unfold and my heart started thudding in my chest. Wasn't it enough for my life to be in this desperate place? Now it was finally pushing me into a dead end and forcing me to choose.

I climbed the stairs slowly, quietly. I walked down the hallway feeling as though I were floating outside of myself, just as I'd felt when I was carrying Mother's dead body in my arms. I stopped at the door and pressed down on the handle. It wasn't locked. As I'd expected, Auntie wasn't in my room. A bunch of keys was on my desk. The sliding door was closed tight; air should be coming through if they were open even a crack, but I didn't feel anything. The journal was open. She'd moved swiftly in the ten minutes she had.

I approached the sliding door and peeked through. She was standing outside, holding her mobile phone, my slippers on her feet, facing the pergola. Her reddish-brown hair rustled in the wind. Her narrow shoulders were quaking. I could tell she was agitated; what should she do?

Meanwhile, Mother was sitting on the swing in the pergola, looking up at the sky, her Joker lips wide open, tapping the deck with her toes. Her white nightgown fluttered in the breeze. She didn't look half bad; that is, if anyone else could see her.

Auntie tucked her hair behind her ear. I stared at her, half pleading and half threatening: it's not too late. Please come back inside. She turned to the pergola and moved towards it, putting a foot on the first paving stone. She moved to the second one. She paused on the third. She raised her mobile and looked at it for a while. Maybe she was trying to decide whether she should call the police or keep looking around.

I meanwhile was trying to decide if I should call her in or go outside. My future would be determined by which I chose. Confess or flee. The former appealed to my reason and the latter to my instinct. Either way, I wouldn't be able to take it back. There was no room for compromise. I was running out of time. I had to decide during the time she crossed the remaining five paving stones. I watched her, whispering for her to turn back. Or maybe I was whispering to myself. I did wait for as long as I could and give her as many chances as possible. The only thing I did wrong was getting fooled by 'honest' Hae-jin and leaving the flat for a few minutes.

Finally Auntie stepped onto the pergola and stopped in front of the table. I looked away for a moment to take my padded vest off. I put it on my desk. I took the razor out of the desk drawer. I moved across and opened the sliding doors, feeling lighter. The wind was blowing loudly now. My bare feet touched the cold, hard stones and something odd happened. Mother, who had been swinging non-stop since yesterday, began to vanish. She contorted, crumpled and melted like a rubber doll on fire. Soon even her melted form disappeared in a wisp of dark smoke, and her toes, scratching the floor of the pergola, finally stopped their lengthy performance. The squeaking stopped. A leaf settled gently on the empty swing.

Auntie also disappeared. She was no longer standing by the table with her back to me. She was prey, treacherous prey at that, which had frightened, agitated, soothed, and forced Mother to ruin my life. My body began to quieten down. My head stopped throbbing and my breathing and heart rate slowed. The knot in my stomach vanished. My senses sharpened. I could hear her frightened, damp, rough breaths, even though there was still a few metres separating us. The world had offered her up, defenceless, and everything had opened up and filled with possibility.

I stepped onto the second paving stone quietly, but I didn't care if the prey heard and turned around. She'd have to notice me at some point, and I was excited to see her expression when she did. What would she say? What would she do? Would she attack me? Run away? Scream?

I paused on the last stone. Only one footstep separated me from the pergola, but the prey still didn't look back. She was so focused on the problem in front of her that she hadn't detected my presence. She was frozen, standing still, not even breathing. Just like the girl two nights ago.

Finally she began to breathe again. She reached out to the table, touched the edge and stepped back, startled, as if she'd touched something hot. She seemed certain about what she'd find inside. I folded my hands behind my back. I was going to have to wait until she saw me or found Mother.

She was working herself up to it. She slid her mobile into her back pocket and stepped forward, put both hands against the edge of the tabletop and pushed. With a heavy groan, the table opened. She stood still for a moment. Or maybe it was longer than a moment.

I knew what she was seeing. First she would see clear plastic, a sack of fertiliser, a hoe, pruning shears, a trowel, a saw, empty planters and small pots, coiled rubber hose, a blue tarpaulin. Maybe a few drops of blood. I'd washed the tabletop but I hadn't bothered with the inside; I hadn't had time and I hadn't expected someone to be looking at it so soon. She leant against the edge of the table and took things out with both hands, moving fast. The clear plastic, the sack of fertiliser, the saw, the hose. She bent over again and shoved a hand in. I heard the tarpaulin being removed. She gasped. Her hair fell forward. Her shoulders began to shake and she started breathing loudly. She had probably come face to face with the Joker. Maybe she'd met her eyes the way I had yesterday in the living room. If she had turned to look at me before she moved the tarpaulin, I would have given her some advice: take out the pots first, that's the feet.

The prey swayed as though she couldn't feel her legs. She managed to straighten up, gripping onto the edge of the table. She let out a moan. She took her phone out of her pocket, but it slipped out of her hand and fell hard onto the floor, dividing into two pieces and scattering in separate directions. The main part flew over to the swing, and the battery landed by my feet.

She went to the swing first and picked up the metal case, then turned around to look for the battery and came face to face with me. Her frantic gaze stopped at my eyes. She actually looked almost confused. The phone slipped out of her hand again.

I flicked the razor open behind my back. 'What are you doing?'

The prey shook her head, her mouth tight as she spotted what I was holding.

I picked the battery up from in front of my feet, my eyes still fixed on hers. 'Weren't you going to call the police?' I stepped onto the pergola.

She jerked backwards, her eyes glued to the razor in my right hand. A sound came out of her mouth. Maybe it was a moan? Or a scream? Whatever it was, it was the sound of terror made by someone who sensed her fate.

I felt sad. It would have been so nice if she could have felt like this sixteen years ago. If she'd cared just a tiny bit about that boy's life, this day wouldn't have come. We wouldn't be standing here like this. But it was too late now, although it would have been too soon then.

'It's okay. Go ahead and call.' I held out the battery and stepped towards her again.

She shook her head and retreated further.

'Go on. Call them and tell them everything. That you took on the treatment of a nine-year-old psychopath sixteen years ago and fooled him into believing he was epileptic. That you medicated him with God knows what. That you manipulated his every movement like he was a lab rat. That you stopped him from doing what he truly wanted, and then one day, he really did go batshit crazy and killed his mother, and now he's about to kill you.' I took a large step forward. 'I said tell them, you cunt.'

The prey stepped back again, but her slipper got caught in a crack and she teetered, flinging her arms out to grab something before falling backwards off the pergola on to the stone floor. Instantly she had created two metres of distance between us. She didn't let this small chance go. She leapt up and ran sobbing and screaming towards the steel door to the stairwell. I caught up with her quickly, grabbing her short hair and yanking it back. The prey let out a piercing sound, the last thing she would utter on this earth. 'Yu-min . . . '

A dark forest was opening within me. Time slowed. I watched the movement of my hand holding the prey's head back, the blade running along the taut skin under the jaw, the neck opening like a zipper and the blood spraying in all directions like a machine gun, the red bullets coating the floor. A sticky warmth covered my face.

Yu-min? I let go of her hair. Her head dropped with a thud onto the floor. Why had she said Yu-min?

IV

ORIGIN OF THE SPECIES

'Yu-min!' Father screamed.

My eyes flew open. Where was I? I was in my bed. I didn't know how long I'd been sleeping, but it was no longer night. It was cloudy outside but I could tell it was daytime.

I couldn't remember much about my dream. But Father's voice remained vivid. It was the first time I'd heard his voice in my dreams. Until now, I hadn't even remembered what it sounded like. I'd never thought of it or missed it. Father didn't exist for me after the age of nine, not in my memories or emotions or anywhere else. But in my dream I'd known instantly that it was him, as if I'd been hearing and living with his voice all this time.

But *how* did I know it was him? Why did he say Yu-min, not Yu-jin? And why was it Father who was shouting and not Mother? I raised myself on my elbows and looked at my clock: 1.41. I looked at the sliding doors and the light streaming in. It must be 1.41 in the afternoon.

I'd glanced at the clock just before I fell asleep. I think it was 9.30 p.m. That meant I'd slept for sixteen hours straight, unsurprising as I hadn't slept at all over the past two days. I had lain down to take a little nap before Hae-jin came home. I blinked, opened my eyes fully and got up to walk over to the sliding doors. The sky was ashy. A herring gull flew low in the misty air. There was no sun, but it was clearly the middle of the day.

The swing was empty. Mother seemed to have left for good. I didn't know why she'd been there or why she'd gone, but I felt a strange sorrow, as though the umbilical cord was finally cut, as if I'd crossed over an inviolable border and become an orphan or something more, perhaps a monster. I'd probably left myself on the other side of the border: the me who lived with people in this world, who believed myself to be average. There was no way to return once you'd crossed a line you shouldn't. There was nothing you could do about it other than to keep moving forward.

Now I knew why the two hours and thirty minutes during which I'd killed the first two people had been completely erased from my memory. It was as if I sub-consciously knew that as soon as I remembered what had happened, I would have to leave the world I'd grown up in. The life I had been leading would be over. I wasn't ready to leave or to end my life, and I wasn't able to handle what I'd done. Only oblivion could deal with things that couldn't be dealt with.

On the other hand, I remembered the majority of last night's events. I'd spent a long time next to Auntie, loiter-ing in the dark forest within me, flying through the fog like a newly hatched butterfly. A red light blinked beyond the fog, warning me to be mindful of danger, but I ignored it. A sweet, intense heat took me to a brighter and higher place. The stars came closer and closer.

I snapped back to reality only when my mind instructed: *It's dark, you're freezing, Hae-jin will be home soon, you have to clean this up.* I looked around at the scene I'd created, feeling dazed. I looked at Auntie, lying in a heap and illuminated by the pergola light; at myself, crouching next to her with the razor still in my hand; at the blood covering the floor. Cold, damp fog was settling over it all. The wind was weeping behind me. The stars disappeared. Only their afterglow was scattered by my feet, and even that was disappearing, twinkling like embers.

I tried to launch myself up but sat back down. My legs were cramped; I'd been crouching for too long. I suddenly realised how cold it was and how everything hurt. I was exhausted. I wanted to lie down right then and there and go to sleep. There was a large rubber bin to the right of the pergola, and I laid Auntie to rest inside, choosing a practical solution like I'd done with the girl with the earring. The roof had become my family's grave site, with Mother in the middle and Auntie to the right. A thought popped into my head: what would go on the left?

I turned on the tap and used the hose to wash the floor. I rubbed my tired eyes. I collected the remains of Auntie's mobile phone. By the time I took off my blood-spattered clothes and stepped into the shower, my body was so cold and stiff that I couldn't even reach for the shampoo. I had to spend ten minutes under the hot water before I could flex my fingers. I showered, washed the razor and put it away in my desk drawer, then went downstairs to put the bloody clothes in the washer-dryer. I folded up the blanket I'd washed earlier and put it back in Mother's linen cupboard.

Next, I put on disposable plastic gloves to deal with Auntie's traces. I used a wet wipe to erase my fingerprints on her phone, then put it back together, and slid it into her handbag. I wrapped her padded coat around her handbag and shoes and hid it in a small suitcase in Mother's dressing room. I tidied Mother's bed, pulling the sheets and blankets taut. I wondered whether I should switch mattresses again. If Auntie hadn't said anything to Hae-jin, he wouldn't look, would he? Honestly, I didn't even want to think about dragging the heavy mattresses up and down the stairs again.

By this point, I was able to move only because my brain was ordering me to. I was so tired that I was nearly comatose. I couldn't really remember how I cleaned up the last bit. Did I take my clothes out of the washer-dryer? Did I lock Mother's bedroom door? Did I put the keys back in the cabinet? It was impossible to stay up until Hae-jin came home; I was already half asleep as I climbed the stairs.

Was Hae-jin home now? He'd said he would be back last night. But how had he got into the building? I hadn't had a chance to go through Auntie's handbag last night, and I didn't believe her story about following someone in. If he'd given her his entry card, as I suspected, he would have had to ring me from downstairs. I didn't remember buzzing him in. Maybe he'd asked someone else, or called Hello's owner. Maybe he'd come upstairs to my room because he was so pissed off at me for not taking that DVD to Yongi's, but had seen me asleep and gone back down. Had he gone straight to bed?

I was suddenly starving. I headed downstairs to check on the things that were nagging at me. I'd also eat something. Yesterday I had felt heavy and clumsy, but today I was feeling much better. Nothing had been solved and I hadn't decided what to do, but I felt quietly optimistic that everything would turn out the way it should. Anything was possible if I wanted it enough.

It was quiet downstairs. I could hear conversation from Hae-jin's room; he was probably watching a film or working on some footage he'd taken yesterday. Mother's door was locked. The keys were in their place. In the kitchen I smelled the delicious scent of bean-paste soup; Hae-jin must have made lunch. A small earthenware pot was on the stove. I went to the laundry room and opened the washer-dryer. My clothes were gone. I went back into the kitchen. Did I dry them last night? Did I take them out and bring them to my room?

'You're up,' said Hae-jin, standing at the entrance to the kitchen.

I stopped next to the sink. 'When did you get home?'

'Maybe around ten thirty? You were already asleep.' He went to the stove and turned it on. 'You didn't budge even when I came in to check on you.'

As I'd suspected. What had my room looked like? Was there anything lying around that shouldn't have been?

'Will you take out the side dishes?' he asked. 'Let's eat. I thought I was going to die of hunger. I was waiting for you to wake up.'

'You go ahead. I'll eat later. I don't feel hungry right now.'

Hae-jin was about to wipe the table clean with a cloth, but he paused. 'You're not hungry?'

I was. But I wanted to avoid a long conversation even more than I wanted to eat. 'I came down because I washed some clothes yesterday. They're not there, though. Did you take them out?'

'I found them on the counter here and hung them to dry on the balcony. Since there were just a few, it seemed a waste to run the dryer.'

I nodded.

Hae-jin asked the question I least wanted to answer. 'Have you heard from Mother?'

'No, not yet.'

He cocked his head. 'Still? Do you think something'd happened? Like a car accident or—'

'If there was an accident, we would have got a call, don't you think? She left her car here, too.'

Hae-jin's gaze followed me, perplexed. 'She's never been unreachable for so long.'

'I'm sure she'll call today. Or come home.' I walked out of the kitchen.

'Did Auntie say if she'd called her, at least?'

'I don't know, I didn't ask her.'

Hae-jin kept asking questions. 'So Auntie came round yesterday? I saw the cake in the fridge. What time did she leave?'

I stopped in front of the stairs and turned to look at him.

'It's just I can't get in touch with her either. Her mobile's turned off and she wasn't answering her home phone.'

Since when did they talk on the phone like that? 'Why do you need her anyway?' I snapped. 'To get your key card back?'

'What?' Hae-jin came out and stood facing me.

'She called you two days ago, so you went to her clinic. To give her the key.'

'Who told you that? Did she say that?'

I didn't answer.

'Don't make assumptions. You always talk as if you know what's going on, but you don't. She did call me, but I didn't go to the clinic. She was asking me all kinds of things, like did I see Mother leave, was I home yesterday. Then I mentioned that you'd passed your exam, and she said she wanted to throw you a little surprise party. She asked me for the code to the front door, so I told her. She told me not to tell you, that it was a surprise.'

'So that was why you asked me to run that errand?'

'You didn't know? Didn't she say anything?' Hae-jin suddenly looked flustered.

I didn't answer.

'I wasn't trying to fool you. Honestly. She said you were watching TV in the living room, which made it impossible for her to set everything up. I said I'd get you to leave for a little bit. I thought she was going to plan something fun. I felt bad I wasn't able to celebrate with you. I just thought Auntie was taking care of it since Mother wasn't home. I did think she was overdoing it, but still . . . '

She did overdo it, I thought. She ran around like an

insane bitch. She held me and Mother hostage for sixteen years and did whatever she wanted with us. I needed to find out exactly why she'd done that. I needed to go up to my room.

'But when I got home, I saw that the cake was still in the fridge. The box wasn't even open. I know you don't like Auntie, so . . . I was actually a little worried. I wondered if you'd had a fight, but you were sleeping. So I called Auntie, but she didn't pick up. It's weird, isn't it? Auntie going incommunicado when we still can't reach Mother?'

The family cemetery on the roof came into my mind. I didn't know what to say. 'I don't know. Maybe Mum wanted to go somewhere without telling us.'

'What about Auntie? She wanted to go somewhere at the same time?'

'Why are you asking me?' I snapped again. 'What do you want me to do about it?'

Hae-jin stared at me with his mouth open. 'I don't want you to do anything about it. I'm just worried. I want us to think about it.'

'I'll think about it starting from now.' I turned around and went upstairs.

Hae-jin didn't say anything; he just watched me go.

I slammed the door behind me so that he wouldn't disturb me for a while and sat at my desk. I was running out of time. I had reached the end of the road. Tonight would be the critical point. I just had to do what I could until then. I had to decide what to do. And I had to act quickly once I made my decision. But I still felt as if I were perched on a slide leading straight to hell. I opened my drawer to take out the journal again.

Psychopath. The inside of my head went blank with shock and Yu-jin's eyes from That Day flashed before me. The way they were when he turned to look at me as I called his name in front of the bell tower. His pupils were dilated, like an excited beast's. They shimmered, flickering with something like flames.

Hye-won said that psychopaths understood the world differently from normal people. She said they didn't have any fear, they didn't get nervous, they didn't feel guilt, and they couldn't empathise with others. But what they could do was read other people's emotions and use them. She told me that was just how he was born.

I wanted to put my hands over my ears. I almost screamed at her. There was no way that this could be true. Why my child? Hye-won said That Day wasn't an accident. That it was the first harmful thing Yu-jin had done. That if we ignored it, it could be repeated at any time. She said I had to go to the police and tell them the truth, and that he would need to be isolated while they intervened medically.

Isolation. I gripped my hands together in my lap, forcing myself to remain seated. I couldn't repeat the mistake I had made three years ago, but I couldn't tell the truth either. No matter what Yu-jin is, he's my son. He's my responsibility, and I have to protect him. I have to find a way to help him live a normal life.

I begged Hye-won, saying I would do anything. I would make it my life's goal to be responsible for him. I would take care of him to the end. I'd live longer than him to make sure that happened. I wanted to show her how much I meant it. I wanted to cut my chest open and take out my heart if that would convince her.

Hye-won gave in on one condition: that I didn't hide anything about Yu-jin from her. She said treatment would take a long time, maybe even his whole life. She would try everything from medication to individual therapy to hypnosis to cognitive treatment to group therapy but she couldn't guarantee that any of it would work. Even if it did work and everything looked fine, he would have to be over forty before we could relax; she said statistically these tendencies lessened a little bit in middle age.

The point of the treatments wouldn't be to nurture ethical concepts. She said that would be impossible. No matter how much we taught him that something was bad, he wouldn't comprehend it. We had to show him how to calculate profit and loss from every situation, and I had to stick to that attitude.

I started to shake. I'd got a promise out of her but I didn't know what to do. I was scared. I felt hopeless. Could I do all of that? Could I forget what had happened? Could I love him as I used to? I was overcome by fear, which was larger than the despair I felt.

I glared at the last sentence. It wasn't just Mother who was afraid; I was scared to turn the page. I couldn't believe I was afraid of something after everything had gone to shit like this. But I couldn't stop now. You couldn't leave a boat in the middle of the Pacific because you felt queasy, could you?

Sunday 30 April
   Yu-jin is sleeping peacefully, deeply. I still can't sleep. It's been two weeks. I left my job. I spend nearly all day at home. I don't do anything other than go to the market, make food for Yu-jin, and lay his clothes out for him. I don't clean or wash or answer the phone. I don't see anyone.
   After the funeral, Min-seok's parents went straight back to the Philippines. I haven't seen Hye-won since then either. I spend time sitting in Yu-min's room. I keep thinking about the sixteenth of April. What if we hadn't gone on that trip? Would we have been able to live a normal, happy life?
   It was our first family trip in three years, a celebration of our eleventh wedding anniversary. I was looking forward to it. We had to take an hour-long ferry after a four-hour drive but I wasn't tired. Everything was going well for us. Min-seok's business was growing, and I'd just been promoted to head of European literature at my publisher's. People always wondered how I could bring up two boys who were only a year apart and work full-time, but it wasn't as difficult as they imagined. The boys were growing up according to their own personalities. I thought of them as colours. Bright, warm, impatient and sloppy Yu-min was orange; calm, polite Yu-jin was a slightly cold blue.

Yu-min ran around the deck, making his father nervous, and Yu-jin sat in the cabin as the ferry heaved, looking silently at the sea. He finally opened his mouth when we got closer to our destination. 'What's the island called?'

Tan Island had become popular because of its rock formations and awe-inspiring cliffs. Holiday homes and restaurants were slowly being established, making it a new tourist destination. It was still isolated, though, and retained a primal aura, with rocky islets jutting out of the murky sea, steep cliffs and windbreaker trees surrounding the island, birds flying through the breeze and white petals scattering like snow from the crab apple trees.

We were staying at a wooden lodge built at the top of a small U-shaped cliff. It was just us there, even though it was the weekend. Maybe because it wasn't peak season yet. It was situated at the end of a road where there were no other lodges or restaurants or even a village. All you could see was the muddy water below and the cliffs thick with pine trees. All you could hear was the crashing of waves, the cries of seagulls and a bell clanging from a bell tower.

The lodge and the bell tower were on either end of the cliff. They were about the same height and faced each other. You could see clearly across, from one to the other, as if looking into the living room of a flat across the street. The bell tower was very old, and next to it was a church with a nearly collapsed roof and a ruined outer wall. The manager of the lodge told us there was

246

also an abandoned village somewhere amid the forest, further back from the cliff.

In the afternoon, the sea retreated from the small space created inside the U shape of the cliff. Below was a long, narrow beach covered with grey pebbles and rocks. We went down and dug for clams and conch. We brought back a lot, enough for dinner. Min-seok took the boys to look at the bell tower on the other side of the cliff, and I laid the terrace table for dinner.

As the sun set, the four of us sat around the table, Yu-min next to me and Yu-jin next to Min-seok. We celebrated the last eleven years of fighting and making up and keeping things going. We high-fived, laughing that we should try for fifty years more. We were loud and happy. It was a good place to be loud; the entire ocean was just for us. A half-moon hung in the night sky, and a gentle westerly wind was blowing. The boys, sitting amid the scene, glowed. Min-seok was tender with me. I got drunk. Later, I fell into a deep sleep for the first time in a while.

The bell woke me. It wasn't a gentle ringing in the wind. It sounded like someone was yanking on the cord with all their might, making the bell clang in a rushed and careless way that sounded like my older son's feet when he got excited. Maybe that was why, still half asleep, I called out to Yu-jin, Make your brother stop. He didn't answer, and the bell rang faster and louder.

My eyes flew open. Intuition pushed drowsiness away as I ran out onto the terrace. The sun was rising and I could see someone ringing the bell across the way.

By now, the ocean had risen halfway up the cliff. The bell tower, tilting towards the ocean, looked even more precarious than it had done yesterday. I could make out the person leaning on the railing, yelling, ringing the bell – his outline was unmistakable to me. It was Yu-min, my elder son.

I felt faint. I thought my eyes would pop out of my skull. My hair was standing on end. Why was he up there? He was a curious child, but not one to put himself in danger. Why was he ringing the bell like that? I went to shout: Yu-min, come down! Come down. But strangely, the word that came out was 'Yu-jin!'

Surprised by my scream, Min-seok ran out of our room in his underwear. Yu-jin appeared in that instant on the bell tower. I immediately recognised his silhouette too. He bounded up to his older brother as though he had heard me. It was a miracle. A flash of relief. Yu-jin would stop him.

But in the next moment, Yu-jin began punching Yu-min. Then he raised a leg and kicked him in the chest. That one kick was enough. Yu-min screamed and plunged from the bell tower. His slim body drew an arc and disappeared below the cliff. I froze. I couldn't breathe, as though my throat had been cut.

Min-seok dashed out of the lodge, calling for Yu-min. I hurried after him along the forest path. Before I realised it, I had twisted my ankle and tripped and fallen. I also realised my feet were bare and bloody. I got up and hobbled on, panting, chanting like a crazy person: Yu-min is fine. Even if he isn't right now, Min-seok will make sure he is fine. When I get there, the three of them will be standing side by side in front of the tower, waiting for me.

The forest, thick with pine trees, felt long and endless, and it seemed I would never reach the tower. When I finally got there, Yu-jin was the only one I could see. He was leaning against the railing and looking down at the ocean without moving. I stopped running. Where was Min-seok? Why was it so quiet? What had happened? My body was shaking and I said weepily, 'Yu-jin . . . '

He looked down at me. His face was covered in blood. His pupils were big and black. I thought I saw flames in them.

I ran to the edge of the cliff, hoping against hope. The water had come up higher. Yu-min was nowhere to be seen. Min-seok was thrashing in the waves alone, pulled under, then thrust above the surface.

My ears buzzed. The moment when Yu-jin had thrown his first punch at his older brother, when he'd kicked him into the ocean – the scenes flashed past my eyes. I needed to call for help but I couldn't open my mouth. My vocal cords strained but nothing came out. I watched stiffly as the waves pulled Min-seok up to the crest and threw him several hundred metres further out. I watched the ocean as it held him in its mouth and took him away.

There is a stretch of time I can't remember: between my standing there and somehow being able to alert the lodge manager. The marine police arrived and rounded up the villagers to get fishing boats on the water. The fishing boats roared between the cliffs, people shouting onboard. The manager suggested we wait back at the lodge, but I didn't move from the edge of the cliff. I thought Min-seok would suddenly appear, dripping wet, holding Yu-min under one arm. If my mind had been sound, I would have realised that it would be impossible for him, let alone Yu-min, to survive the sea during high tide, even if he had been a national swimming champion.

That afternoon, they returned two hours apart as corpses. The villagers found Min-seok and the marine police found Yu-min. The lodge manager called my father-in-law, who flew in from Cebu and took over. My mother-in-law keened and fainted when she arrived and had to be taken to hospital.

I just sat there, dazed. The police came and the reporters came, but I didn't answer any questions. Yu-jin didn't do anything either. After the incident he slept for twenty-four hours straight, a deep sleep closer to a coma. He didn't go to the bathroom, he didn't eat. He didn't open his eyes even when I shook him.

Hye-won came down late after hearing the news. She said Yu-jin was in shock, that it was too much for him to have seen his brother and father die in front of his eyes. I was frozen and couldn't tell her anything about his part in it. She said that I should leave him alone until he woke up on his own, that I shouldn't force him awake.

I couldn't accept that. I didn't feel like watching him sleep angelically. I wanted to wake him up and ask, Why did you do that? Why did you do that? After Hye-won left, something in me snapped and I grabbed the front of his shirt and shook him. I wanted to drag him outside and throw him into the ocean. He opened his eyes as though he sensed it. His big black pupils probed mine hesitantly. He whispered, 'Mum, I love you,' in a small, low voice, like an abandoned baby bird. I understood. It wasn't *I love you*, it was *Mum, don't abandon me*. I stopped breathing. My heart sank and my rage turned to confusion. I felt the curse of the ties of blood, and somewhere among the fury, and losing my mind, I realised anew how much I loved him. I suspected I would never be able to forgive him. I would live the rest of my life in guilt and fear. But I realised who I was. I was Yu-jin's mother. He was my child. That's a fact that can't be erased no matter what. I felt paralysed with feelings and tried for weeks to push everything away.

On the day of the funeral, Yu-jin woke up on his own. The coffins were to go to the cemetery that morning. As always, he moved quietly and discreetly. He ate the food he was served and changed into the mourning clothes I handed him. As the chief mourner, he carried his father's portrait and climbed on the bus to the crematorium without a word. He didn't look sad, exactly. Neither did he look regretful. He sat there, his chin resting on the portrait frame, looking out of the window.

I watched him all day long. I had questions for him – questions I had pushed away but could no longer hold back. Had I seen correctly? Why had he done that? I didn't have a chance until we got to the crematorium. There were too many people around. Once the funeral was over, we were alone, just the two of us, on a park bench. Yet still nothing came out of my mouth. I was afraid to hear the truth. I was scared of myself: if I confirmed that I had indeed seen what I thought I had, I felt I would have to kill my own boy.

That same day, the police came to see us with questions. I began to shake, so I pressed my hands on my knees, hoping they wouldn't be able to tell. Yu-jin looked calmly at the officers. I couldn't tell what he was feeling. His eyes didn't betray fear, anxiety or guilt. He was so expressionless that it blew me away. Was he always like this? Was he always this indifferent and brazen? How had I not realised this before? It was like I was looking at him for the first time.

The police officers asked why the boys had gone all the way to the bell tower. Yu-jin explained that they were playing a survival game while their parents were sleeping. His brother had arrived first and rung the bell, but while he was ringing the bell, the cord snapped and he slipped and fell into the water. Yu-jin had stretched out to grab him, but he was too late.

That whole time, he was calm. He didn't look away or stutter once. Sometimes he took a moment to think before he spoke. I started to doubt myself. Maybe I hadn't seen what had really happened. Yu-jin said he'd reached out. He'd stepped forward to grab his falling brother. I thought of the scene looping through my head. The more I thought about it, the more I realised a simple truth. Yu-jin, a mere nine years old, was calmly lying to the police.

I was no better. When asked who had first discovered what had happened, I automatically lied and said it was

Min-seok. I said I had been asleep. They asked if I had seen anything. I looked at Yu-jin, who was sitting beside me. I was met with those eyes, the eyes I had seen in front of the bell tower, with the dark open pupils and a strange glow inside. I felt like screaming. For the first time, I realised how many thoughts could be mixed up in someone's head – the awareness that Yu-jin was all I had left, the criticism that would pour down on me, Yu-jin's future plucked before it had a chance to bloom, doubt about what I had seen, uncertainty that I would be able to live with the secret I was hiding, Yu-jin's voice whispering, Mum, I love you. I love you. I love you.

I finally said I hadn't seen anything. That was how we joined forces. A cowardly voice in my head tried to make me feel better. I'd just lost my husband and son, I couldn't give up my only remaining child to the police, I wasn't sure I could stand the shame that would come my way. More than anything else, I loved Yu-jin. He didn't have anyone he could trust.

Later I learned that the lodge manager had said the same thing I did. I do believe he didn't see anything. We were the only family at the lodge, and he had only come out as I ran past the office. The incident was determined an accident.

I am thinking about Hye-won often. Rather, I am thinking about Yu-jin's problem that Hye-won had mentioned three years ago. Yu-jin is still my son, but he's not the child I knew. He's now something unfamiliar and unknowable. A fallen meteorite.

I closed the journal and put it down. Just because something seems self-evident doesn't mean it's true. As Mother admitted, she wasn't there when it happened. She didn't know the whole story. She insisted she'd seen what happened clearly, but it wasn't necessarily true. Maybe she believed what she wanted to believe so she could accept the outcome and reduce the weight of her own sins. After all, the tragedy began when she got drunk and fell fast asleep. How could she sacrifice me like that? Because of that she lost her life and destroyed mine. She'd committed an unforgivable crime. If she had believed me, if she'd given me a chance to explain myself, the incident could clearly have been explained as an accident. Then a nine-year-old boy wouldn't have been labelled a psychopath who needed to be isolated from society, and she wouldn't have had to die at the hands of that 'danger to others'.

Mother had never mentioned That Day in the last sixteen years. She never even mentioned Yu-min. She'd cut off all other possibilities and believed firmly that I had killed my brother. Sure, my own memories weren't flawless. I was only nine at the time and it was a long time ago. Still, there was proof that I was right; I was the victim of the accident. I had dreamed the same thing over and over again, reliving that day the way I had experienced it as a boy.

The dreams and the truth were different in exactly one spot: it was always night in the dreams, but the actual events had happened in the early hours of the morning. The rest was detailed and clear enough to make me wish that I could forget it all. Each moment was vivid and immediate: Yu-min's voice, eyes, expression, actions, what I saw, thought, felt, sensed. I remembered it all. I could even remember every detail of the terrace at the lodge. It was a long, wide area with a green metal banister and there was a large outdoor table with benches attached. Over a dozen beer cans stood along the table; a champagne bottle lay on its side; cigarette butts swam in a half-filled water bottle; clam and oyster shells were piled up, along with blackened pieces of meat and sausage; and the grill was filled with white ash. The anniversary cake, uneaten, was cut into four slices, covered entirely with black ants. A bouquet of roses fluttered in the wind, and burnt sparklers and deflated balloons were strewn about. My parents giggled drunkenly as they stumbled towards their bedroom.

The following morning, the two sons of the drunkards sat out on the terrace, having woken in the early hours. We had nothing to do inside, but there was nothing to do out here either. Yu-min looked bored to death. He leant against the wall, playing with his BB gun, glancing at me every now and then, signalling, Should we sneak away and go and play?

He was obsessed with survival games at the time, the way I was obsessed with swimming. Every day he went behind Mother's back, waging fierce combat indiscriminately, at school, at the art studio, or in neighbourhood parks, with a BB gun, slingshot or water gun, with friends, acquaintances or whoever else he could find. If Father hadn't told us yesterday that we couldn't leave the lodge on our own, he would have dragged me to the bell tower as soon as we woke up.

That morning, I sat on the railing, my legs dangling over, watching the ocean as it swept in and out. Mother would have been horrified if she'd seen me, because it was the easiest way to tumble off down the cliff. But that was what I liked about it – the sensation of the wind wrapping around my ankles and tugging, the tension of my body as I balanced. I liked how the waves pushed in and receded. I felt an urge to leap into the water. Yu-min wouldn't be able to, but I could easily swim to the horizon.

I heard the bell across the way. Dark clouds swelled from the horizon and thunder growled behind the clouds. Birds flew low through the damp fog. It was quiet otherwise. Not a single person walked up the unpaved road to the lodge. No other guests were in the surrounding area.

'Yu-jin,' Yu-min finally said. 'Want to go and play?'

I pretended not to hear him. Yesterday we had walked along the beach beneath us; Yu-min had been fixated on the smooth black pebbles strewn along the sand. When Mother wasn't looking, he stuffed handfuls in his pockets. I remembered thinking that the animals in the area wouldn't be spared once Yu-min had added these pebbles to his secret weapon, his slingshot.

'Come on, let's go,' he whispered. His brown eyes were wide and twinkling, indicating that he had, in his words, a killer idea.

There was no guarantee that a killer idea for him would be a killer idea for me. I kept ignoring him. Mother and Father kept sleeping. They fought a lot yet they had produced two sons almost twelve months apart. We were in the same class in the same year in the same school. We were compared to each other in every aspect at every moment of our lives. Yu-min was superior in terms of appearance and intelligence, as Mother acknowledged. He was always a leader in class, surrounded by clamouring followers and worshippers.

As for me, I was a loner. I didn't need a playmate; I was used to playing by myself. Explicit rules and tacit promises were involved in playing with others, and it was easier to be alone than to try to understand or follow them. I was branded as weird everywhere I went. A child at school once called me crazy to my face. He didn't know any better because he didn't know who my brother was. Yu-min forced him to kneel in front of me to apologise. Yu-min was my protector and sometimes tormentor.

'Watch out,' he threatened, jumping up as though he'd shove me off the railing.

If it were me, I wouldn't be so obvious about it; I would just approach silently and push. I didn't say anything, though. I calculated which would be worse: what would happen when our parents caught us, or what would happen if I refused to go along with Yu-min's idea. I knew he wanted to play Survival. I didn't really want to. Yu-min was better than me at everything except swimming, and survival games were the only time we were evenly matched. He had never acknowledged me as his equal, but the record spoke for itself – over dozens of games, we had each won about half the time. That was the problem, though: he was generous only when his superiority wasn't threatened. But I didn't want to lose on purpose; once a match began, I always wanted to win.

'What do you want to play?' I hopped off the railing. I shouldn't have asked; at the time, I had no idea that this one question would completely derail our lives. Then again, how could I have known? I wouldn't be human if I had.

'Survival. Up to there.' He pointed to the bell tower. It wasn't entirely unexpected. Over the years, our survival game had morphed. The winner used to be the one who took the fewest hits. Now we raced each other to a landmark via two separate routes, trying to slow the other guy down by firing at him until the BB pellets ran out.

It wasn't that far. The U-shaped cliff that linked the lodge with the bell tower was carpeted with pine trees, crab apple trees and grass. There were also beehives, blackened slash-and-burn fields and an old abandoned village in the forest. We'd gone there yesterday evening with Father before dinner. When we'd got to the other edge of the cliff, the red sun was halfway below the horizon, dyeing the sky a dark bloody crimson and shining a red path to the restless sea. The bell tower and the vines that covered the ruined church were glowing as though on fire. I felt that we had arrived in outer space. If I stood on that red path, the ocean would push me into another world. It was the most beautiful thing I had ever seen in my life.

Father had slowed down and stopped at the edge. I noticed goose bumps on his arms. He looked from the ocean to the rock formations to the sky and back again, perhaps entranced by the view. But Yu-min was transfixed by the bell tower and tore off towards it. Caught off guard, Father ran after him and grabbed him by the scruff of the neck just before he scampered up the steps. 'You can't go up there.'

'Why not?' Yu-min looked so innocent. 'Can't I ring the bell? Just once?'

Even then I knew what he was doing, but adults often got fooled by Yu-min and his sweet expression. Father carefully explained why not, though even a two-year-old would know why. First, the bell tower was on the edge of the cliff and you could fall into the water. Second, the tower was old and dilapidated, and part of the ceiling had collapsed. 'You boys aren't allowed to come here by yourselves. And don't play Survival in the forest either, okay?'

Yu-min gave his word, but here he was, just half a day later, wanting to do the very thing he'd promised not to do. 'The person who rings the bell first wins. The loser does the winner's homework.'

I met his eyes. 'For how long?'

'One month.'

'How many shots? Three hundred?'

'Two hundred.'

We counted out forty plastic pellets each and loaded them into our guns. We put the remaining one hundred and sixty pellets into cartridges. We grabbed our goggles and crept out of the back door to the narrow, winding path lined with pine and crab apple trees that led to the bell tower.

We played rock-paper-scissors and Yu-min won the right to choose his base. He chose the pine grove. It was an obvious choice, since it had tall trees from which he could launch attacks without having to reveal himself. That

259

meant that the hill beyond the crab apple trees was my base. It was exposed and further away from the bell tower; I would have to run at top speed through the forest and the hilly terrain along the outer edge of the U-shaped curve to be in with a chance of reaching the bell tower first. It was as if he was starting with a hundred additional pellets.

We stood side by side on the path. He stood to the right, closer to the pine trees, and I stood to the left, near the crab apple trees. I began to review the path we'd taken yesterday, thinking back to where everything was, whether there had been anything I could use as cover, where the pines ended and what the terrain was like at that point. Maybe I could use that area to fight for victory.

'On your marks!' Yu-min shouted.

I lowered the goggles over my eyes. The world turned blue and my breathing calmed. Everything disappeared behind my consciousness: the cloudy sky, the breezy forest, the birds flying in loopy curves, the sound of the waves, my thoughts, and finally my awareness of myself. Only the shape of Yu-min's body remained and my low, regular heartbeat. The way to the bell tower unfolded like a map before my eyes, and the places to stop and seek cover lined up.

'Go!' I yelled.

Instead of running, he immediately started spraying pellets at me. A pre-emptive ambush. It was a tactic I used often, though that day I'd decided not to. I wasn't going to shoot until I got closer to the tower. I fled down the left side of the path, dashing through the crab apple trees until I stopped behind a long rock. I surveyed the damage.

My goggles were cracked, my lip was split, my nose was bruised and my jaw throbbed. The smell of blood filled up my body in a flash. I was angry. I'd foreseen all kind of things; how had I not anticipated my brother imitating me? I took off the stupid goggles and hurled them against the rock. I rubbed the tip of my nose with my thumb. The spring breeze gently tickled the back of my neck, as if to soothe me.

Of course I didn't believe that all competition had to be fair. Winning was the goal for everyone. But I couldn't stand it if someone else won. Then they deserved to pay for it, even if it was my brother.

I took my shirt off and tied it around my waist, and my body sprang into gear. I ran onto the ridge of the field piled with dried corn stalks, my first stopover spot. Yu-min began firing from the opposite side. I didn't return fire. I focused only on running until I got past the yellow water tank and fertiliser shed, behind a thick grove of trees. I ducked my head and lay on my belly behind a tree. The gunfire stopped immediately. I heard faint clicks, the sound of Yu-min refilling the magazine. He was down forty pellets.

The next stop was the beehives. It was quite a distance, across an open meadow. I would have to focus and trust my cheetah legs. I bent over, my head ducked low, and sprinted through the pellets raining down on me. A few sailed above my head, some grazed my face, and others hit me elsewhere, but I wasn't dealt a finishing blow. Yu-min refilled his magazine twice. He was now down to eighty pellets.

I ran towards the abandoned village. Using the beehives as cover, I made up the distance towards Yu-min. Pellets began whizzing past my ears again but by the time I got to the steel-roofed house at the edge of the village, I had finally overtaken him. Yu-min arrived on the opposite side a few seconds later. I plastered myself against the flapping, rusted wall and heard him change his magazine for the fourth time. He was down to his last forty pellets.

I stuck my head out, trying to get him to use up all his pellets. He didn't disappoint. Forty pellets instantly blasted towards me. I heard a clicking sound and everything became quiet. Now he was all done. He would be grimacing and looking in the last magazine. He was so consumed by his desire to take me out that he'd probably forgotten how far we were from the bell tower, otherwise he wouldn't have used up all his ammunition this early.

I smiled. I hadn't even used my weapon yet. I moved away from the wall, pointed my gun in front of me and walked carefully out to the middle of the path. It was my turn now.

When I got to a small creek in front of a thicket, I heard something whizzing towards me. Before I could react, something had exploded at the centre of my forehead. My head snapped back and my knees folded. I fell, holding my forehead. Something warm trickled through my fingers. I heard someone running towards me, giggling. A moment later, a pair of eyes was looking into mine. They were innocent and happy, asking, *You're still not dead?* 'See ya!' He waved and took off. I saw his slingshot waving in the air. The world turned dark. Blood was covering my eyes. I managed to sit up. I took my shirt off my waist and wiped my eyes and face with it.

I felt my way down to the creek. I sat in the icy water and washed the wound. I thought back to how he'd bugged me to join in the game and how he had played along until he'd let the pebble fly into my forehead. Of course. He was, after all, experienced at this game. Using up all his pellets was just a cover so that I would walk into his trap.

The bell clanged. It wasn't the wind. It was clear that someone was ringing it. It announced the end of our game and declared Yu-min the winner.

I crawled out of the creek, tied my shirt back around my waist and picked up my gun. I started running towards the cliff. The soles of my feet burned. My sweat dried up and I tasted sourness in my mouth. I didn't feel any pain. I even forgot I was hurt. A solution was bubbling up from somewhere deep in my heart. I had to correct this unfair result.

The bell stopped ringing when I got near the tower.

'Stop there,' Yu-min commanded.

I didn't. I didn't stop there and I didn't stop running. Panting, I kept racing towards the bell tower.

'I said stop!'

The blood kept flowing down over my eyes, making it harder and harder to see. The boundaries between sky and sea and cliff were disappearing. The bell tower loomed like a long red ladder. In the middle was Yu-min, who looked like a shadow.

'Stop, I said!'

Something flew past my ear. I was sure it was a pebble. It grazed the side of my head. Then another whizzed overhead.

I kept going, nearly leaping, as though readying myself for a run-up for the long jump. One step, two step . . . I grabbed the railing and vaulted up and over. I leant forward and yanked the slingshot out of his hand. He gasped and tipped back towards the ocean. Before I knew what was happening, everything was over. He wasn't in front of me any more. Only his scream rang out in my ears. 'Yu-jin!'

His voice slowly vanished. A terrifying, dreadful quiet. I couldn't breathe. Blood whooshed in my ears. My head was burning, and my body felt as if it was being ravaged by spreading wildfire.

I heard Mother calling, 'Yu-jin!'

Gripping tightly to the slingshot, I glared out at the ashy sea. It wasn't me, I didn't do anything. I didn't even touch him. Mother called again, right behind me. 'Yu-jin!'

Father Perishes Trying to Save Son

On the morning of 16 April, a father from Seoul trying to rescue his son, who had fallen into the ocean, lost his life in Tan Island, Sinan-gun, Jeonnam Province. Both Han Min-seok (40) and his son Yu-min (10), who were staying at a lodge on the seaside cliff with their family, drowned. Han jumped into the water to save his son, who had been playing on the bell tower of an abandoned church and had fallen fifteen metres. Both were caught in the rough tide. The police said they were investigating the precise details of the accident.

I kept rereading that sixteen-year-old newspaper article at the pergola table. I'd found it stuck on the last page of the journal. Mother must have cut it out and saved it. Why did she want to keep this? As a souvenir to look back at the incident? To remind herself that it was a lie? To remind herself that I'd killed my brother? If she had believed me, if she'd believed that it was an accident, would everything have turned out differently? Would I have become an average harmless person in her eyes? Would we have lived together for a long time?

I flicked the lighter and set fire to the article. I threw it in the barbecue. I pushed the pages of the journal on top of it, one by one, taking my time. I burned it all. I felt as if I had cremated myself alive. The past lives to which I couldn't return bobbed above the dying fire. Rage and despair and self-pity churned violently in my head. The sorrow that had been pressed deep in my stomach erupted like heartburn. My body grew limp. All of it was awful.

Reality opened up once the embers died down. The moment I could no longer put off had arrived; I had learned all there was to learn and got all the answers I could. I had to make a decision. What was I going to do? A chill ran down my back. I closed the barbecue and came down from the pergola. I stared at the ground as I walked, moving slowly to delay the moment of decision by even a few seconds. What would Hae-jin do if he were me? I leant my head back and squinted at the sky. Light snow flurries were coming down. The pale winter sun was sinking below the heavy clouds. I drew in a breath and let it out in a long sigh, and I could see my breath before me in the air. Another chill went down my back. The cold dug into my teeth. Darwin's maxim came to mind: adapt or die.

I thought about dying. That was certainly the easiest solution. I could hang myself, jump off the building, or cut my own throat with Father's razor. It was also the neatest solution. I wouldn't have to be cuffed, embarrassed or face judgement. I wouldn't have to face Hae-jin, who would be disappointed and afraid of me, which would be the worst thing. The only problem was that I didn't want to die yet. At least not next to Mother. I didn't want to be forced to die; I wanted to be able to choose the time, place and method of my demise.

But neither did I want to confess. Just thinking about sitting across from a police officer and trying to explain what I didn't want to talk about – it made me feel like shit. It would be better to die now rather than to be cross-examined and read about the crime scene in the newspapers. I dismissed this option without thinking any further about it. There was only one way left – vanish as soon as possible. It was now or never. I could think about the rest after I'd gone.

I went back into my room and sat at my desk. Every summer, we went to see Father's side of the family in Cebu. My grandmother would embrace me each time, tears streaming down her face. I remembered her embrace, which was soft and smelled nice, and what she would say as she stroked the back of my head: 'You look just like your father the older you get.'

I took out my passport. I still had over a year before it expired. Would she hug me like that this time? Would she hold me in her embrace even if she knew what I'd done? Maybe. Hope fluttered its wings. I wanted to remain in that hope.

I took Mother's mobile from my drawer. I took her credit card out of the phone case. I turned on the computer, and heard the familiar sound of it booting up. But my mind had to go and ruin it all: *Are you serious? As soon as they find out what you did, your grandma's going to pick up the phone and call the police. She'll hear it on the news. Even if she does hide you, how long could she stand the pressure? It's better to go somewhere you don't know anyone. Then you won't have to reveal your true identity. Find somewhere like that.*

I went to an airline website and clicked randomly on all the countries and cities to which there were flights. Kathmandu, Jakarta, Manila, LA, Dubai, Rio de Janeiro. I suddenly remembered my birthday eight years ago, when I was a high-school senior. All I did every day was go to school and come home, immersed in studying for my college entrance exams. That day was a Sunday; not that it mattered, as I woke up at dawn anyway. Sundays were reserved for a special extra study course that finished late in the evening. But that morning Hae-jin had texted me. *Get ready to be at Yongsan station at 10.*

I immediately understood what this was about. A few days before, he'd asked me what I wanted to do on my birthday. I told him I wanted to go on a day trip to the furthest place possible without getting caught by Mother. I hadn't thought it was possible, but here he was, having planned something.

I smiled despite myself. Yongsan station! I packed my

267

bag with the usual contents in case Mother became suspicious. Pens, notebook, reference books. As I left my room and went downstairs, Hae-jin came out of his room with a camera. Mother was making breakfast. She'd already laid out the traditional birthday meal of seaweed soup, along with the grilled mackerel that I liked, and the glass noodles that were Hae-jin's favourite. Hae-jin and I sat across from each other. Hae-jin raised his eyebrows, which I took as a reference to his text, and I nodded.

'Can you boys come home early today? Let's celebrate tonight,' Mother said, placing a bowl of rice in front of me.

I picked up my chopsticks and shook my head. 'I can't. I have to study.'

Hae-jin dipped his spoon in his soup and shook his head too. 'The club's going to Daebu Island. We're going to find a place to shoot our graduation film. Sorry.' He bowed his head further, trying to hide his flushed face.

'You don't have to be sorry. It's not my birthday.' Mother looked at us, her lips pursed. She was obviously disappointed. She paused, giving us a chance to change our minds.

I swirled the glass noodles around my chopsticks and Hae-jin shovelled the hot soup into his mouth.

Twenty minutes later, Mother dropped Hae-jin off at the bus stop. Ten minutes after that, she pulled up to the school gates. I opened the car door and Mother handed over a 10,000-won bill, my daily allowance.

'I'll pick you up at eleven?'

'Okay.' I got out, and Mother turned the car around and drove off quickly.

When she was gone, I waved down a taxi. My heart began to pound once we were racing towards Yongsan. It wasn't really important what Hae-jin was planning or where we were going. The very fact that we were going somewhere was key.

Hae-jin was waiting for me in front of the Honam Line ticket booth. He handed me two tickets, one for the 10.37 a.m. train to Mokpo and the other for the 6.57 p.m. train coming home. Just as I had wanted, this was the furthest we could manage in a single day. 'Are you excited?'

I nodded. I *was* excited, but I also felt a little like an idiot. Why had I never thought about trying something this simple? Maybe it was because I was beaten down by Mother's rules. It could also be down to the different ways we received our allowances: Hae-jin got a weekly allowance, as he had more freedom, while I was handed a 10,000-won bill in front of school every morning. According to Mother, it had to be this way because I used money thoughtlessly. You couldn't do anything with 10,000 won; it was barely enough to buy two snacks at the supermarket. So my allowance usually disappeared the same day. That might have been Mother's plan all along; she might have thought: he can't do anything if he doesn't have money.

'Let's get something to eat,' Hae-jin suggested.

We went into a fast-food restaurant and I ordered a shrimp burger with fries and coffee, and he got a bulgogi burger with a fountain cola. We barely talked on the train, but it was still awesome. I felt peaceful and free just sitting across from Hae-jin and looking out of the window. The train zoomed through hills covered in cherry blossom and shimmering green barley fields and big cities and small villages before arriving at Mokpo.

We had four hours before we had to get on the train back home. We only had 20,000 won left after having paid for the train tickets and food. There were maybe three things we could do with that amount of money and time: eat a late lunch and relax in a park, take a cab to the beach, or find a cinema and watch a film. We didn't have to discuss it; we agreed on the third option. At a nearby cinema, *The Bucket List* was playing. Hae-jin liked Morgan Freeman and Jack Nicholson, and the film would begin in fifteen minutes. We could share a bag of popcorn with the remaining cash, too.

Carter, a car mechanic, and Edward, a billionaire, are lung cancer patients who meet in hospital. They decide to create a bucket list for their last few months alive in order to figure out who they really are: this includes hunting in the Serengeti, getting a tattoo, sky-diving, laughing until they cry, and having their ashes scattered in a scenic place. It was hilarious, even with death as the subject. It would have been perfect if it weren't for the bastard who kept kicking the back of my seat. Hae-jin was quiet the whole time.

On the train back home, he blurted out, 'I don't like how they made light of death.' It was just as we passed Gwangmyeong station.

I took my eyes off the dark window. 'Why not?'

'It's just dishonest. It's sugar-coating the facts.'

'You don't have to be so serious,' I countered.

270

He stared out of the window, looking blank for a moment, the way he did when he thought about his grandfather. 'I read once that there are three ways to protect yourself from the fear of death. One is repression, forgetting that death is approaching and acting like it doesn't exist, which is how most of us live. The second is never forgetting about it, living every day like it's the last day of your life. The last is acceptance: people who truly accept death aren't afraid of anything. You feel peaceful even when you're at the point of losing everything. But do you know what the three approaches have in common?'

I shook my head. It would be easier to just keel over and die rather than worry about this.

'They're all lies. They all are manifestations of fear.'

'Then what's true?'

'Fear itself, I guess. That's the most honest emotion.'

I didn't ask what the point of all of this was. Hae-jin had given me a perfect gift, and I'd liked the film, especially when Edward said, 'The simplest thing is I loved him and miss him.' If fate called Hae-jin first, I thought I'd say something similar, and I was pretty sure he would feel the same way about me. 'Let's do it too,' I said.

'Do what?' Hae-jin looked at me.

'Let's write down one thing we want to do before we die.'

Hae-jin grumbled – why would we do something like that, that's stupid – but when I took out two scraps of paper and a pen from my bag, his demeanour changed. He covered his note with his hand and wrote down his wish as though he thought I would peek.

'Hand it over,' I said, folding my note four times and giving it to him.

He folded his and passed it to me.

'One, two, three,' we said, and opened each other's notes and put them side by side. *Going out on the ocean in a yacht for a year. Celebrating Christmas in the favelas of Rio de Janeiro.*

The yacht was mine. Rio was his. We smiled at each other. We knew exactly what the other meant.

'Happy stories aren't usually based in reality.' That was what Hae-jin had said after we saw *City of God*. I wanted to ask him what truth he was hoping to find in Rio, but didn't. The train was already crossing Han River; we had to get our things together.

Mother never found out about our secret. She was so focused on her own hopes and dreams that she probably didn't even know what mine were, or that I would be able to grant Hae-jin's wish with her credit card.

I took out a USB drive from my desk and plugged it into my computer. I was the one who made the airline reservations for us to visit my grandmother in Cebu each year, so everything I needed was in here – the certificate of authentication for online banking and copies of our passports. I reserved a round-trip ticket to Rio, connecting through Dubai, the return valid for six months. My Christmas gift to Hae-jin. I would go on my own trip and disappear forever, and the truth of what had happened in this house and where I had gone would remain a mystery. I forgot about my situation for a moment as I thought about Hae-jin's face when he saw this electronic ticket in his inbox. I grinned, imagining how he would explore the alleys of the favelas, camera in hand, tanned from the sun.

But now someone was pounding on my door. Had he seen the email confirmation already? He was supposed to spot it only after I left. I shoved Mother's credit card into my desk and closed the browser. 'One sec!'

Hae-jin was outside my door, looking not surprised or happy but pale and nervous, almost confused. 'We need to talk.' His voice was cold and stiff.

My smile faded. 'I'll be down soon.'

'No. Now.' He stepped closer.

I moved aside grudgingly. 'Come in then.'

He stood in front of my desk, shaking his head. He seemed confused.

'Do you want to sit on the chair?' I offered.

'No, I'll just sit here.' He sank onto the corner of my bed, looking flustered. He put his hands on his thighs and breathed deeply, then bent over, his elbows resting on his knees. He gripped his hands together before opening them.

I perched on the edge of my desk.

'I . . . I have something to ask you.' Hae-jin's voice was shaking.

I hoped he wasn't going to ask about the airline ticket. I was going to have to give him an answer; maybe I would say, Do you remember when we took that trip on my birthday and we wrote our last wishes down? This is my present to you.

'I don't know why, but what you said earlier bothered me. That Mother left her car. She never goes anywhere without her car. Especially when she goes somewhere far away.'

I shoved my hands in my pockets and looked down at my feet. So what?

'So I went downstairs to see if I could find anything in the car.'

My chest was tight. I suddenly felt cold, dark and lonely. I had a hunch that I'd arrived at that very moment I'd been dreading.

'And I found Auntie's car next to Mother's.'

I felt him looking at me. I heard him take in a deep breath and let it out. When did he go to the basement? When did he come back? I hadn't heard him open the front door. Was it when I was burning the journal on the roof?

'I thought it was weird that they would both leave their cars in the garage and go somewhere. It's too strange to be a coincidence, right? But for some reason I didn't want to follow it up, so I worked on my film, cleaned my room, stuff like that. Then I went into Mother's room.'

My brain whirred. I could make up some kind of excuse. Auntie had gone to meet someone, and since it was late and they were having drinks, she left the car here. She'd said she'd be back late but she hadn't come back at all, and whatever she'd done with whoever it was last night wasn't any of my business.

'In the cupboard, in one of Mother's suitcases, I found Auntie's handbag and shoes. I don't get it. Why would Auntie's things be there when she supposedly left yesterday afternoon?' Hae-jin rubbed his palms on his thighs. 'I suppose Mother could have gone on a trip without her wallet or car, and Auntie could have left her things and gone home barefoot, and you could have decided for the first time ever to lock Mother's bedroom door.' He got up and stood in front of me, his hands shoved in his pockets. His brown eyes looked hard as they stared me down. He was impatient, suspicious, angry, disbelieving, wishing for something else. 'But no matter what, I couldn't stop imagining the worst.'

I sensed what would come next. I was screaming in my head, *Stop. Stop there. Just shut up.*

'I thought . . . I thought maybe something had happened in Mother's bed, because when Auntie called me yesterday, she said she was lying on Mother's bed because she was tired.'

I wanted to close my eyes. I felt as though I was falling. Why didn't you wait a little longer? Why couldn't you have waited until I left? I was making a plan to leave too. That would have been good for both of us. You wouldn't have had to speak about these things, and I could have left safely, believing that you were still on my side.

'So I looked under the covers. The rest – well, you explain.'

We stared at each other, not saying a word. He refused to back down, defiant. It felt tense in the room, as though everything could come tumbling down around us.

I felt dizzy. How would I start the story? What should I say? I couldn't excuse my actions rationally and logically, and I honestly couldn't decide what my attitude should be. Losing his trust was worse than killing someone.

Hae-jin swallowed. He looked fearful and expectant, as though he was hoping he'd misunderstood everything;

that I would say, No, you have it all wrong. I gritted my teeth so I wouldn't say that. I didn't want to be a coward.

'Sit down. It's a long story.' My voice was unexpectedly calm and cool.

Hae-jin shook his head, crossing his arms.

'Two days ago . . . ' I started.

Hae-jin's eyes slowly scanned mine as though they were as vast as the solar system.

' . . . I woke up smelling blood.'

Hae-jin didn't say a word in the two hours it took me to tell him everything. He seemed not even to take a breath. He stood like a statue, looking at me so that I couldn't hide behind lies or rationalisations. But I didn't even want to make myself look better. I didn't want to minimise the situation, deceive him, get him to pity me or try to wriggle out of this. I just did my best to clearly explain what had happened over the last few days. I tried not to say what I wanted to say, but only what I had to say. I suppressed the desire to argue, excuse or deny. I couldn't say I was completely honest, but I was more honest than I had been in a long time. 'I still feel like I'm living a nightmare,' I concluded.

Hae-jin's eyes changed every moment; they were burning, then cold, then dark. I stopped talking. I didn't want to keep explaining myself or ask for his understanding or bring up our friendship. The silence between us continued for a long time, thick and impenetrable. It made me feel suffocated. It was a harsh, terrifying silence, the kind where all you can do is wait for it to pass. Despair began to seep into me. I'd hoped that he would stand by my side no matter what anyone else said, no matter what I did. I kept waiting. He had to say something. Even if it was something like: Okay, or: You piece of shit, I wish you were dead. Then I could leave and go on my way.

He walked past me and stopped in front of the sliding doors to the roof deck.

Even though I knew there was no use pleading with him, I reached out and grabbed his elbow. 'Can't you look later? After I leave?'

He shook me off. Or rather, he shuddered. He glanced back at me, his eyes revealing his disgust clearly. A chill descended over my body, and my arms and legs stiffened. Hae-jin opened the door. My stomach dropped as he stepped outside. I had the urge to dash out of the room. What are you waiting for? I thought. Just leave.

'Stay right there,' ordered Hae-jin, his voice trembling.

Outside, darkness had fallen. He walked quickly across the roof deck and paused in front of the rubber bin. He snatched off the lid, almost angrily. The gasp he let out reached my ears. The lid fell out of his hand and clattered to the ground.

I thought of Auntie sitting in the bin. Her cheek would be on her knees, and her eyes would be closed, as though she were sleeping; I'd pressed those eyelids down so that her judgemental stare would never look at anyone again.

Hae-jin turned away, looking pale. He hesitated, afraid to check on the next thing. I wanted to yell, Stop! If he hadn't gone straight to the pergola, I might have run out to block his way and ask whether he really had to do this.

277

He pushed the tabletop open. I thought back to the morning I'd found Mother's body in the living room, that moment of shock when my feet seemed to slip out from under me, when everything turned dark and I couldn't move. I remembered how I'd spent all that time kneeling beside her, waiting for a light to turn on inside my dark head so that I would be able to do something, anything. Hae-jin seemed to be going through each of those moments in a similar sequence; maybe he was hearing his own screams exploding inside his head, thinking it all had to be a bad dream.

He stood in front of the table under the pergola, shuddering as though he were standing on top of a truck hurtling at full speed. I could read his devastation even though his back was facing me and I was watching from inside my room. I didn't move, still perched on my desk. I couldn't do anything but wait, though it made me feel as though I couldn't breathe. I had tried my best but I was free-falling into hell. And at the very bottom was a small boy who above all else wanted to be understood, whining futilely, *But you're on my side, right?*

By the time he turned round to face me, my tongue was stuck to the roof of my mouth. I didn't know why I was sitting there looking at him so desperately. What, specifically, was I waiting for?

He stepped back into my room and closed the sliding door behind him. His eyes were not focused on anything and he didn't look dazed or angry. He certainly didn't appear to be sad. I'm sure he didn't know what to do, but shouldn't he say something to the person he had just ordered to stay put?

'I'm going to leave now,' I announced.

Hae-jin finally looked at me in shock. 'You're going to leave?' His jaw tensed and I imagined him thinking, Who says you can, and where do you think you're going to go?

'Look after yourself, Hae-jin.' I stuck my hand out.

His gaze went down to my hand and came up to my face again. I could hear him breathing loudly. His eyes seemed to be getting wider and his face was turning red. I remembered seeing eyes like this before, not Hae-jin's, but Mother's, two nights ago. *You . . . You, Yu-jin . . . You don't deserve to live.*

I lowered my eyes and nodded to indicate that I understood. Mother had been Hae-jin's saviour, someone who'd welcomed him after he'd become an orphan and loved him for the last ten years. After two days of confusion, he'd finally seen the corpse of the woman he considered his mother. Of course he was shocked. I got that it would be hard for him to understand me at this moment.

'Okay,' I said. 'Let's not do this. I'm just—'

His fist slammed into the side of my face, with all his weight behind it. I heard a loud bang inside my ear and my chin was jerked to the side. I staggered.

'Look after yourself?' He punched me in the chest. I felt as though my ribs were collapsing. A groan erupted from my throat. I couldn't breathe. I hugged my chest and bent forward. A sharp, heavy pain radiated up the side of my body and my back. 'Look after yourself?' Hae-jin's voice was brimming with rage.

I managed to look up at him. I wanted to say something but I couldn't make any noise. The third punch caught me in the throat. Sourness spurted up into my mouth. The world twirled below my feet. I fell over.

Hae-jin launched himself on top of me. 'Is that really what you're going to say to me, you bastard?'

Punches poured in from all directions. My left cheek, right cheek, eyes, nose, lips, chin. The punches were frenzied and fearless. My eyes swelled instantly. I couldn't see anything. Warm blood covered my whole face. My teeth felt loose. I let go. I lay down and didn't resist or defend myself. I gave myself over, letting him hit me as much as he wanted to. My thoughts slowed as he punched. My anxiety subsided. Everything was fucked up, but I felt strangely relieved. It almost felt like penance after a difficult confession.

'How can you say that to me, you bastard?' He grabbed me by the front of my shirt and shook me violently. My ears buzzed. I was dizzy. His face became faint and formless. I realised he was crying. His mouth was twisted, his eyes were red, and he was letting out guttural sobs. 'Why did you do this? What made you do it? What are you going to do, you fucking piece of shit?'

I gritted my teeth. Hae-jin had been a brother to me. The one who had given me the freedom to be who I was. The only one.

He was sobbing harder, 'Your life . . . you . . . ' He threw me aside and collapsed.

I was the one who was pummelled, but he was the one who was spent. He lay on his back, his limbs askew. I closed my eyes. Listening to him, I thought about his question: *What are you going to do?* I wanted to believe that these sobs, which were more wretched than when his grandfather died, were for me.

I swallowed the blood that had pooled in my mouth. The smell of it filled the air. My heart began to tick. It was dark outside. The snow was getting heavier, and delicate flakes were sticking to the sliding door, but it was quiet except for Hae-jin's weeping. We both lay there and soon Hae-jin grew still.

The living room clock broke the long silence. Once, twice . . . six times.

Hae-jin sat up. 'Get up. I have something to say.'

I raised myself. Blood covered the floor.

Hae-jin got up and handed me some tissues. His hair was drenched in sweat, like he had just run a marathon. I was soaked in blood. It wasn't fair, but that was okay. This was fine. I obediently took the tissues and shoved them against my nostrils.

'I'm going to give you two hours,' Hae-jin said.

I looked at him with shock.

'Have a shower, get a grip on yourself, and come downstairs by eight.'

I faced him. What did he mean, get a grip on myself? What was he planning?

'I want you to tell the police.'

My ears rang, just the way they had when the pebble hit me sixteen years ago, as if my head had been smashed in.

'That's the only way,' Hae-jin said.

I looked at him. His eyes were still teary. Weren't those tears for me? Wasn't he wailing for me? Didn't he beat

281

me up because he was so frustrated with me? Or had I misunderstood?

'That's the only way we can sort this out.'

What was he going to do? How could we possibly sort it out? Find a lawyer? Beg for a reduced sentence by confessing? Would he send me packages until I died of old age in prison?

'You'll get caught if you run.'

I knew that. Of course I knew that. But I wanted to forge my own path. 'All I need is for you to do nothing,' I tried. 'If you could look the other way, just for one day . . .'

'If you leave, I'm going to call the police.' Hae-jin's voice grew cold.

I tried to get up.

'You can't sneak out, either,' he warned. 'I'll be by the front door and the dog will start barking if you go out through the roof.' He held out his hand. 'Give me the razor.'

Laughter almost escaped. Why did he want the razor? Was he afraid I'd cut his throat? There were tons of things I could cut his throat with: the saw on the roof, Mother's beloved chef's knives hanging in the kitchen. I could break his neck with my bare hands if I wanted to. Did he think this was easy because I'd let him hit me a few times? I threw the tissues across the room and wiped the stream of blood with the back of my hand. I opened the drawer and held out the razor. I sensed him hesitating.

'Two hours. I'm not waiting more than that.' His voice was low and steely. This was a new side to him, but it wasn't unfamiliar; it was just as if Hae-jin were possessed by Mother.

'You mean this?' I asked helplessly.

'I do.' He was serious. He put the razor in his pocket and left my room, his heavy footsteps disappearing downstairs.

My legs gave way and I crumpled to the floor. I leant against my desk. Confess? I didn't even want to consider it. But I gave up the option of fleeing overseas. It would be hard to sneak out of this neighbourhood, let alone through the airport. Hae-jin, true to his word, would call the police the moment I disappeared. It wasn't that I'd thought it impossible that he would react this way, but it confused me now that he had. I would consider confessing if that made my life easier, but there was no point if it all ended the same way whether I confessed or was caught.

If there was anything to consider, it was the weight of guilt; not mine, but Hae-jin's: his guilt that all this had happened without him being able to stop it, his guilt about Mother's death. I couldn't shake the feeling that he was trying to deal with it by forcing me to confess. Maybe he'd been seized by a foolish sense of duty or ethics. Or maybe he was so angry at what I'd done that he couldn't just let me be. I realised that any sympathy he felt towards me would have disappeared as soon as he'd seen Mother and Auntie's bodies.

In the end, I had to decide: Hae-jin or me? The answer was obvious, but it wasn't an easy choice. Of course it wasn't, given my feelings towards Hae-jin. If I got rid of my feelings, it would be as easy as deciding which pair of shoes to put on. The problem was that I wasn't deciding between different shoes. Hae-jin was purely and wholly an emotional consideration for me. No matter which option I chose, I knew I would regret it until the day I died. I was trapped.

Time trickled by. The clock passed 6.30 and headed to 7. I yanked myself out of the thoughts swimming under the surface of my consciousness. I needed to make a decision.

I stood up. I stopped debating what I should do. A complete picture drew itself in my head, as though it had been planned by my subconscious all along. The only variable I needed to keep in mind was the patrol car that circled the neighbourhood regularly.

First I picked out the stuff I needed to throw away – Mother's mobile phone and credit card, the pearl earring and my roof key. I put on latex gloves and rubbed the fingerprints off each item with a tissue. Next I grabbed the *Private Lesson* jacket from the wardrobe and pushed them all into the pockets. I took that outside and shoved it into the pergola table. I grabbed a towel and wiped the fingerprints from the outside tap and the bin, then tossed the towel and gloves in the barbecue and set them on fire.

When I got back to my room, the clock indicated 7.47. I had to hurry. I took out two 50,000-won bills I'd hidden in my bookcase for emergencies, along with Mother's car key. I pulled on loose jogging bottoms and a checked shirt, though I didn't fasten the buttons around the wrists. I heard the doorbell ring downstairs. I paused. I heard Hae-jin's footsteps going to the front door, then heard the door open. My mobile began to ring. I answered. 'Come downstairs,' Hae-jin said quietly.

Hae-jin was leaning against Mother's door, his arms

crossed, watching me descend the stairs. Only when I got to the bottom step did I realise that there were two other people in the flat – the two detectives who had visited yesterday, sitting side by side on the couch. I paused awkwardly, one foot on the last step and the other on the ground. In my head I was searching for the quickest escape route; I could run upstairs, slip out the roof door . . . but there might be twice as many policemen outside, surrounding the block.

Panic began to spread in my stomach. I was dizzy. I hadn't ever imagined this scenario. I would be handcuffed and dragged out in front of everyone before I'd had a chance to work something out. I looked at Hae-jin from under my swollen eyelids. How could he have done this to me? After promising he'd wait. It wasn't even eight yet.

Hae-jin glanced at the island, as though to tell me to go there. The two detectives stared at me and then at Hae-jin. Probably because I had been beaten to within an inch of my life. It must have looked even more gruesome because I hadn't washed the blood off yet. It was obvious who must have done it, unless I'd gone crazy and tried to beat myself up. I was embarrassed. If I turned and ran away now, I would be a wimp and a coward. And when I inevitably got caught, I would be a wimp and a coward and an idiot who didn't even know how to flee.

I turned and walked towards the island, head held high. I tried to breathe calmly and not reveal anything on my face.

Hae-jin moved from the door to the wall dividing the kitchen and the stairs, and spoke without looking at me. 'They say they're from the police station.'

They say? Why was he talking like that? I leant on the island and crossed my arms. The clock began to chime. Once, twice . . . eight times.

Hae-jin looked back as the men stood up and approached. 'So what's this about?'

The middle-aged detective took out his badge and flashed it at us. I didn't catch the details other than that his name was Choi I-han and he was a lieutenant. He addressed Hae-jin. 'Is your mother Kim Ji-won?'

'Yes,' Hae-jin replied.

Why was he talking about Mother, not me? What was going on? And why had Hae-jin asked what this was about? That wasn't something a person would say after inviting someone to their home. It was what you would say to someone who burst in without notice. So were these cops not here to arrest me?

'What's your name?' Lieutenant Choi asked Hae-jin.

Hae-jin answered. This time Choi looked at me. Neither he nor his partner seemed to recognise me. Then again, I was bruised and bloodied. I opened my swollen mouth and slurred, 'Han Yu-jin.'

'Then you must be the one who was home when we came by about the theft report made by Kim Ji-won.'

Hae-jin stared at me, puzzled.

I said yes. So they hadn't been summoned by Hae-jin. That made more sense. That wasn't the sort of thing he would have done, no matter how shocking the situation. I was relieved, but only for a moment. It didn't matter in the end. It just delayed the inevitable. My life was still hanging in Hae-jin's hands.

'Where's Kim Hye-won?'

I flinched. That I hadn't anticipated. I nearly said, Auntie?

'Auntie?' Hae-jin asked.

'She said she was coming here yesterday? Where is she now?'

Hae-jin turned to look at me.

'She came around two and left around five,' I answered.

'Five? Who was here then? Both of you?'

'Just me,' I said.

'Does your aunt come by often?'

'No.'

'Then she must have come for a reason. Can I ask why she came?'

I glanced at Hae-jin, who still had his arms still crossed and was looking down at his feet. I took that to mean that I was to answer. I tried to be as concise as possible; I explained why she'd come and how we'd celebrated.

'Did she say anything out of the ordinary when she left?'

'No.'

'Do you remember what she was wearing?'

I thought for a moment. Grey padded coat, jeans, black sweater, long necklace. 'I think she was wearing jeans and a sweater, but I don't know for sure. I didn't really pay attention.'

Choi looked at Hae-jin. 'Where were you?'

'I was in Muan for work.' Hae-jin looked up. 'What's this about, anyway?'

Choi continued. 'Business trip?'

'Something like that.'

'When did you get back?'

'A little after ten. What's this about?' Hae-jin was growing impatient.

'What kind of work do you do? Do you work in an office?'

Hae-jin stopped answering, as if to indicate that the detectives needed to explain themselves first.

The other officer had wandered over to the key cabinet in the hall. 'What's this smell?' he said loudly. 'It's like bleach and something metallic . . . ' He had his back to us as he looked at the family portrait on the wall, the one we'd had taken when we became brothers.

I glanced at him before looking back at Choi. There wouldn't be any blood there. I'd wiped everything I'd spotted. If I hadn't caught something, I wanted to believe the detective wouldn't either.

'We're here because we can't reach Kim Hye-won.' Choi finally relented. 'We called her with some questions about a report she filed, but her mobile was turned off. We tried her at home and the housekeeper said she'd gone to her sister's house. That's why we came here, to talk to her in person. It's not that common for a robbery call and a missing persons report to come in from the same family around the same time, is it?'

'A missing persons report?' Hae-jin straightened up, looking surprised.

'Kim Hye-won filed it around noon yesterday. And now you're saying she came here after calling it in. Did she say anything to you?'

Hae-jin looked at me and I looked back at him. Now I understood what had happened. Auntie must have figured that filing a missing persons report was the only way to find out where Mother was. The only issue was that the police didn't do anything when an adult was unreachable for a few days. She would need something else in order for them to move quickly. The false robbery report was therefore an effort to create more suspicion. She must have figured that the police would be interested in the fact that a woman living in a neighbourhood that had recently experienced a murder had called in a report about a burglar, then the very next day was found to be missing. Maybe she'd thought they would investigate immediately. She must have imagined that when she came in here bravely by herself, they wouldn't be far behind. But the police had started their work a day later than Auntie had anticipated.

'So your business in Muan? What kind of work do you do?' Choi asked Hae-jin again.

Hae-jin said he worked in film, and then they made small talk. What do you do in film, what films have you worked on, are they in the cinema, did you go to Muan for another film? Hae-jin answered each question politely, explaining when he had gone to Muan, which train he had caught home, what time he had arrived.

'So you were done at two, then you were by the Yeongsan River harbour,' Choi concluded. 'Were you with anyone?'

'No, I was alone.'

'And you took the train back by yourself too.'

'Yes.'

Choi nodded. 'Then let's talk about your mother.'

Now? When was this going to end? I glanced at the

clock. Where was the other guy? Had he gone into Mother's room? Even though I knew that couldn't logically be possible, I called loudly, 'Where are you going?'

The other detective poked his head out from the staircase. 'Oh, I've never been into a two-storey flat, so I was looking around.' He came back into the living room. 'What *is* this awful smell in here anyway?' He walked past Hae-jin and paused at the entrance to the kitchen, muttering to himself, 'It's like a corpse is rotting in here or something.'

I looked at Choi with annoyance. He needed to control his partner. Choi ignored me. 'Exactly when did your mother leave the house?'

'The morning of December the ninth,' I said. 'I don't know exactly when. She wasn't here when I woke up.'

I could feel Hae-jin's eyes on me. I repeated the story I'd told him initially. I couldn't tell the truth, so there was no reason to be ashamed about telling this story; feeling ashamed wasn't going to change the situation. Choi listened, nodding. Did you notice anything strange about her behaviour, does she often go on retreats, does she always go alone, did you get in touch with her, didn't you think it was strange when you couldn't reach her?

'Not really, because she usually keeps her phone turned off when she's at a retreat,' I explained.

'It's strange,' he commented. 'Why would a woman who doesn't even live with her sister call in a missing persons report when her son, who does live with her, thinks nothing is wrong? Why wouldn't she at least discuss it with you?'

290

I didn't answer.

'Where do you think your mother is? Is there somewhere she's always wanted to go?'

'I don't know.'

'Does she have close friends?'

'She's close with some people from church, but I don't know if she went with them.'

'Do you have their contact details? Did you look in your mother's address book or anything?'

'No, it would all be saved in her phone.'

'And you don't know any of their numbers?'

'No.'

He stared at me in disbelief. I wanted to ask him if he knew his mother's friends and their contact details.

'And you didn't see your mother leave either?' Choi asked Hae-jin.

'No.'

'Why not?'

Hae-jin began to flush, uncomfortable under my gaze. I didn't look away so that he wouldn't change his mind and say something incriminating. 'I slept over at a friend's studio in Sangam-dong the night before.'

'So your friend was there too.'

'No, he doesn't live there. I was there alone.'

'So you weren't home when either your aunt or your mother disappeared from this flat?'

Hae-jin was about to say something but stopped. His face and even his ears were red. Choi observed his discomfort. The other detective was standing by the key cabinet again, pretending to look at its contents.

'So nobody sees your mother leave the house,' Choi summarised. 'The older brother is out and the younger one is asleep in his room. That afternoon, someone who claims to be Kim Ji-won files a false robbery report. The next day her sister files a missing persons report, then she visits this flat and falls out of touch with everyone. The older brother is not home, but the younger one is. Did I get that right?'

'Yes,' I said.

'So you're here because nobody knows where Mother or Auntie is?' Hae-jin asked.

'You must have heard about the murder two nights ago?' The other detective came to stand next to Choi.

Neither of us answered.

'And around the same time, two women who live nearby, sisters at that, disappear, one after the other. Doesn't that mean it could somehow be linked with the murder? I'd like to ask you something,' the detective said, looking first at Hae-jin and then at me. 'I'd like to take a look in your mother's room. In your presence, of course.'

I almost staggered. I couldn't breathe. Hae-jin was the last person to have gone in her room. There was no way he took the time to straighten things up before running upstairs. Auntie's belongings would be spilling out of the suitcase, the blankets and sheets would be flung off the bed, the bloody mattress would be peeking out.

'Why?' Hae-jin asked.

'A living space tells you a lot about a person,' Choi explained. 'It could be helpful in figuring out this situation. Whether there is something going on, or if she really has gone on a retreat like you say.'

292

Hae-jin stared at Choi. His face was getting redder. I felt like I was suffocating, as though I was hanging from a noose on a tree. Hae-jin held all the power. Even if I said no, if Hae-jin said go ahead, they would go right ahead.

'Mother's not going to be happy about this when she finds out,' Hae-jin said.

Choi looked disappointed.

'If something has happened to your mother—' the other detective began.

Hae-jin cut him off brusquely. 'Go and get a search warrant first.'

'Okay—' Choi said, but was himself cut off by his radio, instructing them to report back to the station for an emergency. The detectives looked at each other, then around the room. 'We will, but don't even think about going anywhere, the two of you. We won't be long.'

They walked out quickly and I could hear their radios on the other side of the door.

'Put your coat on and then come back down,' Hae-jin ordered. He was sitting at the island.

I looked back at him on my way out of the kitchen.

'We have to go to the station so you can confess.'

Was I hearing him correctly? The detectives had left not even five minutes ago. Confess? So he hadn't chosen me over the police after all. Or had he changed his mind?

'You mean it?'

'I just didn't want you to be arrested here and dragged out,' Hae-jin said. He had a pained expression on his face.

'You really mean it?' I asked again.

'Wear something warm. It's cold out.'

It's cold out. Was he being serious? I nodded and looked down at my feet. I suddenly remembered the U-shaped cliff. How I used to think, each time I woke from the dream, that if I could go back, I would make sure that pebble never hit me. But now I understood. Life meant living through cycles of similar events. My variation this time might be that I needed to make a slingshot first.

'Okay.'

Hae-jin opened his mouth but closed it without saying anything. He looked like he wanted to punch me again. I knew he wouldn't, though; he had settled on a course of action.

'I want to eat something first. I'm hungry.' I went back into the kitchen, took out the cake, found a fork and started to eat while leaning against the sink. I chewed carefully and slowly, calming myself down. I didn't need bravery, nor did I need to make a decision right now; I just needed some more time. And luck. I saw Mother's kitchen knives to the right of the sink. I knew Hae-jin was distracted.

Hae-jin spoke in disbelief from somewhere behind me. 'How can you eat right now?'

I wanted to tell him about a concept I'd heard about a long time ago: that like other creatures, mankind had survived because it could adapt to various situations. *Look at me*, I thought, *I'm adapting shockingly well to the idea of betraying you.* I put down the cake and the fork and pulled out the car key from my pocket. I placed it on the island.

'What's this?' Hae-jin looked down at the key. He knew what it was; he'd driven the car countless times.

294

'You drive.'

He took the key and stood up, his face cold and expressionless. The Hae-jin I knew, whose face was so transparent, was no longer in front of me. It was as if our years of friendship and decade of living as brothers had vanished. All the trust, consideration, understanding, sympathy we'd shared, all our brotherly love.

'It's snowing outside. Get your parka,' he ordered, sliding the car key into his pocket. The other pocket contained something long and bulky. Was it my razor?

'It won't be cold in the car,' I said. I turned to walk to the front door.

Hae-jin followed me, also not stopping to get a coat. In just a sweater and jeans, he shoved his bare feet into his shoes. He couldn't let me flee, so he was going to shiver in the cold with me. I put on the trainers I'd worn two nights ago. They were still damp and caked with mud. My feet were cold.

Hello began barking as soon as we left the flat. It sounded like he was in the hallway; he must be going out. I pressed the lift call button and stood with my hands behind my back, pushing my right hand into my left sleeve and grabbing my wrist. Hae-jin was pulling the backs of his trainers over his heels.

The lift arrived. I stepped in first, my hands still behind my back. I moved awkwardly and leant against the left wall so that the CCTV wouldn't catch my back. Hae-jin followed me in and pressed the button for the car park. He stood next to me. The lift stopped at the seventh floor. The door opened and Hello, held in his red-lipsticked owner's arms, got in. The owner looked over at us with a smile, which quickly stiffened as she took in my swollen, bloodied face. She glanced at Hae-jin, who tensed. I sensed that he was about to reflexively say, *Oh, I didn't do this to him*, before realising a second later that in fact he had.

Hello's owner turned to face the door, looking down, and I could tell she was uncomfortable. Hello seemed to sense something too; he began to bark loudly over his owner's shoulder, growing more and more insistent. By the time we got to the car park, his barking was so loud inside the lift that my brain felt like it was going to explode in my skull. The moment the doors slid open, Hello's owner shot out and disappeared through the emergency exit.

'Come on,' Hae-jin said.

I didn't move. He dragged me out by my arm. When he let go in front of the emergency exit, I stopped.

'What are you doing?' Hae-jin opened the door and pulled on my elbow. I stumbled through. The ridiculous scene of me stopping, then dragging my feet a few steps when he tugged at me, and then stopping again when he let go continued until we got to Mother's car. Hae-jin seemed to think I'd had a change of heart. Holding onto my elbow, he opened the passenger door and shoved me in. I made a show of resisting before crumpling inside. He slammed the door behind me. It didn't take more than ten seconds for him to walk around and get in the driver's side.

'Put your seat belt on,' he said, buckling his own.

I did so, sinking deeper into the seat and taking off my shoes.

He started driving. We encountered Hello's owner's car by the exit. Hae-jin flashed his lights to let her go first, but she didn't move.

Once we were out of the car park, Hae-jin said, 'We're going to the Gundo Patrol Division.' That was in District One. It would take less than five minutes to get there; it was just on the other side of the bridge after the junction.

'I don't care,' I said, looking out through the windscreen. It was snowing. The first real snow of the year. It was really coming down, but it fell slowly. Hae-jin turned the wipers on. The clock read 8.36. I wondered about Yongi's. Would Mr Yongi close early today? The first snow of the season had to be a reason to shut early, right?

Hae-jin drove towards the back gate. I looked at the side mirror; the lights of Hello's owner's car flashed as it emerged from the garage. We made a right towards the junction, and she followed; she must be headed to the sea wall.

'You're doing the right thing,' Hae-jin said, glancing at me. 'It's the best option at this point.' He looked sure of himself, but I could also sense guilt, nervousness that I might try something in my defeated and desperate state and the responsibility he felt to get me to the patrol division. He was probably saying this to reassure himself. The right thing, for me, wasn't always the best option. The right thing also wasn't the obvious thing; the right thing now was to hold on to my life. That would be the best option for both of us.

'Whatever,' I said, glaring out through the windscreen. Red light.

'I never imagined this when I got home yesterday,' Hae-jin said. We stopped at the lights and Hello's owner stopped behind us instead of pulling up next to us. 'Or even this morning,' he continued. 'I never thought you and I would be in Mother's car like this, in this situation. I could tell something was wrong. When I was waiting for you to come downstairs earlier, I was thinking, is this a dream? None of it feels real.'

I bit on the inside of my cheek. It sounded so much like the kind of things Mother had written in her journal – *I love you but I have to do this, this is harder for me than it is for you, even though you're the one this is being done to, and I want you to know that.*

'And now I'm driving you to the police station.'

The light turned green.

'I have a request,' I said as he pulled away.

'What?' He checked the rear-view mirror.

'Can I just have twenty minutes?'

He glanced at me suspiciously.

'I want to go by the observatory.'

'The Milky Way Observatory?'

What other observatory was there? 'Don't worry, I'm not going to run away. You're the one driving anyway. I won't get very far.'

'I'm not worried about that, it's just—'

'I just want to stop there before going to the police station.' I remembered the countless nights I had suffered from headaches and tinnitus. The countless mornings I'd sprinted to the observatory. The railing along the cliff, Yongi's across the way. That was when I didn't know anything, when I still dreamed of declaring my independence from Mother. The bridge came up ahead. 'Just one last time. I won't be able to come back here again. I don't need to get out of the car; we can just drive past it.'

Hae-jin drove past the bridge. At the sea wall, Hello's owner turned right towards Incheon and we turned left towards the marine park. The road was darker and emptier than usual, with hardly any cars. The bus stop was deserted too. I glanced at Hae-jin. He could let me out here and I could do us both a favour and vanish. I knew he could feel me looking at him, but he just kept staring straight ahead. I looked at Yongi's, still brightly lit even though it was closed. Mr Yongi would be inside, transforming himself into a businessman coming home from a trip. The patrol cars that had been parked in front of the ferry dock weren't there now.

Ten minutes later, we were on the suspension bridge; we had entered the point of no return. We passed a patrol car halfway across the bridge, on its way out after circling the park. Hopefully it would continue without paying attention to us. It disappeared behind us. But when we entered the park, it appeared again and began to flash its lights.

'They want us to pull over,' Hae-jin remarked.

A bitter taste spread inside my mouth. This was the variable I'd been worried about. It was going to get harder. The sign we'd just passed indicated that the cliff was less than five hundred metres away, down a stretch of road as straight and wide as an airstrip. It was time.

'Gun it.'

'What?' Hae-jin looked at me.

I opened my window. 'I said gun it, bastard.' The wind whipped through the window and snow rushed inside.

The patrol car switched its siren on.

Hae-jin put a hand on the window buttons. 'They want us to—'

I rammed my left elbow into his eye. He gasped and let go of the steering wheel; his head and upper body snapped back. His foot slipped off the pedal. I shoved a leg into the driver's side to slam down the accelerator, pressing my upper body into his face and torso. I grabbed the wheel and held him down. One, two, three . . .

Mother's car, with its powerful engine, let out a low roar and sped up. Hae-jin struggled under me but I didn't budge. We raced towards the cliff. The yellow metal railing came towards us. I took my foot off the pedal and slid back into my seat just as we smashed through the railing and burst into the air, swirling white with snow.

I felt myself levitate. Time slowed to a crawl, just the way it had done when I'd killed Auntie last night. All the nerves in my body became eyes, reading the situation moment by moment. Then the seat belt caught me as I lurched forward, and my head and neck snapped back. There was an enormous crash. The car pitched. The airbags deployed, then deflated as water poured in through the open window.

Darkness and quiet descended on us. The car was nearly vertical in the water, about to flip over. The waves coursed in. The water was up to my neck. A chill seeped into my bones. I could hear the siren above us. Soon more would assemble, summoned by radio. It would take a little longer for them to get down to the water though, or for the marine police to mobilise. The car would sink before then.

I unfastened my seat belt and escaped through the open window. I braced myself against the body of the car, held onto the roof, and took off my shirt and trousers. The searchlight cut through the water. That helped me figure out which direction I had to go in. It would have been easier if the police hadn't shown up; I could have just climbed up the cliff. Then I wouldn't have had to swim through open water in a snowstorm.

I breathed deeply a few times, then closed my eyes. This wasn't the ocean; it was a swimming pool. I was about to begin the 1,500 metres, my main event. This was the last competition of my life. I ignored the fact that I hadn't trained since I was fifteen. I forced myself to forget that I hadn't actually been in the water since last summer, in Cebu. I trusted the alluring voice of the optimist in my head: *You can do this. At most it's two kilometres. That's nothing. Take your time.*

My heart settled down, beating regularly as it always did. I watched the ocean as it swelled. The tide would be rising at about seven to fifteen kilometres an hour, two to three times faster than my pace. If I rode along with the tide, it wouldn't take me more than half an hour.

Right before I took off, I looked at the darkened car, sinking below in the depths. Hae-jin was already underwater. I could see thick fog and snow above the surface. I didn't have time to wait for the searchlight to loop back. The cold air felt like an axe. I pushed off and began my strokes.

There was a long way to go, and my entire body felt like ice. I felt a sharp pain in my side, but I tried to breathe normally. Getting tense now would mean death. If I pushed myself too hard, I would sink before getting halfway to shore. I had to keep calm, not rush, and ride with the water. The searchlight approached me gradually and went past me. Then it became even darker. The blackness was so thick that I wondered if I could scoop a mound of it out of the air. The fog grew denser. I couldn't see. The ocean sloshed heavily over me. I felt myself growing weak. I went under the surface often. I was having a hard time breathing. Cold salty water rushed in every time I opened my mouth, and my limbs stiffened. I wasn't swimming; I was just splashing. My mind skipped through time and space, rushing towards the past.

I was back at the cliff on that island, playing Survival with Yu-min. I was on the ground after being hit. I heard his laughter ringing out behind me as I held my head in my hands. And his voice: *You're still not dead?*

Just you wait, the voice inside me answered. *I think I'm going to die soon.*

I could hear the bell ringing from far away.

Stop there! he yelled. *I said stop!* A pebble flew past. Everything was disorientating. The bell was crashing in my ears. *Stop, I said!*

My body rose and crested over a black wave. My head dipped underwater and managed to resurface. Yu-min's voice disappeared. As did the cliff, the pine trees, the sound of the bell. Lights were moving quickly in the fog. I thought I could hear a faint motor. That must be the police boat, going out for rescue.

Darkness pressed in on me. The ocean rushed over my body. The last breath of air leaked out of my lungs. My body was depleted, and I felt my will to live subside. Was this what it felt like for Yu-min and Father? Was this how they gave up? The waves turned me over. I let go and lay back in the shifting water. It had stopped snowing. The sky opened, and light from the stars poured down on me. As it touched my forehead, a voice whispered, *Mother was right.*

EPILOGUE

That night is still as vivid as though it was yesterday. Only the moments when death seemed imminent remain foggy. I'm not sure if I lost consciousness. What I do know is that I smacked my head on something and lost consciousness. When I woke up, I was draped on a mooring cable at the dock, like the girl with the earring. The sea was covered in white, the fog so thick that you couldn't tell which way was up. I could hear the sirens in the park and boats criss-crossing out on the water. Patrol cars rushed back and forth along the road by the sea wall. The dock, though, was deserted. I had managed to return to the cold, dark banks of life.

I didn't have time to congratulate myself for coming back from the brink of death. I felt heavy, as though I was wearing cast-iron armour. It was hard to pick myself up out of the water. Everything was dark, and I couldn't feel anything. My teeth were chattering and my joints creaked. Cold air slashed the inside of my throat. The same words were still ringing in my ears. *Mother was right.*

Dozens of fragments floated by: me running deter-
minedly towards the bell tower, Yu-min yelling at me to
stop as he rang the bell, me leaping over the railing and
throwing a punch, Yu-min staggering, one hand still on
the cord, me kicking him in the chest, him arcing below
the cliff, the cord fluttering in his grip. The ocean that
opened its mouth to swallow him whole, how I felt as I
watched him disappear. I remember what I was thinking:
Don't kid yourself. The person who stays alive is the winner.

The street lamp by the dock was glowing yellow. I
gripped the metal railing of the steps and forced my legs to
climb them, breathing heavily. It was as if I were climbing
the Himalayas while battling altitude sickness. Yongi's, just
above me, might as well have been Pluto. I kept going. It
wasn't a matter of will, and it certainly wasn't a miracle.
It was the power of simplicity; I concentrated solely on
where to place my foot next. When I got up to the sea wall,
the dark shack greeted me. I was grateful that Mr Yongi
had gone home. I was moved by my luck: no cars or people
were on the road when I emerged. I broke into the shack.
It was easier to breathe in here. I was overwhelmed with
relief. I was going to make it.

I searched and found a thin lighter shaped like a gun. I
clicked the trigger and a flame sprang up. Now I could see.
I spotted Mr Yongi's uniform hanging up as usual. I dried
my hair and body with a rag and put on his trousers, jacket,
cap, disposable mask, thick hiking socks and rubber boots.
The trousers were too short, but now was not the time to
worry about style. I was just grateful I managed to fit into
the clothes at all.

I dragged myself onto the intercity bus to Ansan, where I spent the night in a twenty-four-hour bathhouse, washing off the salt, sweating it out, and taking a deep nap in a room with a heated floor. The next day, at dawn, I caught the train to Mokpo. Twelve hours later, I boarded a shrimp boat as an apprentice. For the next year, I roamed the sea, sleeping in the belly of the boat, cooking, cleaning and helping with the nets.

All I knew about what had happened to Hae-jin was what I'd seen on YTN News on the train. The police had recovered the car and his body. It appeared that he had tried to escape from his seat belt. So in that last moment when I looked back before swimming for shore, he had been struggling in the dark by himself. I took this in more calmly than I'd expected, though a lump remained lodged in my throat for a long time. What were we to each other? Were we brothers? I still didn't know. What I did know was that if I had left just a little earlier, or Hae-jin had figured it all out just a little later, we could have kept our relationship intact.

Beyond that, I was in the dark about the investigation. The boat had a radio, of course, but I didn't have time to listen to the news. For the very first time in my life, I was scraping by, focused only on surviving.

Early this morning, I stepped on shore with the little money I'd earned in my pocket. First I went to a public bath for the first time in a year. I washed, shaved and moisturised. Then I bought new clothes and a hat and trainers, ate something and drank a coffee. Hae-jin loved coffee. I went to a nearby internet café. Sitting among pathetic gamers, I scrolled through the news from a year ago.

They'd called it 'the Razor Killings'. Hae-jin had been pegged as the killer. The police concluded that he'd killed a stranger, his adoptive mother and her sister before trying to flee overseas. When he failed at that, he killed himself. All the evidence supported that conclusion, including the razor in his jeans pocket, the *Private Lesson* jacket discovered in the table on the roof of the flat, and the ticket to Rio he'd reserved with his mother's card. A neighbour had reported seeing Hae-jin forcing his adoptive brother, who'd clearly been beaten up, into a car and driving him to the park. The brother was deemed missing. They searched for three days but couldn't find anything other than his clothes. They thought it was possible he'd survived, since he'd once been a competitive swimmer, but no clues or witnesses had turned up to give credence to that theory. Reflecting the shocking nature of the crime, several hundred headlines had been posted over a couple of days, and each article had thousands of comments. The substance of many of them was the same: *What do you expect when you bring someone else's child into your family?*

I closed the browser. While I'd been roaming the seas, the shock had worn off, and by now everyone had forgotten about the missing brother. I was about to turn off the computer when I decided to log into Hae-jin's email. It wasn't hard to remember his password. There were hundreds of unread messages, most of them promotional offers. I flipped back twenty pages or so before I found the email that had been sent around this time last year, confirming the purchase of an e-ticket to Rio.

Passenger name: KIM HAE-JIN
Booking reference: 1967-3589
Ticket number: 1809703202793

He had never opened the email. He wouldn't have had the time before he left the flat. And he wasn't able to open it afterwards. If I could have said my goodbyes the way I had planned, I wouldn't be opening it now either. The Christmas present he never received had been embedded deep in my consciousness over the last year. Many nights, as I floated out in the ocean, I thought of our final wishes. If he'd let me go that day, what would have happened? Would he have been in Rio for Christmas? But he hadn't let me go, and because of that, only my wish came true. Granted, it was a shrimp boat, not a yacht, and I'd worked myself nearly to death every day. Still, I had found peace. For the past year, I'd lived like an animal, without a thought. Now I'd returned to the world, but I wasn't so sure I could live as a human, among other people.

I closed the browser and left the café. I walked around, looking for somewhere to sleep. The streets were deserted, the night was still and the sea air was wet with fog. Up ahead, in the mist, someone was walking. I heard her footsteps. The smell of blood wafted towards me with the salty wind.

You-jeong Jeong was born in Hampyeong, South Korea. You-jeong initially trained as a nurse and is now South Korea's leading writer of psychological crime and thriller fiction. She is often compared to Stephen King and Raymond Chandler. You-jeong is the author of four novels including *Seven Years of Darkness*, which was named one of the top ten crime novels of 2015 by the German newspaper *Die Zeit*. Her work has been translated into Chinese, Japanese, French, German, Thai and Vietnamese. *The Good Son* is the first of her books to be translated into English.

Chi-Young Kim is the translator of the *New York Times* bestseller *Please Look After Mother* by Kyung-sook Shin, as well as fiction by Sun-mi Hwang, J.M. Lee and Young-ha Kim, among many others. She lives in Los Angeles, California.